Sailor In Paradise

A novel
by Robert Hein

Review —
"The best sea passages I have ever read."

Books by Robert Hein

The Bangkok Survivor's Handbook
(Third Edition)

Sailor In Paradise

Published and manufactured
in the United States of America.

Visit www.SailorInParadise.com

***This book is dedicated
to the love of my life,
my wife, Bianca.***

Chapter One
The Royal Suva Yacht Club

I had the hostel to myself when I awoke from my post-lunch nap. The afternoon quiet was broken only by the housemaid singing as she hung clothes in the back yard, and the nagging voices of the Finance Committee holding an emergency meeting in my head.

'We don't want to sound like alarmists, bud,' said the Chairman, 'but you had better start considering your future. In less than three hundred dollars you will have reached the nadir of your monetary existence on earth. Stone broke, if you missed the drift.'

The Accountants began projecting how long the money could last. It had become a daily exercise to worry about the future. This session was the mid-afternoon Anxiety Rush that I coped with by stretching out on my bunk and blowing smoke rings toward the top bunk. Some of them made the two-foot distance then stuck against the bottom of the mattress where they spun into wide circles and dissipated. Others didn't go more than a few inches before they stalled in the muggy air, floating like bent, abandoned halos.

'If we stay in Suva, we only have enough money for a couple more weeks,' the Committee reported.

"I didn't miss your point. It's been poking me in the butt for days. I'll make some moves today, okay?"

They droned on like an unwanted pop-tune stuck in my Thinkman. No siesta today, not with that mental Muzak playing. I sat up, stubbed my cigarette, "Okay, lighten up. I'll go look for work at the yacht club."

I grabbed my hat and walked out of the hostel into the hot, Fijian sun and headed for the docks. I didn't really expect to get a "job," but hustling in the heat might keep the Committee quiet. After a ten minute walk through the city to the market and a five minute, shoreline bus ride, I arrived at the edge of town in front of a one-story, white wooden building with the sign, "Royal Suva Yacht Club" nailed to the wall. I walked through the open front door into a large room with an office at one end and a low bandstand at the other. No one was in sight but my ears caught the sound of clinking bottles and led me to the lounge where I instinctively knew my way around. Three men leaned on the far side of the U-shaped bar, the only customers.

I sat down opposite them and ordered a Coke from the Indian bartender. The men and I glanced at each other out of eye corners. No one seemed eager to check my membership status so I began to relax. After a while, I noticed the tallest of the trio staring at my forehead.

"G'day, mite," he said, raising his beer in greeting.

"Howzit," I answered Hawaiian style.

He smiled, "You'll have to buy the bar a round if you insist on wearing your hat. One of the club's rules. You're lucky there's only three of us here."

"Sorry. Forgot I had it on." I took off my leather, truckin' hat.

"We'll let it pass for now. You're new around here, aren't you? Just get in todie?"

It took a few moments to translate his Aussie accented "todie" into "today."

"I've been in the islands for a month, the last few days in Suva. I'm from Hawaii."

"I've heard Hawaii's beaut. What brings you to Feejee?"

"Just wanted to see more of the world, Fiji sounded like a good place to start."

"I s'pose it is. We're going to throw some darts. Care to play?"

"Not right now, thanks."

I wanted to check the place out while I had the chance, getting in here might not be so easy next time. I had been warned about the Tongan bar manager who challenged new faces to prove they were either a member, invited guest, or on their way out the door.

Barney and Bo, American yacht sailors I met while wandering around the islands a couple of weeks before told me about "job hunting" at the yacht club. They were on holiday from their boat in Suva, staying in a village where I was invited also. That night, we sat around in our host's thatched hut, talking. After the usual American discussion about Fijian food and its effects on our digestive system, we switched the topic to sailing.

"I owned a seventeen-foot sailboat in California," I said, "sailed it to Catalina Island a few times but never did any blue-water cruising like you guys are doing."

"Well, if you want to try it, check out the Suva Yacht Club," Bo said, "someone is always looking for crew members."

"Especially now," Barney added, "since the overseas boats want to be out of here by the end of the month, before the cyclone season starts."

"What do they pay?"

"Nothing, usually. But sometimes the owner will give you enough for an air ticket back to where you signed on."

"How do I go about it?"

They filled me in on how to look for a crew position and it sounded easy enough, but I hadn't come to Fiji for that reason and put the idea on hold for the first few days I was in Suva. I just wanted to live in the South Pacific for a couple of months, to fulfill a dream, a teenage fantasy that had faded in the reality of following the middle-class, credit cards-on-a-stick. Now with the cards gone, the stick was starting to prod me.

I left the bar and wandered through the empty meeting room. A trophy case stood along one wall, surrounded by gray photos of past commodores and racing yachts. The folding doors on the seaward side opened to the view of the manicured lawn and shade trees with sturdy, outdoor furniture clustered at their bases. A seawall hemmed the small yard, beyond which the club's docks extended, filled with the day sailors and outboard powered fizz boats that make up the yacht club fleet. A hundred yards from shore, the larger, guest yachts from overseas lay anchored.

A bulletin board hung from a post at one end of the room, covered with notices of items for sale, postcards, personal messages and crew ads, some faded and curly, stuck and tucked where space allowed.

EARTH COUPLE NEED PASSAGE TO ANYWHERE
Veggies -- No-smokes -- Love
Leave Message for Guiding Star or Twinkle
c/o Poste Restante GPO, Suva

FREE CRUISE TO ROMANTIC NOUMEA
Fun-loving females only.
MUST COOK!!
See Chip on trimaran WILD TIMES

NAVIGATOR NEEDED IMMEDIATELY
For 85' trawler to New Zealand. Departing mid October.
Inquire at the Y.C. Office.

My imagination went ballistic on that last one and sailed for a few minutes as a navigator in the South Seas. I moved to the edge of the room and scanned the anchorage for the trawler, though not sure what to look for. Loud cheers and guffaws from the lounge broke the spell and I went back to the bar. The dart game was over and the men noisily reclaimed their seats. They quieted down after awhile.

"Do you guys know of any boats that need crew?"

Mr. Tall looked over at me, "Going where?"

"Uh, anywhere," I hadn't thought about it.

They sipped beers, puffed cigarettes and pondered.

"How about that American couple, the ones that fight a lot," one said, "I heard them say they needed a hand."

"What's the name of their boat?" I asked, though the idea of sailing with a scrapping domestic duo didn't appeal to me.

Mr. Tall walked to the end of the lounge where windows faced the anchorage and motioned for me to join him. "It's that white ketch with the orange awning," he said, "The dinghy's alongside, so someone's on board."

"How could I contact them?"

"Well, you could wait until they come ashore, or ask someone who's going out there for a lift."

He returned to the bar and I headed out the back door of the lounge. A path led across the yard to the seawall where a wooden ramp went down to the docks. I sat with my legs dangling over the edge of the wall and studied the pontoon where a dozen, tethered dinghies squirmed like feeding puppies for space at the dock. Fact and Fancy found an empty room in my head and began debating soon after I got comfortable. The Committee of Reality reported that besides the cash, we had an air ticket to Honolulu. It suggested I stay in Fiji as long as possible, return to Hawaii, get a job, save up, and get in the wind again. Even this conservative voice liked the low-level travel game of the past month, it just wanted more security while doing it.

'That sounds a lot like prostitution,' said the newly formed Coalition for Fanciful Schemes, 'What kind of job is a skill-free man in his late thirties likely to get? Putting on a plastic smile and going back into sales? And it'll have to be sales or you'll never cut the rent. Keep your options open for awhile. Sometimes, not to decide is to decide.'

I didn't want to go back into selling. I no longer craved money enough to be any good at it. For the time being, I only wanted to keep that nagging feeling of Impending Doom at bay. I had been following the Coalition's hunches the past few weeks and they turned out good, but it was easier when I had more money.

'Besides, that's all you would be going to Hawaii for, a job. There are jobs everywhere.'

I looked up to see a young man approaching. He nodded, smiled, said "Howdy," then continued down the ramp to the dinghy dock. He wore a finely woven, Tahitian planter's hat and a black, Van Dyke beard triangulated his face. Thin, tanned legs poked from his homemade canvas shorts into hand decorated, red, white and blue, starred and striped sneakers. He tugged one of the dinghies to him, tossed his bag inside, then fished a pack of Pall Malls from the pocket of his Mexican vest.

"I wonder if you can help me," I said.

He looked up at me sitting on the wall, "Maybe, what do you need?"

"I'm trying to get out to that boat with the orange awning. A guy at the bar said they were looking for crew."

He tipped his hat back, scanned the anchorage, then turned to me, "That's Mark and Lucy's boat. They were looking for crew last week. I don't know about now."

"Oh. You from the States?"

"Yeah, New Hampshire. And you?"

"Hawaii for the past five years. California before that. I'm Max."

"I'm Mike. So, are you on vacation?"

"Sort of," I briefed him on my story, "...Barney and Bo said I could probably get a crew job here."

"I know them," he said, "they sailed for New Zealand a couple of days ago. That's where we're going next. Whenever Pere sobers up or runs out of money."

"Who's Pere?"

"The owner of the boat I'm on. I got on board a year ago in Puerto Rico."

"Oh. Are you a professional sailor?"

"Not really. This is my first time and I don't get paid."

He told me of his beachcombing life in Puerto Rico with his girlfriend, making "pajaritos," little birds, out of palm fronds and selling them to tourists. "One day, Pere sailed into our cove and anchored near my hut. We got to know each other and when he left, I went with him."

"Do you still like boat life?"

"No big complaints, but it'll be good to live in New Zealand for a few months. I'm going to rent an apartment while I'm there. Where are you heading?"

"Uh, New Zealand," might as well go with the flow.

"Come on, I'll take you out to Lucy's boat. I'll be coming ashore in an hour or so, I can bring you back then."

I climbed into the dinghy and we putted out to the anchorage on a perfect, tropical afternoon. This is the way to look for work. Much better than rereading the classified ads in a coffee shop or filling out applications for jobs I don't want. I counted fifteen yachts flying foreign flags, including the trawler, a black, long-range fishing boat.

"They're taking on crew," Mike said, "but they charge."

I turned to ask how much and saw him looking at an old schooner festooned with bedding and clothes hanging on lines stretched across the deck in the lower rigging. "They must be broke, they're taking in laundry."

"Nah, it's because the boat leaks a lot when it rains and they're always drying out. The other day a big blast of wind came through the anchorage and blew their clothes over the side. Had everyone diving to save their stuff. There's about twelve people in the crew and most of them were nude at the time. There are some foxy ladies on board."

"Oh? How much are they asking?"

"I think it's five dollars a day. You'll meet them if you hang around the yacht club."

He pulled alongside the Tahiti ketch, *Kahuna*, cut the motor and called out, "Yoo-hoo, anybody home?"

A tall, tan and attractive young woman came up on deck wearing a pareau, shoulder length, blonde hair and a smile, "Hi, Mike."

"Howdy, Lucy. Are you still looking for crew? Max, here is ready to go cruising."

She looked down into my grinning face, "Mark hasn't decided and he's not here right now, but I'm sure he'd like to meet you. We'll be in the club later if you are still around."

"I'll try to be."

"Right," Mike said, "see ya, Lucy." He started the outboard and steered the dinghy through the maze of anchored yachts to the sloop *Simba*, and tied alongside.

"That's an African word, isn't it?" I asked.

"Yeah. Pere brags that we're the most international yacht here. Made in Germany, christened with an African name, owned by a Swede and crewed by an American. Come on board for a cup of coffee."

He unlocked the hatch, slid it open and disappeared below. I stayed on deck, amazed at where I ended up after only an hour of job hunting. At 35 feet, *Simba* was twice as long as the boat I once owned, but certain things stay the same on sailboats, only the size changes. I walked the deck recalling the parts of the wind engine — headstay, backstay, shrouds, halyards, winches. Sail bags and plastic jerrycans stood lashed to the lifelines while wire milk crates, stuffed with miscellaneous gear, nearly filled the cockpit.

"Coffee's ready," Mike called, "c'mon down."

Below decks, the cabin arrangement followed a common design with the galley and saloon table on one side and the navigation station and cabin berth on the other. Forward, the bow section held the vee berths and the "head." But in contrast to yachts' interiors displayed at boatshows — which exemplified gracious, seaborne living with a vase of long-stemmed flowers and a wine & cheese setup on the saloon table — this boat resembled a staircase closet inhabited by fraternity brothers.

An unplanned montage decorated the mast from table top to overhead with snapshots of posed people, vast seascapes and distant islands tacked to the decorative ropework that surrounded the spar. On the bulkhead, a Schatz clock and barometer competed for space with a native spear, cowry shell and candlenut leis, palm frond hats and Hinano beer labels. I studied a native ceremonial mask hanging in the center of this wall. It wore a John Deere hat, a pair of sunglasses and a cigarette plugged into the mouth slit.

"That's Bruno. He gets us through," Mike said, "I traded some rice for him in the Tuamotus and we've had good luck ever since."

He set the cups on a table littered with the flotsam of life at anchor — a swollen deck of cards, a few Fijian bank notes, empty SP Lager bottles, tattered yachting magazines and a week-old Fiji Sun paper with the crossword puzzle half worked. Books on everything from astronomy to ZAP KOMIX filled the shelves lining the cabin, and two beer crates full of paperbacks sat on the berth.

"You guys sure read a lot." I scanned the titles.

"Those paperbacks are for trade. If you see any you like, help yourself."

"Thanks. Do you have any on how to crew on a yacht? I've only made overnight cruises. You know, a couple of days fishing and party. I've never really lived on a boat."

"Do you get seasick," he asked.

"Sometimes, but it doesn't last long."

"Can you navigate?"

"I used to be a fair coastal pilot, but it's been awhile since I've done it. I studied celestial navigation too, but never tried it out."

"How about cooking? I don't mean cordon bleu, more like Boy Scout Jamboree."

"I'm a passable cook."

"Then I would stress that point. You can always get a berth as a cookie."

"Oh, yeah? What's the usual routine for a cook at sea?"

"It varies from boat to boat. I do all the cooking here. Pere can't even eat below deck without getting sick. But he does all the dishes. That's the general rule on most boats, the cook doesn't do the cleanup or the meals start getting pretty common. Know what I mean?"

"Sure do. Is that it for sea duties?"

"You'll have to stand helm watches, as well."

"How does that work?"

"It depends on how many people are in the crew. Pere and I do six hours on and six off. But I wish we had another guy, at sea I'm always sleepy."

"Doesn't look like you have room for any more crew."

"It's a jumble right now. We've been here two months and keep dragging more stuff out of stowage. We haven't had this much gear out since the Customs men in Samoa searched the boat."

"What were they looking for?"

"Booze. Pere thought it would be cool to serve them drinks when they came on board to give us clearance. They drank all we had, got nasty drunk, and demanded more. When Pere said we didn't have any, they searched the boat, I mean thoroughly. They were scary."

He seemed happy to talk and rambled on with stories when I asked about some aspect of life at sea or one of the souvenirs in the cabin. Topics ranged from engine problems to receiving mail six-months old. His longest stretch at sea was a forty-day passage between Panama and the Marquesas Islands. Cruising on a boat, far from land for a long time, that's the ticket.

"How long would it take to sail to New Zealand?"

"About two weeks."

"Man, I'd sure like to make an ocean cruise like that."

"There'll be boats arriving here for the next month. This is a favorite port-of-call before going on to Australia or New Zealand for the cyclone season. You'll get a ride." He glanced at the clock, "Time for Sundown Hour at the yacht club."

Mike tidied up the galley while I went on deck to give my imagination some room. That talk was as seductive as a visit to a navy recruiter in peacetime. Any one of these boats would do for me — that ketch, that schooner, that trawler. I could pack and report on board in an hour. Where do I sign?

On the way to shore, Mike pointed out the clues that identified the transient boats from the local ones. "Cruising boats have radar reflectors and chaffing gear in the rigging and stuff piled on the decks." In contrast, the few locally owned yachts were clean as submarines.

At the club, we joined other yachties arriving from a day in town and others coming ashore for the first time that day. Most were planning a night of Chinese dinners, movies and debauchery at one of Suva's dancehalls. The conversation flowed easily around tables full of drinks, snacks and ashtrays, but by seven-thirty the party had peaked and people were leaving. I got up to go.

"Have you put a notice on the bulletin board?" Mike asked.

"I'll probably do that tomorrow."

"Well, keep in touch. Hey, there's a barbecue here on Saturday, costs two dollars. You ought to make it if you can since most of the yachties will be here. I'll sign you in as *Simba's* guest."

"I'll see you Saturday for sure."

The busses had stopped running so I walked back to town. The yacht club is on the Queen's Road, the last building in a line of soap factories, breweries, bakeries and truck fuel stations. Diesel fumes, copra odors and the thick smell of fermenting beer mixed in the night air. The only sound came from the brewery's second-shift churning out crates of Fiji Bitter. The only street lighting came from the flood lamps atop the walls and at the entrance to the nearby Suva prison. The darkness heightened the theatrical effects of the cinema in my excited mind where a full color adventure was projected complete with stout ships, stormy seas and plenty of romance in foreign ports. During intermission, Fact and Fancy met in the lobby.

'What about money?' the Realists asked.

'Hey, Mike said we can live on a yacht for five dollars a day,' replied the Adventurers, 'room and board.'

'No, we mean in the future,' the Skeptics insisted.

'We're not done with today, yet.'

'You're not even sure where New Zealand is.'

'True, but the captain of the boat will know.'

Chapter Two
The Coconut Inn, Suva

At three dollars a day the Coconut Inn was the budget travelers' haven. The two story, masonry hotel dated from the 1940's and had since been converted into a youth hostel by Canadian Ken, the owner who lived on the top floor in an apartment decorated like the headquarters of an explorers' club.

On one end of his desk a squad of carved Fijian warriors stood glaring at the framed photos and sketches arranged on the other end, grisly scenes of cannibal feasts when Fijians relished roast "long pig." Spears, clubs, lances, cane knives and a relic Snider rifle stood in racks along the walls, reminders of Fiji's violent past.

"Got any shrunken heads?" I asked on the day I signed in.

Ken's face went serious, this ex-Mountie was not much of a laugher, "No, you get those in South America. Here, the old Fijians ate just about everything."

The bottom floor was divided by the front foyer and staircase into two wings. The kitchen, dayroom, two dorms and a bathroom lay to one side, four bunkrooms and a bath occupied the other. The bunks were World War Two surplus, eight to a room, with mosquito nets around them which helped to keep out other pests as well, like the drunk German I met on my first night. It was after midnight when I awoke to the sounds of grunting. While it took a few moments for my eyes to adjust to the darkness, my nose detected the odor of a nearby beer-breath. Then I made out a man's face and arms entangled in the mosquito netting that surrounded my upper bunk I lay still for a few moments watching him until I was certain that he was trying to climb into my bunk, then I said, "Hey, this is a one-person bunk, man."

The surprise of my voice froze his actions. "Ach, escuse me. I thought no one vas here."

"Well, someone is here now, so this bunk is taken." He backed off, mumbling "Escuse me, escuse me." A few seconds later I heard the sound of creaking bedsprings followed by a steady snoring. I turned my alarm system off and went back to sleep.

He apologized profusely the next morning, saying that he sometimes used my bunk because it was usually vacant and his was so small. I didn't know him well enough to point out that it was smaller because of the two rows of paperback books arranged full length on top of it. Besides, he obviously had a storage problem since the nearby window sills held more ranks of books arranged in Teutonic order and three-volume clusters were pinched in the wrought iron scrollwork which covered the openings. Several more stacks lurked under the bed.

"How long have you been here?" I asked, awed by this large, personal collection.

"In zis hostel? About two months."

When I returned from the yacht club, he lay in his bunk next to his books, reading.

"Hi, Lothar. Have you seen Megan around this evening?"

He didn't bother to look up, "Yes. She left with some other hostelers to the movies and a disco."

I put my pack down, grabbed a towel and a bar of soap and was headed for the shower when I turned to him. "By the way, I know a guy who has a hundred paperbacks to trade, are you interested?"

His attention centered on me like a cat's on a passing mouse.

"Really?"

"Yep."

"Yes! Of course! I would like very much to see them. But I will only buy them. I don't trade my books. They are my friends."

"I'll tell my friend that you are interested in his friends."

"Yes. Please do. Thank you."

He was the first traveling book-junkie I'd met. Most backpackers carried only their favorite thought-volume, the small edition of *The Prophet* was a popular choice. Those engrossed in mega-novels often tore out the pages as they read them.

Later, I went into the kitchen, made a grilled cheese sandwich and joined in the debate between Lars, "The Wiking Who Lives In The Willages," as he introduced himself, and Yoshi, the long haired, love-beaded cab driver from Yokohama. The topic was coffee vs. tea.

"Americans don't drink very much tea," I said, "Not since the Boston Tea Party."

"Vat vas dat?" Lars asked.

"Amelican Tea Celemony," quipped Yoshi as he raised his hand to cover his giggles.

I thought it was funny, too, but it would take an explanation for Lars. I left Yoshi with the job and went into the dayroom where hostelers lounged on the overstuffed furniture and the floor like cats. In one corner, South African Simon strummed a guitar, softly accompanying a couple of young ladies who liked to sing. At the desk, Captain Bamboo wrote in his journal, occasionally glaring towards the noisy spectators of a nearby chess game. On one wall hung a large Air France world map, I studied it for the first time.

Fiji lies three thousand miles southwest of Hawaii and New Zealand was another twelve hundred south of Fiji. That's a long way from the USA. What happens if I run out of money down there? I better have a talk with the Auckland school teacher.

Although the Coconut Inn was nominally a "Youth Hostel," at thirty-six, I was not the oldest youth there, that honor went to a vigorous woman of fifty whom I'd met in the kitchen that morning when I went to make coffee. She was stirring up a batch of trail mix — nuts, dried fruit and some kind of fodder.

"Good morning," I said, "would you like a cup of coffee?"

She looked up to see if I was talking to her. "Yes, thank you. Would you like some cereal?"

"That's a deal. I'm Max."

"Hello Max, I'm Margaret. Bring a bowl and spoon with you."

We started small-talking. "I'm going on to the New Hebrides," she said when I asked what her travel plans were.

"I don't know anything about them, except that they are a group of islands somewhere around Fiji, right?"

"About one thousand miles west." She launched into a lively talk about the islands starting with their latitude and longitude coordinates, physical characteristics, history, politics and economy. She topped off this mini-lecture with a background of the natives and their curious cults.

"It sounds as though you've lived there."

"Not at all," she laughed, "I've never been out of New Zealand. I'm a teacher of South Pacific Studies in Auckland on my first sabbatical to the islands. How about you."

"This is my first time here, too, but I'm not planning on going any farther. Maybe I'll move back into the villages again, I enjoy that life."

"I've been staying in them as well. Wonderful people, the Fijians. Friends advised me that Fiji would be a good place to start, but now I'm ready for the New Hebrides. They're not as civilized there, you know."

"No, I didn't know."

"Oh, yes. Some tribes are quite wild. I hope to live with them. Study them. I've been in training a year for this chance. Did you like the muesli?"

"Yes, thanks a lot."

"And thank you for the coffee. I must be off to the post office now, perhaps we'll talk again." She cleared the dishes and tidied the kitchen with the efficiency of a farm wife and strode out the door humming a tune.

That night, I found her seated on the front porch and asked if she would tell me about New Zealand.

"I'd be delighted," she said, and for an hour filled me in on the cost of living and life there in general. "You can rent a room in a house easily enough and live well on the farmer's market groceries, provided one cooks at home, of course."

I had trouble believing this low overhead, a week in New Zealand wouldn't cover one day in Hawaii. "How's your New Hebrides adventure coming along?" I asked when she finished.

"Very well, thank you. The Suva library has many books on Melanesia which I've not seen before. And, oh, I found some incredible photos of the natives, would you care to see them?"

"Sure."

We went to her dorm where she fished a half-dozen postcards out of her backpack and handed them to me. "These are the tribes I hope to study."

The description on the back identified the subjects as men of the Big Namba and Little Namba tribes. These frizzy haired Melanesians dressed simply in an animal tooth necklace, a spear, a sneer, and a four-inch wide, made-in-Paris, patent leather belt with a large, gilt buckle. And although the color combinations of red, white and blue were eye catching, this girdle served more than cosmetic purposes. It anchored the tribesman's athletic supporter. Below the belt, was the namba, a skillfully woven tube of coconut fibers which covered the man's penis. From the end trailed a few inches of sennit which was tied to the buckle and kept it pointed upward and limited its motion. Even without a college degree, I could see that. And the difference between the Big and Little Nambas, besides their height, was right up in front. But, for a spinstered specialist of the South Pacific, I guessed photos were not good enough.

"They're beautiful men, aren't they," she said.

"Uh, yeah, but they're probably married."

Later that night, I wrote a "crew position wanted" notice.

The next morning, I tacked my blurb on the yacht club bulletin board.

FREE, TO A GOOD HOME ON A YACHT
One, multi-purpose biped, male, fully trained to paint,
scrape, polish, operate capstans, winches, bilge pumps. Can cook,
wash dishes and play harmonica. To find out how you can own this

handy shipboard tool, call Max at the Coconut Inn, Phone 25230.
American made and equipped with passport, return air ticket
and plenty of time for a voyage to New Zealand.

The exaggerations of my skills I could live with since I knew enough about boats to be useful, but one part of the claim toyed with the truth a little since I had barely enough money for a return flight to Fiji only if I departed right away. All South Pacific countries require proof of onward passage from travelers, no beach bums allowed. If the crew member doesn't have it, the owner of the yacht becomes the guarantor. They don't like the position, so Mike advised me to mention that I had everything necessary for getting into and out of New Zealand.

I bought a Coke and took it to a table under the trees. After awhile, Mike rowed up to the boat ramp, hopped out and dragged the dink up a little ways. I walked over.

"Howdy," he said, "did you put your notice up?"

"Just now."

I looked into the dinghy where the outboard motor rested on cushions in the bow, "Taking your Seagull for a ride?"

"To the hospital, it's sick. Pere came back last night with two, big, Fijian maramas, all drunk, and when they tried to get on the boat they swamped the dinghy. I got a ride out earlier and was asleep when I heard all this yelling and looked out to see Pere clinging to the rail. When I go to help him I see these two women hanging onto his legs, floating alongside. The dinghy had sunk but Pere managed to get it tied to the boat. I spent most of the night trying to hoist those two mamas on deck. If the dinghy had been floating I would have towed them ashore like barges, but I didn't get it up until this morning. Now I gotta work on the engine."

We talked as he tinkered on the motor in the workshop.

"By the way," he said, "I spoke with Mark, he wants female crew, and I found out the hippie boat charges five dollars a day. But they don't know when they're leaving or where they're going."

That afternoon, I sat in the Coconut Inn dayroom mulling over my future and talking with Lars about Australia.

"Living there vas quite easy," he said, "I got a job in construction only two days after I arrived."

"Can tourists get jobs in Australia?"

"Vell, they stamp 'Employment Prohibited' on your wisa just like Fiji does, but you can still find vork."

"Is New Zealand the same?"

"Yes. I have met travelers who have vorked there, but the pay is not so good."

Our conversation broke off when Captain Bamboo strode into the room like a young, pukka sahib of the British raj. His narrowed eyes glanced at me and though his no-lips mouth didn't move, his chin pruned, as usual. He wore a quasi military shirt with button-down epaulettes and the sleeves rolled neatly to just above the elbows. Khaki, knee length shorts, beige stockings and brown sneakers completed his costume. I hadn't really met the Captain. We passed each other in the hostel a few times, but he avoided eye contact. He was like that with everyone and wouldn't say crap to another person if they were standing in it, without a proper introduction. The only way to meet him was as a potential member of his crew.

"Hello, Lars. Did you make the travel arrangements?"

"Yes. We catch the bus at —"

"Why don't you tell me at the desk so I can make notes."

The Captain's office was open. He was organizing a river rafting expedition to be made in the manner of the upland Fijian tribes who use bundles of bamboo poles lashed together to float goods and people to downstream markets, half submerged all the way. One of the hostelers nicknamed him after his first aborted attempt a couple of weeks before. Then, the expedition members deserted the idea at the end of a four hour bus ride and the start of a mountain hike to the village where they would build their rafts. They took the same bus back to Suva. The undaunted Captain simply recruited a new group of sterner stuff.

"Haroo, Bamboo Captain," Yoshi called as he entered and walked to the desk, "I have news, Bamboo Captain."

He sounded like a palace page, even looked the part in his flowing Indian clothes.

"It's Captain Bamboo, Yoshi," he corrected in a tone freighted with the weariness of the white man's burden.

Yoshi nodded his understanding and though his face remained impassive his eyes sparkled with mirth. He didn't come to town on a sampan. Their interaction had me mentally scripting the movie "Son of The Bridge On The River Kwai."

A couple of nights before, I met Megan, the expedition's American member, and we went out for a pizza dinner. As ex-Southern Californians we had a lot in common and the conversation never lagged. She suggested I join the rafting venture. I said I'd let her know. Until I went to the yacht club, my interest in her was quickly displacing my distaste for Captain Bamboo. I felt a light pinch on my neck and looked around to see Megan. She smiled and sat on the arm of my chair.

"Are you going with me? Today's the last chance to sign up, we leave tomorrow."

"Something's come up," I told her of my visit to the yacht club, "...and the barbecue tomorrow is a good chance to meet the yacht owners."

"Well, maybe I'll see you when I get back."

"I hope so. When will you return?"

"Tuesday is the plan. But you know how the last one went."

"How about dinner, tonight?"

"Can't. We're having our victory celebration in case we're not friends afterwards." She laughed and went on to conjure up catastrophes which would happen to them. Maybe I should go with her. My mind was made up until she laughed. I like partners with a sense of humour. While we talked, she loosened her long, blonde hair and shook it like a mane, and then stretched her arms over her head in a beautiful motion that nearly pushed my wavering decision over the edge. "Well, I'm going to see what the great Captain has going. I'll see you later, okay?"

She joined the others at the desk and I grabbed my hat and harmonica and headed for the "Sundowner Hour" at the yacht club.

At six o'clock on a Thank-God-It's-Friday evening, the members' cars filled the parking lot while inside the clubhouse their owners unwound from the work week. They were joined by yachties gearing up for a night in town after a week of doing very little. I found Mike at a table with four friends.

"Howdy, Max, pull up a chair. This is Pere, my owner."

Pere, a thin man with hair to match, smiled and said, "Not really his owner."

"Max knows what I mean," Mike continued, "and Ingrid, Jim and Dave, the trio from the trimaran *Allegro*."

"But Dave is trying to make it a foursome, aren't you Dave," said Ingrid the Tease.

"I'm not leaving Suva alone," he said, "you two will just have to wait until I find a sea wife."

They explained their in-joke. The men had been cruising the South Pacific and in Tahiti, Jim met Ingrid, a lovely French Canadian traveler. They had been together since.

"Too bad you're not a girl," Mike said to me, "you could sail with them."

The conversation drifted through topics finally settling on which boats might need crew and the ones to steer clear of.

"...And find out what kind of food they're taking on the trip," Ingrid cautioned.

"Speaking of food," Jim said, "let's go to the boat and eat."

Pere declined, but Mike said, "I thought you'd never ask. C'mon, Max."

The sun had dropped behind the mountains when we climbed onto *Allegro's* spacious decks and everyone moved quickly. Ingrid went below to the galley. Dave started a fire in the brazier. Jim and Mike secured the dinghies and made a final deck-check in the fading light. The calm anchorage reflected the sky's sunset pastels and insects buzzed like high-tension wires in the mangroves. This was the setting for my favorite, childhood fantasy in which I crewed on a sailboat. In those days, adventure was the essence of the dream, not boat ownership. But as I grew older, that changed to a hope that I would own a voyaging boat when I retired. Now, I again felt the tingle that accompanied that old mind-movie. This boat could take off for thousands of wind blown miles and I could be on it, if I were a female, though I would make a lousy sea-wife, or husband. I could never get it straight who was supposed to take the garbage out.

"Soup's up," Ingrid called.

I joined Mike and Jim in the cockpit.

"Where are you off to next, Jim," I asked.

"We're going to the New Hebrides then to Australia for the cyclone season."

"There might be a sea-wife at the Coconut Inn who wants to go to the New Hebrides. I'll put a notice up if you want."

"Great idea," said Dave.

We shared dinner, some Fiji Green, jokes and sea stories for a couple of hours.

"...We were sailing to Tonga with humongous following seas" Dave said, "I was in the galley writing a letter when a wave landed — WHAM — on the stern window and blew it in. Then a stream of water, thick as my leg, poured onto the table in front of me. I thought we'd had it."

Afterwards, Dave, Mike and I walked into Suva. We passed the waterfront bars packed with beer drinking, machismo sweating stevedores and headed to the small hotel across from the brightly lighted telegraph office on Victoria Parade, the city's bayside avenue. Its fourth-floor night club was originally a roof garden covered with tin and walled in glass which gave a mini-view of the city. A narrow stairwell added on to the front of the building led up to the disco and at each landing full length glass panels faced the street. There, the upward procession of Fijian ladies provided a mini-skirt review for the Indian cab drivers parked across the street.

We danced and chatted with girls whose faces alternately disappeared in the shadows then glistened in the lights of the dance floor. After a couple of hours Dave came back to our table, glancing over his shoulder.

"Hey, you guys. I think we ought to go."

"Why? What's up?" Mike asked.

"A fight. This girl I was dancing with said that her village and a rival one were here and they would fight. What do you guys think?"

"If a brawl does break out we'll be trapped for the duration," Mike said, "I got stuck in a dance hall rumble a couple of weeks ago where the cops locked everyone inside until it was all over."

"I don't want to get into a fight and be interviewed by the police," I said, "I've got enough problems."

A powerful voice came from the back of the darkened room. It spoke in clear Fijian and carried over the music and hubbub. The strong rhetoric soon silenced the nightclub as people rose from their chairs to stare in the direction of the faceless voice.

A girl came to our table, "Dave, you boys better go now or you won't be able to when the police come."

I took her hint and turned to leave when the voice shrieked wildly, raising the hair on the nape of my neck. I looked back, Dave and Mike were right behind me and for the moment we were the only ones moving. Suddenly, the air sparkled as a volley of glasses and bottles flew through the glare of the spotlights. Chairs, serving trays, table candles, and a guitar made up the second salvo. The people trying to get in didn't know what was going on and we had to push our way down the stairwell. When we reached the ground, the clang of a plate window breaking overhead sent us running across the street away from the shower of glass shards. We watched the melee from there. Shadowy forms struggling, screaming, erupting onto the small balconies, like two, hard-rock bands sharing a hotel room. The place was trashed by the time the cops arrived. It took them five minutes to climb the stairs but once inside, they busted heads and sent the injured down to the waiting paddy wagons. The crowd on the street cheered loudly each time a truck loaded with warriors left for the jail.

"That's Fiji," Mike said, "no television but a great fight every weekend."

But while the Fijians play hard-ball with each other, they watch over the travelers in their islands like brood hens. This troop of trekkers needed that extra care, I thought as I watched the International River Rats leaving the hostel on Saturday morning. Captain Bamboo led the parade, kitted out in his British army tropical fatigues. Lars marched behind him wearing his usual sandals, shorts, lumberjack shirt, Queensland hat, and humping a backpack the size of a Volkswagen. Yoshi hovered in the Viking's shadow, wearing gauzy clothes and toting a half-packed JAL flight bag. The two women strolled behind, Megan in jeans, Hawaiian silky blouse and straw hat, Margaret outfitted from pith helmet to jungle boots in a cross between a hunter and an anthropologist, with pens bristling from the bullet loops in her bush jacket.

Later that morning I was brewing coffee in the kitchen when a young guy poked his head in the doorway and said, "Hey, man, is that real coffee I smell?"

He's a Yank. "You're just in time. Grab a cup." I made a lot of friends with my coffee habit. "You just get in?"

"Yeah, man. Got here on this morning's boat from Koro."

"That's out in Central Fiji, isn't it?"

"Yeah, that's it, dude. Have you been there?"

"No, but I went to an island nearby."

"I didn't think so. I've been the only honky there for three months. I'm Chris, man, from Oakland."

"Glad to know you, Chris, I'm Max from Hawaii."

I sat at the table, stirred my coffee, "What did you do on Koro for three months? Didn't it get boring?"

Chris joined me, "No way, ho-say, I played with the people during the day and told them stories from the *Lord Of The Rings* at night. Have you read it?"

"No."

"Neither have they. They asked me what a Hobbit was and I said it was this dude who ate five times a day, slept a lot and didn't like to travel. You know what, man? They identified! 'Hobbits are just like us,' they said. I love 'em."

He launched into some anecdotes of his life on Koro, telling them with lots of animation and enthusiasm. "I only came to Suva to renew my visa and buy supplies for my village."

Later, I helped him shop and carry his purchases back to the hostel. "Come to Koro if you want to kick back for awhile," he said as I left for the yacht club.

"I'll keep it in mind. If I don't get on a boat in the next couple of days, village life will be all I can afford."

At the yacht club, a large gate was opened so members could back their trailer boats into the water. I watched the activity for a few minutes as mum, dad, Buddy and Sis rigged and launched the family dinghy. Nearby, a score of eight-footers were racing, skippered by the members' kids. Cries of "STARBOARD! You silly bastard!" rang out as young captains demanded right-of-way. Sailboat racers are as keyed-up as bomb defusers. I learned that when I crewed a few times on friends' boats in California.

Once the boat was launched, the immaculately dressed mum stood on the seawall shouting directions while the kids desperately attempted to sail out of earshot. She then flitted off to greet friends on the lawn while Dad headed for the bar to join his mates, and I located the yachties anchored to the chairs under the trees.

"Howdy, Max," Mike said, "Glad you could make it."

He introduced me in a general way. Mark and Lucy were there. She smiled and said "Hi." He waved in my direction and sulked. An Australian yacht owner was going to Brisbane but charged ten dollars a day. At that rate, I would have to swim part way. I met the skipper, Noah, and some of the crew from the *Gonowhereboat*, as the yachties called the leaky schooner. Nine nationalities made up their crew list, all headed for the same goal, not clearly defined to me, though it was obvious they were on a different course than I. "Esoteric," one of them called it. The members and yachties mingled around the braziers, sharing boat notes, passage tips and dreams with each other.

"So you like your ketch, do ya, Bob?" a club member asked a guest.

"Well, Alf, she don't go upwind without the motor," the yachtie replied, "but she's roomy, and just loves the trade winds."

Alf glanced at his watch, "Only three more years here, then me an' Audrey'll be cruising around the same as you."

"Three years," the yachtie repeated, thinking on it, "by then I should be in Rio for the Carnival."

They were so self assured in their plans that the Aussie predicted how much money he would have and a general picture of his health, "...Enough for a forty-five footer. I'll be fifty-five then, that's not so old." The yachtie listed his future ports-of-call as though he had already made the trip, "...Six months in New Zealand, then on to Australia and Singapore the following six months." I flashed back to when I used to project ahead like that. Lately, I hadn't planned more than three days in advance.

The afternoon of observing their apparently secure family life, financial success and dreams realized caused me to look at both the members and yachties from another angle. I didn't belong there at all. Although the party raged on at the yacht club, I felt funky, alienated from the people, like I mistakenly got on the wrong deck of a ship. I didn't know where I fit, though right then I felt most comfortable with the hostelers down on "D" deck. I should have gone with the River Rats. Maybe I'll go with Chris to Koro on Monday. Village life was so timeless that an identity crisis seldom arose.

That evening, I heard a guitar as I entered the hostel and went to the dayroom where South African Simon sat on the couch with Andrea, his favorite singing friend. They were clearly a couple, but had not yet formalized their relationship by staying a night at the bayside, Grand Pacific Hotel. This was a Coconut Inn hostelers' custom since handholding was the usual top-level of intimacy shown at the hostel. Anything more was definitely not for shy lovers. With up to eight people in each room, any "Midnight Bedspring Concerto" was bound to attract an audience, instead, couples honeymooned with a night at the romantic GPH.

I sat down with them, took out my harp and we jammed. Other hostelers drifted into the room with cups of coffee or cocoa. The party livened up when Chris made a bowl of kava. Twin brothers from Arkansas chatted up a French girl while Lothar discussed philosophy with a runaway Jesuit priest from Canada. Chris rapped with a fellow he just met.

"Where are you from, man?" Chris asked.

"Auckland."

"Oakland? Hey, I'm from there, too! What hospital were you born in, man?"

"Auckland Hospital."

"Oakland Hospital! Heavy coincidence, man! That's my mother hospital, too!"

"Well, I'm not sure it was my mother's birthplace," the New Zealander said.

Chris studied the guy for a few moments, puzzled, the accent had thrown him a curve. "What part of Oakland are you from, man? Didn't you have no bloods living around you?"

Sunday morning I walked through a city of shuttered shops, few cars, fewer pedestrians. Only the peals of church bells echoing through the streets. The deeply religious Fijians would keep a low profile today. Then I stopped for coffee, cake and thirty minutes of shrieking Indian music at a milk bar crowded elbow to elbow with the roti and curry for breakfast crowd. I hadn't slept well and when I woke up, the Committee on Consternation was waiting for me. It had been up all night in my head worrying over the crewing idea.

'You're not going to fit in with the people,' said the Chairman.

'What are you really going to do for money?' the Treasurer asked.

On and on. I thanked them for sharing, promised to consider their anxieties and told them to take the rest of the day off, especially since I could barely hear them over the sitar at twenty million decibels. A friend turned me on to that mental trick. He said our minds are like radio receivers but since the intellect would rather debate than take directions, it gets stuck on the cross-talk station. If we can change the channel, we may find an information program called Intuition. I am not sure this theory brings guidance, but it does give me a measure of serenity. The Indian music was my idea.

I left the shop and walked along the seawall where a muffled roar filtered through the silence like a row of cannons going off. I looked out in the direction of the sound and watched the long, white surfline where the sea threw its weight against the coral reef two miles offshore. Each time a wave crashed, the line broadened and I would hear the explosion a few seconds later. One member of the Committee couldn't resist saying, 'Those are big waves, suppose you get seasick and don't get over it?'

"Hey look, Voice of Doom, I'm not even on a boat yet. Take a break will you?"

At nine o'clock I arrived at the yacht club and except for the Indian caretaker, had it to myself. Nearby, the faded red, tin boatshed appeared picture-postcard perfect. During the week this cauldron of din echoed with the sounds of rust-chipping hammers, screeching saws and shouting men. On Sunday, it's dead quiet. On the calm bay, the anchored yachts sat motionless as the nearby mangrove islands. Only the sometime sparkle of sunlight from a distant wavelet animated the scene. A soft buzzing of an outboard motor split the silence. I sat on a lawn chair and tried to "keep the positive energy flowing," as Chris put it. After awhile, a man in a dinghy putted to the dock. I asked if he knew anyone who needed crew. "Not right now." Two more dinghies came ashore that morning with the same answers. About eleven, a large sloop motored in and moored along the seawall. It was a local boat, flying a Fijian flag at the stern and none of the cruising gear on deck. The two men on board immediately began attending to various tasks, probably getting ready for a charter or fishing trip. Nobody needs crew today.

I left, crossed the road and waited in front of the prison for a bus back to town. It was too hot to walk and besides, I had nowhere special to go, simply felt out of place hanging around the club begging a boat ride. The idea that someone would take an unknown person on a long voyage began to seem ridiculous.

After waiting twenty shadeless minutes at the busless stop, I decided to have something cold at the club, then walk to town. I went back, bought a Coke and carried it out to the yard. The two men still busied themselves on the yacht at the seawall, ducking in and out of the cabin. I walked over and watched them. The older one, a fit man in his fifties, came on deck, looked at me and smiled.

"Hi," I said spontaneously, "do you know anyone who is going anywhere and needs crew?"

He looked me over, "Yes, I do. Have you ever sailed before?"

His surprising answer took a couple of seconds to sink in, "Uh, yes! I owned a seventeen footer for a few years and crewed on friends' boats in California. Day sailing, mostly."

"Can you cook?"

"Reasonably well."

"You've got a passport and all that, don't you? You're a Yank, right?"

"That's right. I'm Max, from Hawaii." That seemed to cover both questions for the time being.

"I'm Gray. I'll be taking my boat to New Zealand on Thursday next, can you make it?"

"Sure!"

The other fellow came out on deck. "Oh, Roger, this is Max," Gray said, "He'll be sailing with us. He's a Yank. See, he's drinking a Coke."

"Yes, and I have a hamburger in my back pocket."

We had an easy laugh together, shook hands and Gray said I could move on board Tuesday morning. He took me on a tour of *Graybeard* while we talked.

"I didn't think you would need crew. You live here, don't you?"

"Since nineteen forty-two. My parents came over with the New Zealand army during the war and never returned home, except for the occasional visit. Now, me and my Fijian princess are moving there for good."

"Will she be going with us?"

"No. Betty'll take the steamer with our household goods, car, and a thousand orchid plants. We're going to start a nursery."

Later, they took the boat out to the anchorage and I floated back to town on auto-pilot, constantly replaying the scene with Gray through my mind to see where the catch was. He didn't ask for money or even to see my passport. Why was it so easy? A short interview changed me from a worried landlubber into a carefree sailor. My joy at this elevated status wouldn't let the doubts get past first base, though I did kick my impatience in the butt for nearly losing me this chance.

That defect will be better or worse at the end of this 1200 mile trip doing six miles an hour. But for now, I was a sailor on the *Graybeard*, rolling down the Queen's wharf past the moored South Pacific cruise ship, *Fairstar*, generously allowing my Committee of Superiority to silently deride the passengers which streamed down the gangways like colorfully dressed white ants.

Chapter Three
Life on Graybeard

Tuesday morning, I left a note for Megan and Margaret at the Coconut Inn, said goodbye to Ken, and walked to the yacht club. I was sitting at the lawn table drinking a Coke when Gray and Roger walked through the gate.

"G'day, Max, having your breakfast?"

"Good morning, Gray. Yes it's the only way a Yank can get any caffeine around here. The instant coffee you guys drink makes me understand why you prefer tea."

"Too right, there," Gray said, "the Americans do make the best cup of coffee I've ever had."

"Have you been to America?"

"Last year for a fortnight. But during the war there were mobs of your countrymen here."

As we rode the dinghy out to *Graybeard* I wondered how long it might be between cups of American coffee for me. We brought the boat to the dock and worked at the numerous projects on the "TO DO" list — service the engine, clean the bilges, fill the tanks, check the batteries — plus the stowing of Gray's household possessions, including his good luck totem, a five foot, wooden statue of a Fijian warrior. Then Betty arrived, a graceful woman not much bigger than the statue. She spoke with a charming, mission school lilt.

"I wish I was going with you this time," she said.

"You've done this before?" I asked.

"Yes, when we raced the boat to Auckland a few years ago."

"Betty steered for thirty hours straight on that trip," Gray said, "We hit a very bad storm and the crew got seasick, couldn't do anything. Betty and I ran the boat for two days."

When we returned to the anchorage, Gray showed me how to operate the engine, then went through the boat with me, pointing out various systems, valves and switches that I needed to know the locations and functions of.

"Do you have it all, Max?"

"Yes, I think so."

"Good, have the boat at the dock tomorrow morning at eight."

"Uh, sure thing, Gray," I said, after all I was a crew member not a passenger.

Gray built the boat himself over several years, using Fijian kauri for the hull and deck and fitting it out with expensive winches, hatches, portholes, mast and rigging salvaged from yachts wrecked in the islands. He enclosed the center cockpit to make a wheelhouse nine feet square with nearly seven feet of headroom. Padded settees lined the sides, and the sheet winches mounted on the aft bulkhead allowing the sails to be trimmed from inside. In the center was a box three feet long and tall. The width tapered like a vaulting horse from twenty inches at the base to ten inches at the top and it served as the motor cover and drop leaf table. With a little padding it became the perfect helmsman's seat since the wheel and compass were mounted on the forward bulkhead within easy reach.

Gray's cabin lay aft of the wheelhouse. Forward, the companionway ladder led down to the main saloon and galley. The sink and Primus stove occupied the starboard side, to port lay the saloon berths. Packing boxes covered the lower one but the upper was clear and had a porthole at one end. The bow section contained the head, two pipe-berths and more of Gray's household cargo. Roger had claimed the upper pipe-berth, a Spartan, frame and net affair located in the darkest and stuffiest part of the boat. I tossed my hat onto the saloon berth with the porthole view and after Gray left, stretched out and studied the outside world from this new perspective.

The porthole matched in size and shape my family's first TV set, a round, seven-inch Admiral. Instead of test patterns, this tunnel vision presented me with a slowly changing view of the nearby shoreline as soft breezes swung the boat on its anchor. Looking at the world through an aperture fascinates me, and judging by the popularity of cameras, I'm not alone. Who hasn't gained some personal secret by looking through a paper tube, a see-through fist, or a hole in a fence? I discovered one that day. As I watched the porthole scene slowly shifting between the distant steamer docks and yacht club, the realization came that I was no longer a part of shoreside life. Though it bustled only a few hundred yards away, whatever happened there had less significance to me than a weather pattern hundreds of miles distant. I had compressed my life inside of a wooden tube and expanded my universe. What's more, anxieties about food, rent or which direction to follow no longer nagged me. I was truly free from the land.

The next morning, I drove the boat to the dock without mishap so I didn't bother to tell anyone that it was the first time I handled a boat this size. Not even Roger, whose on-deck efficiency had us snugly moored in minutes. He knew the ropes. We talked for a couple of hours the night before. This was his first trip away from home and his energy and attitude seemed beaten down by the tropics. "Certainly, the waters around here are clearer than New Zealand," he said, "but they are chock full of sea snakes. And there's no seagulls, yet billions of flies." All true, though I could live without seagulls, Hawaii didn't have any either. He still lived with his folks and followed his father, an army buddy of Gray's, into the insurance business.

"I'll stay with the game for another twenty-five years," he predicted, "and have a yacht like this when I retire."

It sounded like a sentence handed down by a judge, "Are you on vacation?"

"Yes. I've been with my company for eight years and they know that I'm keen on sailing so they let me have time off to make this trip."

"Do you have a boat in New Zealand?"

"No, but I do quite a bit of racing on my friend's yacht. He has a twenty-five footer and we're in every race."

He told me of the rough, wet and cold weather he endured and included a couple of narrow escape anecdotes delivered in the blasé manner of a veteran Hurricane Hunter. His accent kept me guessing, "sailing" sounded like "sighling" and "racing" was "ricing." Despite his pronunciation, he had much more recent and in-depth experience than I. He had also just completed an astro-navigation course and proudly showed me his new, plastic sextant.

We spent the day preparing the boat. That afternoon a young guy stood around watching us while munching a chocolate bar. He was probably sorting out who the captain was, for when Gray came on deck the fellow walked over to him.

"Need any crew?"

"Maybe," Gray said, "where are you from?"

"Canada. I'm Patrick. I'm going to New Zealand to work."

"Well, you won't have any visa problems. Have you sailed before, Patrick?"

"I was in the Scouts. Got a badge in lake sailing and one for cooking."

They talked for awhile then Gray said, "Well, you know one end of the boat from the other, can tie knots and cook. Yes, I can use you. You can move on board Friday, we'll be leaving at noon Saturday."

The new departure date didn't raise the least anxiety, I had already kissed-off my shoreside affairs — well, not all of them. That afternoon, Gray and Roger went to stay ashore leaving the boat to me. I lay relaxing in my berth when I heard the sound of oars passing my porthole and a voice called out. "Yoo-hoo, Max."

That's Mike. I wonder why he doesn't call "ahoy." Maybe it's anchorage etiquette where at a certain distance "ahoy" switches to "yoo-hoo." Sailors like to be ruled by arcane customs, though I hoped "yoo-hoo" was his own personal style. I went on deck to see him standing in his dinghy, alongside.

"These two ladies were looking for a boat to crew on and I thought of you."

Megan tilted her head back so I could see her face under the hat brim. "Hello, sailor," she said, flashing a fetching smile.

"Ahoy, Max," Margaret called.

I had asked Mike to keep a lookout for them at the yacht club. "What a nice surprise! I was beginning to think you were lost in the jungle under the command of a crazed Bamboo Captain and I'd sail away before you were found."

Megan came on board, put an arm around my waist and gave me a friendly tug-hug, "I'm glad you didn't."

I showed them through the boat, then we settled in the wheelhouse for coffee.

"When does the boat leave?" Megan asked.

"This Saturday. We'll be in Auckland in two weeks, or so."

"I'm confused," Margaret said, "is this not the boat to New Hebrides? The one you wrote needed crew?"

"No, that's another one. I guess my note wasn't very clear."

"No, it wasn't," Megan said.

"Well, tell us about the one that needs crew, Megan has decided to go to the islands with me."

Mike filled them in on *Allegro* while I ran film clips through my head of what it would be like to cruise with Megan. If only she had gotten here ahead of Patrick, Gray might well have signed her up. She was a "Surfer Generation" girl and no stranger to sailing.

"I can take you to their boat," Mike said.

"Thank you, Mike. Do you want to go, too Megan?"

"No, I'll wait here with Max."

"Where do you sleep?" Megan asked after they left.

"I have that top bunk in the saloon," I pointed to it.

"It's really narrow, and there's not much room between you and the ceiling, is there?"

"It's a one-person bunk, all right. So you're going with Margaret."

"Yes, it sounds exciting. Did you see the pictures of her natives?"

"Yeah, some real centerfolds."

"Maybe there's enough room on *Allegro* for the three of us," she said.

"I don't think so." I didn't tell her about Jim's prayers for a sea-wife, which didn't include me, "I'm committed to this boat. Tell me about your river trip."

"I had a lot of fun, but then I didn't lose anything when the raft broke apart." She had me laughing as she related the rafting misadventure, "...At the first white water, the lashings on the raft loosened and it disintegrated under us. Yoshi's flight bag floated off and Lars' camera got dragged along the stream bottom. Captain Bamboo's ego was nearly drowned and is now undergoing CPR at the hostel. We had to walk a long ways to the road for a bus back to Suva. That's why we got back a day late."

We talked like old friends, without coy games. Just like our impromptu date a week before when I leaned into the dayroom and asked if anyone wanted to go for a Dutch treat, no-strings dinner. Megan said yes and we went to Biddy's Steak House where we gabbed nonstop for a couple of hours. The evening ended without a kiss but not without promise, it was impossible not to sense each other's chemistry cooking. Thoughts of her crossed my mind over the past few days but I didn't know if she had returned from rafting, read my note, or would answer it. My scenario was that I'd sail away without seeing her, feeling a selfish melancholy for "what might have been." I hadn't scripted for her showing up like this.

Travelers' romances use a lot of vertical space but very little time. Lovers quickly spiral and soar very high to meet and mate like birds, knowing full well that they were in for a dented heart. Though they readily remove their backpacks, during embraces they clutch an itinerary in one hand and a Valentine card inscribed "I'll See You When I See You" in the other. We had mentally shrugged our packs and were moving towards a first kiss when Mike returned without Margaret.

"Hey, come on over to *Allegro*," he called, "We're invited for dinner."

Jim and Dave showed us through their boat then we gathered in the cockpit for coffee and a talk-story session. The setting sun cast a parting amber glow on the trimaran's white decks and ten minutes later all the stars were out. Ingrid rolled up a Fiji Greenie and passed it around. Margaret tried a couple of puffs for the first time in her life, "When in Rome...," she rationalized. We talked for a few hours about islands, stars, sharks and natives we had met. Margaret impressed Jim and Ingrid with her knowledge of the South Pacific, and her agility — the training paid off.

"Do you get seasick?" Jim asked her.

"Not that I know of. It never bothered me when I went on my uncle's fishing boat in the South Island."

"So, Megan, you want to sail with us, too," Dave said. His eyes glowing with visions of sea wives, "we have plenty of room."

"It sounds good," she said, "I'll think it over."

I took the women ashore and stood next to Megan on the dock, "How about dinner tomorrow night?"

"I'll be here at four-thirty," she said, then leaned close and kissed me lightly.

Back on *Graybeard* the ambiance had changed. It was no longer a secure cocoon but a silent, badly lighted, lonely capsule. In addition, the overhead was too close, I bumped my head three times getting up that night. I couldn't sleep. Megan's visit had curled the carefree edge I had about my upcoming departure and I mulled over strange ideas on how to stall this voyage. I hadn't had a love interest in some time and was unused to feeling emotionally vulnerable and insecure. The Whiners in my head carried on with 'Lousy timing. If only...,' but they faded out when I remembered the upcoming dinner date. I'll make it my last night in Fiji party. Where's my tux?

True to her kiss-and-a-promise, Megan showed up just as we finished boat work and went with us to the anchorage. On the way out, Gray said, "There's plenty of food on board, you two can make dinner here if you like. Roger and I will be spending the last night in my house."

Megan stayed on board while I took the men ashore, on my return I found her relaxing in a nest she had formed of cushiony, bagged sails on the foredeck. I came up behind her, "Hey, this is a cozy conversation pit."

"There's room for two," she said with an inviting look over her shoulder, "Join me."

"I'll get us something to drink first." I went below and grabbed a thermos of iced tea and glasses, stalling a couple of minutes to let my imagination and emotions stop racing or at least slow down. They had been running fast all week. Now, while entertaining a girlfriend on a yacht in the South Pacific, they approached hyperspeed. I watched her through the wheelhouse windows for a couple of minutes. She always seemed to be in tune with wherever she was and looked right at home on the foredeck.

"You're radiant," I said when I returned, "you must be happy."

"Yes, I'm happy. Well, at least adjusted. I sat up last night wondering if the decisions I'm making are the right ones. I haven't been traveling much longer than you and I'm still new at constantly having to make choices. Especially when I have to part from people I'd like to know better."

"I think I was tuned to the same station, my mind drama included you."

"Same station. How did yours end?"

"On a high note," I said, "I looked forward even more to seeing you tonight. And you?"

"On a wish that something minor would happen to your boat that would keep you in port for another week."

"That thought crossed my mind, too. Do you want to go out for dinner? Biddy's or the GPH?"

"Not really. Let's eat in. I've seen your gorgeous, grilled cheese sandwiches at the hostel."

She put some music on while I lit the Primus stove and started coffee brewing. We took turns in Gray's cabin changing into sulus, the Fijian wraparound. Music, the hissing stove, clinking dishes, conversation, laughter, the sounds of two people sharing life filled the boat.

"How about cheese and veggie omelets," I called from the galley.

"Sounds good to me."

"Do you want onions or are you kissing someone later?"

"If we both have onions it won't matter, will it?"

I made some hash brown potatoes, toasted the bread and opened a chilled can of peaches, except for the missing sprig of parsley, it was standard California coffee shop fare.

"I can eat breakfast three times a day," she said as we sat down.

"What can I fix you tomorrow morning? Pancakes? French toast? Eggs over easy?"

Afterwards we sat on deck and shared a Fiji Green while watching the harbor lights. I went below to change the tape and refill our coffee cups, when I came back Megan lay on the sailbag nest. I joined her. We couldn't help but end up side by side. I couldn't help but kiss her, tentatively at first. Then her hands went behind my head and held me in a lip-lock that set my ganglia jangling. She loved to kiss and aroused me in a new-old way, a giddy excitement mindful of teenage necking in convertible cars. We broke for a breath, and the scent from her hair lured me to her ear. From there my lips trailed across her forehead, her high cheek bones, around the tip of her nose to her mouth.

"I sure love you today," I said, "I probably will tomorrow, too, but I can guarantee my feelings right now."

"I love you a lot right now, too."

"Maybe that's as good as it gets. So long as you're in love with a person in the present, you always love them, right?"

"I'm not sure. Let's see how we feel about each other in the morning," she said with a teasing smile.

"Right. Philosophizing about love is for lonely people."

We threw our sulus into the air and our arms around each other. Later, we lay like spoons and my mind drifted aimlessly through the alpha zone, neither asleep nor awake.

"Do you still love me?" she asked after awhile.

"Yes."

"Good. I'm horny again."

If this isn't love, it'll do until the real thing comes along. We dozed through the night, waking once to find our desire still warm. At dawn, we crept into the cabin. After lunch, we exchanged future GPO addresses and promises to write. Finally, it was time to trade Valentines and check travel schedules.

Parting with Megan left me funky and I stayed pretty quiet that evening on the boat. The others kept to themselves as well, busy with last minute stowage. Roger lashed his sextant box into the lower, pipe berth. Gray packed spare parts for his radio set. Patrick put his stash of Mars bars in the freezer. I poured some coffee into my new mug, a gift from Megan, went on deck and watched the Friday night party at the yacht club. Just before we turned in Gray opened a bottle of Fiji Bitter and one of Lemon & Paeroa, a carbonated lemon beverage made in New Zealand. He poured four glasses and handed them around.

"Thanks," I took the glass, "what is it?"

"A shandy. Lemon and beer. "Would you prefer straight beer?"

"No, thanks."

Roger accepted his, "At home I have a glass of sherry once a week when I play chess, any more and I can't concentrate on my game."

"Do you smoke?" I asked him.

"I have a cigar at Christmas."

"Can't give it up, huh?"

Patrick drank his shandy and mine. He had the lower berth, beneath mine, and later, in the darkness, I could hear him unwrapping a candy bar.

I wondered if any of us slept. I merely dozed while a review of the week's events flowed through my mind. My negative Committees were silent, after all, we were on a roll. Even the Take-A-Chance gang in my head politely refrained from saying, 'We told you so.'

Chapter Four
Sailing for the Southern Cross

The next morning Gray and I took the dinghy to the yacht club where Gray said goodbye to Betty and friends who came to see him off. Around noon we got in the dinghy and began rowing out to *Graybeard*. When we were about 50 feet from the landing I saw Megan and Margaret coming through the yacht club gate. They saw us rowing out and waved and hollered, "Goodbye."

Back on *Graybeard* we hauled the dinghy on board and lashed it down between the wheelhouse and mast. Gray went to the wheelhouse and started the engine. He revved the motor and studied the gauges, then idled the engine and called out, "Raise the pick, boys. Let's go to New Zealand."

Patrick and I began hauling up the chain. After a few minutes I looked over the side to see the anchor lift clear of the bottom, then turned back towards Gray and called out, "anchor's aweigh." He gave the thumbs-up sign and slipped the idling engine into gear. We cruised through the anchorage passing *Simba*, *Allegro* and other yachts whose crews shouted "good luck" and tooted their canned-air horns. Betty watched from the yacht club lawn while Megan and Margaret waved from the seawall. Dave appeared behind them with a five-mile smile — lucky guy. Then we rigged the boat for sea and stowed the anchor below decks, closed the portholes, measured the water level in the bilges, checked the lashings which held the dinghy, outboard motor and jerrycans on deck.

I poked my head into the wheelhouse. "Everything looks secure, skipper," I said to Gray. I decided to go with the salty talk. After all, it was my fantasy coming true, why not play it to the hilt?

"Good. Once clear of the reef it won't be so easy to walk around and we don't want anything coming loose. There's the pass."

I looked towards the surfline which stretched across the horizon a few miles ahead like a fuzzy white rope with a piece missing where a channel had been cut through the reef. A half hour later, *Graybeard* wallowed her way through the confused waters of this pass while combers boomed on the reef to either side. Once clear of the awesome bottleneck, we set the sails and steered for the cloud capped profile of Kandavu, Fiji's southernmost island.

That afternoon I began my first helm watch in the aft cockpit where steering was done with a tiller like the boat I once owned. The yacht galloped southwards into the twelve knot trade winds, throwing flecks of foam into the air. Overhead coasted a flotilla of small cumulus clouds — fair-weather puff balls that materialize out of thin air. How do they do that? It's funny how quickly the problems of shoreside life are replaced by the questions of the universe when a person goes sailing. My watch ended at six pm and Gray took over in the wheelhouse. Kandavu loomed off our port bow, a purple silhouette blending into the twilight. It would be behind us when I next came on watch at three am.

The helmsman's trick was three hours long, twice a day. Gray took the 6-9 o'clock watches, Roger from 9-12, Patrick went from 12-3, and I had the 3-6 sunrise and sunset watches.

Even in calm weather, the first day at sea is exhausting. Walking at an angle, with legs bent. Hands always grasping. Arms always pushing or pulling. Knees, hips and elbows bumping into corners, objects and hatchways which were never in the way before. All the time hauling one's ashes up and down the short ladders, in and out of the cabins. No one suffers insomnia on the first night. Dinner that night was soup, cheese and crackers. Shortly afterwards I went to bed and quickly fell asleep counting the flashes from the sea beacon on Kandavu Island which beamed through my porthole.

"Max. Hey, Max." Patrick's soft call cut through my sleep. I heard the water gurgling alongside the hull but couldn't separate dream from reality especially with stars appearing in my porthole, tossing around like fireflies in a clothes dryer. A small, galley lamp threw enough light around the cabin for me to pour a cup of coffee from the thermos and climb the three steps into the dark wheelhouse where Patrick sat astride the motor box steering with one hand, a candy bar clutched in the other.

"Boy, you sure get up easy," he said, "you've still got twenty minutes."

"In that case, I'm going back to bed." Instead, I stood on the port settee with my head sticking out of the hatch, facing forward.

Islands no longer blocked the weather and the tradewinds blew with the steadiness of an air conditioner, snapping the edge of the jib sail and raising a low chorus of moans from the rigging. Occasionally, waves smacked the hull sending up spray which turned red in the glow of the port running light. My head was quiet, apparently everyone inside realized that this was not a dream, not a rehearsal, but life, the experience. I ducked back inside.

"Gray said to wake him if there are any big wind shifts or you need help with anything," Patrick said as I took the helm.

"Right. Hey, I'll trade you three cookies for half a candy bar," I offered.

"It's a deal." He went to his stash in the fridge and brought one back.

He stayed with me for awhile and told me about his adventures, "...After graduation, I worked as a carpenter's helper and saved up to go traveling. Then I flew to Fiji a couple of months ago."

"What will you do in New Zealand?"

"I've got a Canadian friend there who says he can get me a job in construction. Anyway, since it's part of the Commonwealth it'll be like living in Canada. I plan to stay for the summer, then head to Australia."

His youthful optimism punched my positive energy buttons and had me repeating to myself, "I'll find something to do there, too." He went to bed and I concentrated on keeping the boat on course. Mike said that because of *Graybeard's* fourteen-foot beam and added-on wheelhouse, the boat was now a motor-sailor. "She'll steer like a sponge," he forecast. Not so, her sails had plenty of drive and her responsive rudder soon had me oversteering. When Patrick was here it seemed easy, after he left I became mesmerized by the compass. During the afternoon watch I didn't give it a glance, now, I dared not take my eyes away from the card as it turned and swayed in the ruby glow of the binnacle lamp. Then I remembered a night sailing trick, use a "star to steer her by." I found that I could stand on the port settee, stick my head out the sliding hatch and steer with my right foot. I got the boat sailing on course then poked my head out and aimed at a star ahead, occasionally changing stars as they moved off my heading. Throughout the watch, the star constellations of the False Cross and the Southern Cross hung in front like two celestial kites pulling us south and Scorpio sunk into the western horizon leaving only its curved tail tip showing when the sky lightened in the east. Then the weaker stars dimmed out, as well as two, small clouds, the only ones in the sky. When Gray relieved me at six am, I felt high, like I'd been driving a space ship through the heavens and made a gentle splashdown in the South Pacific Ocean.

As the duty cook that morning I cooked a large American breakfast as a first day at sea celebration, besides, I was starved. I made patties of hash brown potatoes with a hole in the center where I fried the egg. If you don't put a frame around a frying egg at sea you end up with one as big as the skillet it's cooked in. Toast, sausage, coffee and tea completed the meal. By the time I'd handed the third plate up to the wheelhouse, the judgments were coming back.

"Great brekkie," Gray said, "I like the cheese on top and the onion mixed with the potatoes."

"Yes, that was a mighty feed," Roger agreed.

Patrick was too busy eating to talk. I went to fix my plate when something told me that although I was hungry all I wanted was toast and coffee, if that. The combination of cooking smells and kerosene fumes from the Primus stove filled the galley and sent mixed messages to my brain. Suddenly, I turned off the stove, went on deck and threw up. I didn't go back to the galley but crawled to the aft cockpit and crashed. Awhile later, I awoke, threw up again and dumped a couple buckets of seawater over my head.

Then I heard Roger's voice cutting through my nausea, "What's the matter, Yank, not feeling so good?"

I looked up to see him and Gray sitting on the cabin top, holding sextants. Roger smiled, I couldn't, then he raised his instrument and looked through it as though he knew what he was doing. I envied their gallant appearances, if I held a sextant just then I would have thrown up on it. I dumped another bucket of water over my head, skipped lunch and slept in the cockpit until time for my watch. Patrick lived up to his cooking badge that evening and my appetite had improved, so I downed a plate of sliced ham and pineapple, veggies, a green salad, and a piece of pie with a cup of tea.

"That was a mighty tea," Roger said.

"The food was great, too," I added.

"In New Zealand, tea is the meal," he explained as though I should have known.

"Really? What do you call tea, the drink then?" I was annoyed at his efforts to stay one-up on me by using New Zealand colloquialisms and explaining them in a demeaning tone — "bickies" means cookies, "lollies" are candies.

He copped this attitude from our first conversation that night on the boat in Suva. Once he found out that his sailing resume read better than mine, his manner towards me went up the condescension scale a few clicks. He acted like the voyage was a summer camp scenario where he was a counselor. It was the old Male Pecking Order movie starring himself as First Mate. I had no problem with that. I didn't want to be an authority figure and gave Roger plenty of space for his role playing. But now, he was beginning to believe his fantasy included me, and I had unwittingly taken a small role. I didn't mind him jiving me when I was seasick, I might have done the same thing. But later on, I agreed to do his galley cleanup since he "had to take an important star sight in a few minutes." Instead, he sat and chatted with Gray without even unpacking his sextant or another word to me. I held back from saying anything, which he probably regarded as good manners one expects from sea wives, if he considered it at all.

I steered by the stars again and after awhile the same two, hazy clouds that I saw on my previous night's watch, appeared at the same place in the sky. I showed them to Gray when he relieved me just before dawn.

"Those are the Clouds of Magellan," he said, "The nearest galaxies to earth." He went on to identify some stars and constellations, "and do you see how the long axis of the Southern Cross points due south? So, even though we don't have a pole star like you Yanks, we can still figure out where it is."

"How?"

He got some navigation books and a star chart from his cabin and gave me a tour of the Southern Hemisphere sky. Afterwards, I told him that I had studied celestial navigation and he loaned me his spare sextant, a cheap plastic model. I spent the next two days in the aft cockpit, studying navigation or sleeping in the sun. Roger based his navigation station in the wheelhouse, where he maintained his fish-belly white complexion. We crossed sextants a few times on deck when we simultaneously shot angles on the sun and cast anxious, How-Do-I-Look? glances at each other.

The sextant. The most sensual tool of the sailor's trade. The most stimulating. And like sex, its finest hour is measured in seconds. Its real power lies in the ability to alter a man's personality much like holding a pistol does. Formed handgrip. Telescopic sights. Matte black. No nonsense shape. A man pressing a sextant to his eye, or simply cradling it wearing a serious expression looks like a take-charge individual — that's the theory.

On the third day at sea, a steady procession of swells began rolling in unbroken, serried ranks from the northwest, the same quadrant as the breeze that kept our Fijian flag pointing forward. Every few seconds, a hill of water lifted us high atop its crest where I could see for miles, then the boat slipped into the trough and the view shortened to the inch high, dragon scale wavelets on the swell's massive backsides. Mother Carey's Chickens skimmed the water with scarcely a wingbeat. These tiny birds kick the surface with their feet as they fly, to stir up their link in the food chain. Fragile creatures made mostly from air and with only a ten inch wingspan, booting a disciplined army of Pacific Ocean rollers in the butt for something to eat. I identified with them, scrambling rations on top of an ocean.

A high haze covered the sky, masking the sun. Roger sat on the cabin top, sextant in hand, looking like he was stood up for a date. I watched from my aft cockpit base. This crumple-chinned achiever didn't cope too well with setbacks. "Damn! I need another sight to tell where we were at noon," he said.

"Even if you do find out where we were, we're in a different place, now."

"That's just the point. If I knew where we were I can figure out where we are right now."

"Within reason," I ventured.

"With precision," he countered.

"You remind me of the story of the new naval ensign and the experienced navigator who were asked to determine their ship's position after a storm. The ensign made a dot and said 'we're exactly here.' The navigator made a dot, put a circle with a one-inch radius around it and said, 'we're in here, somewhere.' The point is that it's impossible to verify your position without landmarks."

"Well, the navigator must have been a Yank. I have faith in my lines of position." The sun came out and he raised the sextant to his eye and fiddled with the micrometer drum, then lowered it, glanced at his watch and wrote the time down on a notepad. "There," he announced smugly, "this one will tell me exactly where we were at noon." He went to the galley table to work the solution.

Every time Roger said the word "Yank" it was with the connotation of resentment though I didn't have a clue why. He said I was the first he'd met. Snap judgment? That evening over dinner in the wheelhouse, I asked Gray where he got the old Primus galley stove.

"It's from a Sunderland bomber," Gray said, "a World War Two flying boat. There were a couple of squadrons based in Suva during the war."

"Did you see any action?" I asked.

"No, Fiji was only a staging area and I was too young."

"You can rest assured that the New Zealand army behaved better in Fiji than the Americans did in New Zealand," said Roger The Righteous.

I looked into his face, his pruned chin and stressed lower lip showed he meant it. I checked my reactions, I didn't know where he was coming from and didn't want to start anything. "Yes, I saw a movie about the Marines in New Zealand. John Wayne was in it so it was rowdy."

His face pouted even more. "I'm sure it didn't show how abominably they treated the New Zealand women."

I tried to lighten the conversation with, "No, but then it was a family movie."

"The Americans took advantage of them every way they could while the husbands were overseas."

Gray sensed how serious Roger was before I did, "All armies behave like a pack of bastards overseas," he said, "let it go Roger."

This curious topic explained a lot of Roger's behavior to me and gave me something new to puzzle over during my watch. Did New Zealand ladies resent Americans?

I didn't say much when I relieved Patrick at three am. He didn't mind. He grabbed a Mars bar from the fridge then lay in his bunk, reading. He spent all of his off-watch hours either sleeping or reading and had read three paperbacks in two days. I had been too excited to read but tonight, Roger's attitude got to me. A thick overcast covered the sky, no steering by the stars tonight. The northwest wind blew a steady 18 to 20 knots making the waves steeper. This downwind sailing required constant attention to the compass and anticipating which way the boat was going to twist in a wave. I soon got used to the movements of the boat and began to relax. I had enough time between helm changes to pour a cup of coffee and light a cigarette. Then an off-duty Committee in my mind started wandering around in the future.

'What if the New Zealanders don't like Yanks? Gray and Roger are the only ones we've met,' said one member.

'Well, I guess we'll just have to leave,' said another.

'Where to? That's the same old problem.'

'I'm going to act as if they do like Americans,' a positive voice chirped.

'So? We're still stuck with the problem of what to do. Can't work there.'

'We may not even be allowed into the country,' said Mr. Doom and Gloom.

Then they began talking all at once and I listened.

Suddenly a wave broke over the bow and a wall of water raced along the deck, splashing off the mast and dinghy to wash up onto the wheelhouse windows. I looked at the compass and saw that I was 40 degrees off course, coming around into the wind. I struggled with the helm for several minutes and was trembling from the adrenaline rush when I finally got it back on course.

The next voice I heard in my head was from the Survivalist, 'Don't worry about what will happen when you get to New Zealand. You're not there, yet, and you still have ten thousand waves to go through before you arrive.'

The storm raged through the night and the morning dawned on a gray world. The seas rolled relentlessly, closer together, combining with the northwest winds to push the boat at a steady eight knots. After breakfast, Gray and I went on deck to take in some sail and check the lashings for the dinghy. Wind strength increased throughout the day, so late that afternoon we dropped the regular sails and hoisted the storm jib and trysail. "We may not need this heavy canvas," Gray said, "but if we do, it will be too rough and dark to work on deck."

"Looks like we're in for bit of a storm," Gray said at dinner that night, "the barometer is dropping and there's a depression reported to the northwest of us, moving this way."

"At last! Some action! I was beginning to think this tropical sailing was for poofters," strong words from Roughwater Roger. The news gave me a jolt of excitement mixed with dread that I might get seasick again. No stars danced in the porthole that night, instead, the view was filled with swirling water as the boat's roll increased. When I awoke for my three am watch, the noise of crashing through the sea sounded like we were submerging. I went to the wheelhouse where Patrick gripped the helm, his eyes fixed on the compass. "Man, she's hard to hold tonight," he said as he twisted the wheel first one way, then the other. I went to the hatch and looked outside. The wind yowled in the rigging and seas humped like a honeymoon waterbed under a quilt of low, scudding clouds. With the wind and seas pushing our tail, steering became difficult and critical. I stood at the wheel and got used to the boat's actions, then sat atop the motor box with my knees clamped to its sides and my hands clutched to the wheel. It pitched, bucked and rolled through the night. In my bunk near the waterline I hardly felt these motions. Up here, in the early morning blackness of the wheelhouse, it was like riding a mechanical bull in a space vehicle through a cosmic storm on the dark side of everywhere. You can't buy a ride like that in Disneyland.

I felt exhilarated after my watch and made brekkie for three. Roger didn't get up to eat. The weather piled up as the day went on bringing thick, rain squalls. I took a shower in the first one, then stayed in my bunk and watched the tempest through my porthole. The boat's roll alternated my view like a front-loading washer loaded with dingy, gray clouds then filled with foamy, swirling water. That night I put the lee cloth up to keep from being tossed out of my bunk. This made my space into a loose fitting cocoon, keeping me as snug as a pea in a basketball during a championship game.

"I think the worst is over," Gray said when he relieved me the next morning.

"How bad was it?" I asked.

"I figure it hit around force seven." He used the Beaufort scale to measure the weather strength. Force seven is winds to thirty knots and waves to thirteen feet, a full gale. "How did you boys rest? The stern cabin got a little jumpy."

"I caught a few winks after I knew I wasn't going to be sick and got wedged into my space," I said, "Patrick was so relaxed he read *The Cruel Sea* and ate candy bars while the storm was raging. Where's Roger? I haven't seen him for a couple of days."

"He's sick," Gray said.

Despite a sea lumpy as a bag full of bowling balls, the sky was clearing so Gray and I took some sun sights. He helped me reduce them and plot the line of position. Over the next two days we had long practice sessions and discussions on the theory of celestial navigation, "It's my favorite hobby, Max. It's like a game to me." I played the game with him and kept my own navigation plot going.

Roger would have liked to play, too, but he was still sick. I hadn't seen him for a few days since our helm watches didn't meet and he didn't turn up for meals. Then one afternoon he worked his way out of his pitching berth — the bow section is the liveliest part of any boat — and came up to the wheelhouse where Patrick and I feasted on cookies and candy bars.

"Hi, Roger, care for a bickie?" I asked.

"No, thank you," he mumbled as he slumped onto the starboard settee. A huge, navy peacoat covered him like a carapace, his hands and head poking out like an albino turtle's. I didn't know what Roger's illness was, but assumed it wasn't life threatening or Gray would have radioed for help, but Roger wasn't acting either. He hardly moved at all except to spasm and double up, stagger to the hatch, stick his head outside and retch loudly. He got my stomach's attention. The afternoon sunlight illuminated the gray-green tinge of his gaunt face, classic symptoms of serious mal de mer. I stopped eating cookies and concentrated on steering. For me, seasickness can be contagious.

"What's wrong, Roger?" I asked. Patrick and I looked at him but he wouldn't make eye contact.

"I don't know what it is. I just can't keep any food down. I can't stop throwing up."

"Oh," I said, "haven't you ever been seasick before?"

He flashed a look of shock at me as though I asked if he wanted a bacon, egg, sausage and cheese burger. "It's not that! I've never been seasick and I don't get seasick!"

"Maybe so, but you're not airsick, carsick or landsick."

"Want a candy bar? That might help," said Nurse Patrick.

What a fall, from Iron Tummy to Jelly Belly. I gloated to myself over his loss of face until he crawled to the hatch again and retched pitifully. I well remembered my own pain of a few days before. But I didn't deny my illness. For me, admitting that I'm sick is a survival tactic.

I figured he was stuck with the philosophy of "Manly Denial" which leaves no room for quivering lips. The credo is simply that Real Men don't cry, get seasick, become alcoholic and a thousand other peculiar rules men measure themselves by. If Roger admitted he was seasick, even only to himself, it would change him forever. Better to keep the denial strong. Blame it on the food. Inside the pea coat he shivered like a dog with a bellyful of chicken bones, but then his body heat was low and it had gotten colder since the storm. On the morning of the ninth day we sighted Cape Brett low on the horizon and from then on Roger's health began improving. Lucky guy, he has never been seasick.

Life on board picked up a notch as we coasted New Zealand. Roger kept busy identifying the gulls which flew out to inspect our garbage. Patrick tuned the radio to the pirate rock-music station which broadcast from a ship near Auckland. Gray bought a tiny TV set in Fiji and amused himself by watching Burt, Ernie and the rest of the Sesame Street gang. I studied the ocean's phytoplankton. These plant-life creatures remained invisible during the day, but at night they glowed like dots of radium in the tumbling waves. During their short lives they would swim only a few feet and drift a couple of miles. Occasionally, they became trapped by the swirling water outside my porthole and suddenly set spinning in a tight spiral. Their blue-green lights streaked around the glass until flung out of the vortex and left somewhere down the line, dazed and disoriented. I felt a strong affinity with those tiny creatures.

Gray catnapped in the wheelhouse during the night when we passed islands, headlands and fishing fleets. He stayed awake much of the time and we talked.

"What got you into this backpacker game, Max? You're older than the average hippie."

I stumbled through a glossy version of my economic and social downfall. I hoped in vain that he would say something like, "Mid-life crisis, that's what it is. Had it myself once, back in the middle ages, ha, ha." But then, he, too, faced a daunting life change.

"What made you pack up and leave Fiji, Gray? Tired of the tropics?"

"Not a chance. I worked for a government department for twenty years and intended to retire there. But then, Fiji was given independence from Britain and ruled that only native born persons can work in the bureaucracy. Changed me a hundred and eighty degrees, I'll tell you. The past few weeks have been hectic. Selling the house. Preparing for the voyage. Getting all those orchid plants shipped. This cruise has been very relaxing. I wish it didn't have to end so soon."

"So do I."

"What are your plans, Max?"

"I haven't made any. I'm turning my cards over one day at a time."

"Look, I'm going to need help for a couple of weeks, putting up my greenhouses. I can't pay you, but you'll have room and board and plenty of time off."

I mulled it over for ten seconds, "Sold! Where do I sign?"

On an overcast October morning we sailed past Rangitoto Island, the volcanic cone which marks the entrance to Auckland Harbor. Everyone brought out cameras and took snapshots of each other and everything in sight. We crossed the harbor through a dozen anchored merchant ships and passed close to a bright, red one named *Panama Reefer*. "I gotta get a picture of that one," Patrick muttered. It certainly was the most colorful object around. The city's buildings were dull brick and stone, the waterfront in steel and concrete. The wharfies and ship's crews that stared down at us wore drab woolens. We tied to the Customs Wharf and were immediately boarded by Health Department officers, Customs officers, an Immigration Department clerk and Roger's mum. He left at the first opportunity, seabag in one hand, sextant box in the other and the look of a freed hostage on his face.

"You'll have no problem for a long stay," the clerk told Patrick, "but the American will only get one month."

"That's hardly enough time to see the country," I said.

"Sorry, but since you arrived without a visa, that's all we can give you. Let's go across the street to the Super's office."

I knew nothing about visa regulations and assumed that I would get three months, the same as Fiji. Now I was short on time as well as money.

Chapter Five
Seduction in New Zealand

Gray and I sat in the waiting room at the Immigration Office while the clerk took my passport and Fiji to Honolulu air ticket into the warren of cubicles. The Anglo-Saxon bureaucratic style was light years away from the Fijian. There, the Immigration officer gave me a visa and a ride to my hotel. Here, the stark setting hit my Committee of Consternation like a whiff of ammonia.

'He didn't ask us to show any money,' one member said.

'Even so, we'll probably have to buy an air ticket to Fiji.

'That'll leave us thirty dollars. There's no way we can live on a dollar a day.'

I had not been this broke since high school, half a lifetime ago and my anxieties multiplied like amoebas.

The clerk returned, whistling a tune. "You're lucky," he said, "the Chief's in a good mood. He gave you a three month, renewable visa. That means you can remain here for six months, total. Enjoy your stay."

"Come on, Max, I'll buy you a real coffee," Gray said.

We walked through streets filled with office workers. Business suited men wearing tight, Monday morning expressions scurried like pale vampires racing to their tombs. The women in their high heels cruised slower than the men and I swivel-necked at every pretty girl we passed on the way to the coffee shop. After five years of living in the Pacific islands and two weeks at sea, I was a pushover for apple cheeked, blue eyed blondes, green eyed redheads and gray eyed brunettes.

We moored the boat at Westhaven Marina where Patrick signed off to live with his Canadian friend. Gray borrowed a car and for the next few days we drove around Auckland gathering the materials to build greenhouses. One afternoon as I stood on the sidewalk waiting for Gray, I noticed a young guy staring at my hat. I touched the brim and gave him a nod and he walked over to me.

"G'day, mate. Mind telling me where you got your hat?"

"Not at all. A friend gave it to me in Hawaii."

"Thought so, can't get a hat like that here."

I handed it to him, "Have a look." It was made from thick, flexible cowhide with a deer skin sewn on top.

"Miiighty! Miiighty! Wish I had one."

I nearly offered to sell it to him but I liked that hat. The wide brim and high crown kept the sun and rain off, and it could be sat on, soaked and stuffed into a bag and still pop back into shape. That's a feature my body could use.

On Saturday, we sailed north to Sandspit, a ferryboat landing at the mouth of a small river near the town of Warkworth. Here, Gray had bought a small farm on a hillside overlooking the stream where we anchored *Graybeard*. Sandspit came alive for the morning departure and afternoon arrival of the Barrier Island ferry. For the rest of the day it slept in a rural setting of country roads, scattered houses, hills thick with heather, the air crackling with bird calls. In the afternoons I rowed the dinghy upstream and hiked the lanes trying to catch a glimpse of a Tui, a large bird with a fascinating call. I saw a number of Kiwis. Not the Kiwi bird, the flightless symbol of New Zealand which retired after selling shoe polish to the US Marine Corps, I mean the local gentry. We said "G'day" and small-talked in passing. Then, one afternoon while rowing, I spotted an auburn-crested Robyn. She was perched on the railing of a small bridge which crossed the stream. Nearby was a Mom & Pop store where I usually took a break. She watched as I pulled the dinghy out of the water and climbed to the road. I went to the side of the bridge and looked down to see if the dinghy had walked away. I glanced at her. She smiled.

"G'day," I said.

"Have you come a long way in that little boat?" she asked.

"Just from Auckland," I lied, "only stopped here to get a hamburger and a Coke."

"Well, you may have to settle for fish and chips with L&P. You're a Yank, aren't you?"

"Yes. I'm from Hawaii."

"Hawaii. I always wanted to go there but then I heard it was very commercial."

"It's a paved paradise, if that's what you mean."

"Really?"

"It's undeniable. Everybody there sells joyrides or condominiums. It's like an overpriced amusement park you can buy a piece of." I grinned to let her know I wasn't too serious. Her shoulder-length, wavy hair framed a face which resembled a heroine on the cover of a Gothic novel. "Well, now that I've completely ruined your fantasy, the least I can do is treat you to a bottle of L&P. Besides, I hate to drink alone. Have you got time?"

She looked at me for a couple of seconds, "Yes, I have time."

"I'm Max," I said as we walked to the store.

"I'm Robyn."

The line "when a redheaded Robyn comes bob, bob, bobbing along" tripped through my mind. At the store I bought a bottle of L&P and two paper cups and we sat on a bench in front and talked. I gave her a short rundown on how I started in Hawaii and ended up at this bridge, then asked, "How about you? Do you live around here?"

"No, I just came up from Auckland for the day. You know, a drive in the country," her voice inflected upwards at the end of her sentences like questions.

"I'll be moving to Auckland in a few days," I said.

"Where will you stay?"

"I don't know yet."

"I have a friend in Ponsonby who rents rooms in his house, he might have a vacancy." She wrote down "Kelly" and a phone number. "I'll call and tell him about you. Anyway, once you're settled, drop by the Modern Theater on Gladstone street. That's where you'll find me."

"What do you do there?"

"I've got a part in the play, The Odd Couple. Do you know it?"

"Yes. You must be one of the Pigeon sisters."

We chatted on about plays we knew, and then she looked at her watch, "You'll have to excuse me, Max, time to head back to the Big Smoke."

We walked over to her mousy-brown, Austin A-40 parked near the bridge. "I hope to see you in Auckland, Max," she said, then chugged off down the lane. I drifted downstream to *Graybeard* feeling kind of sad-glad that the Sandspit episode was ending. Living on the yacht in a quiet estuary was an exotic holiday, but a lonely one.

I called Kelly the next afternoon and he had a vacant room, ten dollars a week. A couple of days later the greenhouses were completed and Gray paid me an unexpected fifty dollars then took me to the Warkworth bus stop.

"Feel free to visit me anytime, Max," he said as I boarded the Auckland bound coach.

"I'll take you up on that, skipper."

With a month's rent in my jeans and a couple extra pounds on my frame, I felt secure as a millionaire yet free as the wind.

I arrived at Kelly's house on a quiet Sunday afternoon. It wasn't much to look at with a sagging porch, peeling paint and gaps in the gingerbread trim. Kelly answered my knock. He was in his early thirties with tousled blond hair and a ready smile. He wore a sweat shirt and jeans, his Sunday leisure suit I found out later.

"G'day," he said, "You must be Max, Robyn's friend. C'mon in."

I followed him into a high-ceilinged hallway with bedrooms on either side and at the end a small dining room, tiny kitchen and a toilet/shower stall that gave a precise meaning to the term "water closet".

"Let's have a cuppa," he said as he poured some tea.

We sat at the table and talked for a while. He had been divorced recently and bought this house as an investment, I was his only tenant. "It's a fixer-upper," he said, "You can work off some rent if you're any good at painting or paper hanging."

The next day, I answered a newspaper ad for a salesclerk in a downtown stationery store and was interviewed and accepted on the spot.

"But, what about my visa?" I protested, "Is it legal?"

"Don't worry about it. We can fix that up for you," the Personnel Manager assured me.

"I'll need some time to think it over," I said as I backed out of the office. But my mind was already made up, I couldn't work for lower than low wages, five and a half days a week, not yet. On the way home I went into a leather craft shop where the owner raved about my hat while selling me $25 worth of hide and tools to make more. I'd never made anything out of leather before and my first attempt turned out like a lampshade. I put the stuff in the closet and turned my thoughts to the Modern Theatre.

Live theater was my hobby since high school. It was my escape from reality. When I took part in a production I could hang my daily problems outside the stage door for a few hours and get immersed into someone else's fantasy. Besides, cast parties are a great place to meet girls. One afternoon, I located the Modern Theater in a converted church hall. A sign in front announced "The Odd Couple, opening soon." I went in, stood by the last row of seats and watched the on-stage activity where several people worked on the set. The stage manager was the one giving instructions while chain smoking. He saw me and came over.

"Hello, can I help you?"

"Hi, my name's Max. I met Robyn who told me about your theater. I stopped by to see if you could use me. I can paint, take tickets or sweep the floor, and I'm free."

"I'm Terry the production director. Yes, I think I can find something for you to do." He showed me around and introduced me to Lynn the props girl, Rachel the set designer and Kim, the diminutive brunette who ran the light board. I began painting sets and a while later Tony, the theater "angel," came in with a box of food.

"I hope you like New Zealand tucker," he said to me as he opened packages of sausages, and fish and chips, the Kiwi equivalent of the McDonalds menu. Later, Robyn came for rehearsal and gave me a lift home afterwards. I asked her in for coffee. Kelly was out so we had the place to ourselves and settled at the dining table for coffee, cake and theater gossip.

"The guy playing Felix really sounds American," I said.

"He's Canadian. He was a radio actor there. He's only been here a few months. You must have noticed his little friend, Kim, on the light board."

Kim? The five-foot, two, eyes of blue package with the form and grace of an aerialist? Sure I noticed her and her flirty smile. She's with that hambone?

"Yes. We met," I changed the subject, "The guy who plays Oscar sounds more like a Kiwi than an American, though."

"Derek? Well, he shouldn't. He's Australian," Her chin clenched.

"Did I say something wrong? I'm really lousy at guessing accents."

"No, it's not you, Max. It's something else on my mind."

"Want to talk about it? I'll be your confidant."

"Do you mind? I've got to talk to someone."

"My lips are sealed. Sock it to me." I expected to hear gripes about the director, the actors and the play in general. A common breakdown before opening night.

"Where can I start? Derek and I are, how should I say —"

"You're Derek's little friend," I guessed after a silence. She looked at me with zipped lips, then her face relaxed and broke into a wide smile which involved the corners of her eyes.

"Touché. Except that lately we're not so friendly and we've still got to face each other on stage for three more weeks."

"Are you married?" I asked though I meant "living together."

"No. Well, not to each other anyway. His wife is in Australia. My house and hubby are in the Summerhill suburbs. Cute name, isn't it?"

"Conjures up images of families playing together on sunny days. Front yards littered with rusty children's vehicles, lawn pools and station wagons."

"Right. Very middle-class," she said.

"Not your cup of tea?"

"Not at all. I lived in London all my life until five years ago when I moved here. This is like living in a farm co-op, Max, it's boring, provincial and lonely. I miss the city life."

I refilled our cups, "Why did you come here, if I may ask."

"I'm not sure anymore. To save a marriage? To be a sought after, London trained actress? To prop up my husband's jobless ego? Pick one, they all apply, but only the last has been accomplished."

I thought about the personal direction this conversation was taking, "Why are you telling me this?"

She looked directly into my face, "I need to share this with someone, Max, and practically everyone I know is part of my situation. My instincts tell me I can trust you. I'm only being candid with you because you asked and I felt I didn't need to lie and say everything's hunky-dory. Was I wrong?"

"No, you're not mistaken."

"Well, except for hubby's ego inflation, the move is a failure. There's little work for professional actresses, so my career is on hold. Meanwhile dear hubby has formed a new circle of drinking associates and we don't see much of each other, but then we don't look very hard. Finally, I got into this play and met Derek. Now, that relationship is going through the wringer. I don't think we were truly friends before we became lovers. Have you got a cigarette?"

I lit one for each of us. She used hers as a prop. Actors hate to be empty handed. I smoked mine to cover my nervousness. I couldn't recall a woman leveling with me about the life and love games she played. Probably because I was part of the scenario.

"And that's how it stands today. I'm still totally confused about my situation but I feel better having talked about it." We finished our cigarettes and coffee in silence, then she looked at me, "Thanks, Max," she smiled, "it's life's ironies that make it interesting, isn't it?"

"Yes, that's right," I held back on the corny platitudes.

"Time to go," she picked up her purse and I walked her to the door, "I'll pick you up for rehearsal tomorrow night."

We looked at each other with the same question in our eyes, Should we kiss, or not? We didn't. She already had a lover and a husband, what she needed was a friend, so did I.

That night, my Committee reviewed her story and found it had more similarities than differences with my own. Except now, my emotional slate was fairly clean and I wanted to keep it that way for awhile. Don't fall for anyone with more problems than I have, that's the credo.

As opening night drew near, I was made soundman and sat in the wings, stage right, directly across the stage from Kim at the light board. During a technical rehearsal, we discovered that we could see each other plainly, though no one else could because of the curtains. Our eyes caught and we smiled and waved. We managed to have a few brief conversations, except when Felix hovered over her, now we had a secret, contact channel. The play had only a few sound and light cues giving us time to mug and parody the actors for each other, a favorite pastime of amateur theater crews.

On opening night, I caught a ride with a stagehand to the cast party at Tony's house, a two-story, modern design of heavy timbers, stone and glass. A small sundeck extended from the upper floor. The party was cooking when I got there, fueled on the adrenaline release of the first-night jitters. Actors bellowed anecdotes about forgotten lines, open zippers, wrong costumes or missing props. Nothing exciting like that happened to me, all I did was flirt with Kim during the show. I found her seated on the floor near the fireplace, smoking from a long stemmed, clay pipe, the small bowl, Irish kind.

"Hi, Light Lady. Enjoying the party?"

"Hello Soundman, have a seat," she patted the floor.

"That looks like an Irish peace pipe," I said.

She thought about it for a minute, "I suppose it is, especially since there's a bit of green tobacco in the bowl. Would you like to try some?"

It may have been green but it tasted more Asian than Irish. I took two puffs to confirm my judgment.

"Where are you from, Kim?"

"New Zealand, I was born here. Why do Americans always ask where one is from?"

"I'm not sure. For me, I don't know the Kiwi, Aussie and British accents well enough to separate them. Aussies get mad when you mistake them for Brits."

"I guess it would be. When I visited America, I had a very bad time understanding the people, and found the accent differences from north to south intimidating. I got along better in Canada."

"Is that where you met Felix?"

"Yes. I got a job at a TV station where he was an actor. He wanted to try and make his name in New Zealand and Australia so we moved back here."

"You're not aiming for the stars?" I asked.

"No. There aren't any notable pinnacles of fame in New Zealand's TV advertising business. That's the reason I left in the first place. I'm back at the same agency I started at ten years ago. What about you Max, someone said you arrived on a yacht. Are you on holiday."

"No. I'm retired."

"You look a bit young."

"I'm testing a theory."

The slight tilt of her head, raised eyebrow and beginning smile showed her skepticism, "Oh? Tell me about it."

"Well, I grew up in middle-class America when it was considered shameful if you didn't have a job, unless you were a union member on strike or a paraplegic."

"New Zealand is somewhat like that."

"Probably an English export from when they used to ship their unemployed to remote colonies. Anyway, a few years ago I read G.B. Shaw's essay, *Work*, in which he figures the world would be better off without the Protestant work ethic. So I came up with a formula that would satisfy both the hedonistic and responsible sides of my nature. Work for twenty years, then retire until you're sixty and return to work for the remainder."

"I don't know if that's realistic for most people," she said.

"I'm not even sure if it's realistic for anybody."

"How long have you been retired?"

"Three months, but I still have enough in my retirement fund to last until the play's over."

She laughed, "That's only two more weeks."

"Yeah, I'm finding out that retirement is like love, short and sweet."

"What will you do then?"

"I don't know. Robyn said I could get some work as a reader, taping books for the blind."

"You should come by my agency sometime, we'll make a tape and put you on file. You never know, we might get a call for an American. Excuse me a minute, I'm going to get some more wine."

I watched as she crossed the room. She wore a gauzy, sort of harem fashion which showed the profile of her legs and allowed her soft, rounded curves to jiggle provocatively. It suddenly seemed ages since I'd kissed a woman. I was idly wondering if she played around, when she returned.

"Have you seen the rest of the house?" she asked.

"No. Just got here."

"Come on, I'll show you the view from the roof."

I followed her, glancing quickly around to notice that Felix was politely passed-out, upright, on the couch. We went upstairs and down a short hall which led out onto the sundeck. There, two outdoor recliners were placed side by side, facing the vista of the city lights below.

"This is a nice place to take a break," I said as I sat down.

"Yes, I always come up here for awhile when I come to Tony's parties."

She made herself comfortable, raising the backrest to an upright position and extending her legs. She pointed out Auckland's night time landmarks. I pretended to be interested, but was distracted by the light scent she wore. She seemed to sense my mental direction and trailed off in mid sentence to look over at me. In one slow motion, I moved over to kiss her. I was hungry. So was she. Her arms wrapped around my neck and pressed me into her mouth, "That's for making me laugh during the show."

I took a deep breath in her hair, then leaned down and kissed her again. We didn't come up for air until our senses were filled and our passions had peaked. A voice coming from the yard below brought me back to the reality of where I was and who I was with. "Kimmie — Kimmie, are you out here?"

"That's Felix," Kim whispered. We could see his dim outline as he walked a few feet down the driveway. He called once more, then, satisfied there was no one around, unzipped his fly and relieved himself. "I'll duck inside while he's busy," Kim said, "Thanks for the squeeze."

Felix gave a little shake and cut a big one when he was done. Then walked back into the house singing out of tune. How simple life is before you find out its truths. It felt strange spying on the man I had just cuckolded, like I just had a walk-on part in his life and now stood in the wings.

On the play's second night, Kim and I threw kisses at each other from the wings but at the cast party Felix stayed sober, and close to her. They left early and I walked home shortly after. I was falling for her. It wasn't difficult. The hard part was trying to see what would come of it.

I woke up on Sunday morning feeling tired and funky, the comedown that follows a play's opening weekend. My headspace matched the thick overcast which covered the city. Inside, my Survival Committee had been stirred by the ease with which I counted my remaining cash.

'Hey, Bud,' the Chairman said, 'we're down to less than one hundred dollars. You better start coming up with some ideas on how to keep this movie rolling.'

"Thanks, guys. But your timing's lousy. Come back later."

I crashed for a few hours and that afternoon, after a quart of coffee, a piece of cake and a couple of cigarettes, slid into thinking about a way to make money. At the party, I'd talked with Tony about job possibilities. "You've come here at the wrong time, Max," he told me, "the country's in a depression." Really? Which one? Many of the buildings dated from the 1930's. The street traffic thickened during the peak hours and public transportation was by trackless trolleys and stubby city busses that reminded me of Los Angeles in my youth.

Another time warp was the abundance of new comic books with plots featuring the Spitfire Pilot vs. The Hun In The Sun, and tank duels with Rommel in the desert. World War Two footage took up a lot of time on the nation's only TV station. But the low wages, high taxes and tight money controls told of an economy that probably hadn't changed much since The Great Depression. If I settled for a job, I'd never be able to bank any escape money. I had to sell something. Then I remembered the leather and tools and for the next week I made hats during the day and showed up at the theater each night to meet the sound cues and flirt with Kim. Monday through Thursday the cast and crew went home right after the performance except for the Friday night cast party at the home of one of the actors.

Some of that night's audience were there as well, already loosened up from pre-show cocktails and the wine served during intermission. I got a glass of L&P, pasted myself against a wall and watched the revelers, a vivacious, attractive brunette in particular. She was talking with the host. I sauntered around the room until he couldn't avoid seeing me.

"Ah, there's the Yank," he said, "Max, come join us."

The girl looked towards me and smiled invitingly. "Max, this is Sandra," he said when I walked up, "she loves America."

"Pleased to meet you, Sandra. Have you ever been to the States?"

"No, but I've been a Yankophile since I first saw American movies as a child. What part are you from?"

"Hawaii, recently, Los Angeles before that."

"Los Angeles! That's where I want to live. Have you been to Hollywood?"

"Sure. I lived there a few times. It's a zany place with a personality all its own."

"Do people still throw wild, weekend parties where everyone gets really drunk and does crazy things?"

"You mean like throw each other into the pool with their clothes on?"

"Yes, that's it."

"And when you come out," I went on, "throw your clothes in the air and jump into the shortening pile?"

After a couple of seconds, she said, "Maybe. What's a shortening pile?"

"A heap of nude people greased up with shortening, squirming like a nest of eels on the floor."

"Mmm, sounds delightful. Have you been to many?"

"I'll tell you about them later."

"Are you shy?" She glanced at the two guys who had joined our circle.

"Not at all. I just don't like to boast."

"How's your drink?" She filled her glass from a nearby bottle of wine, "Need a refill?"

"No, thanks."

"What are you drinking, wine?"

"Lemon and Paeroa."

"Only?" She took a sip from my glass, "I thought American men were two-fisted drinkers. Don't you drink?"

"Don't judge them by me. Most of them probably are heavy drinkers. I just didn't like the wear and tear on my body so I turned America's drinking image over to the care of the next generation."

"Just my luck," she said to no one in particular, "the first Yank I meet is a nondrinker."

I lost a lot of points there. A guy who didn't drink was suspicious enough, if he's over thirty, that's strike two. Strike three was to be classified as a poofter. I made a move to the kitchen where I found a bottle of L&P among the flagons of wine and cartons of beer. Not being at Sandra's partying level didn't bother me, I'd had enough dates with heavy drinking women and woke up with more than a few hungover ladies to know what I was missing. There wasn't time to think about it anyway, since Kim came into the kitchen a minute behind me.

"Hello, Soundman."

"Good evening, Light Lady. I was hoping to see you."

"We just got here. Took a few minutes extra to have a spat along the way." She poured two glasses of wine, looked up at me and smiled, "I'll see you in a little while, all right?"

"Sure, I'll be around."

We went back into the living room, and she went to Felix who stood talking with Sandra. I mingled for an hour or so, then Kim walked past me and signaled with her eyes. I watched her go to the kitchen, then followed. She went straight out the back door into the dark yard and settled on a lawn swing.

"This is a nice little hideaway," she said, "A good place to take a break from the party." She wore a black satin blouse and dark, woolen skirt from which she pulled a small pipe with a metal bowl cover. "Have you a light?" she asked. The bowl glowed as she took a drag, held it for a few seconds then let the smoke out in a long, thin stream. "Like to try my latest blend?"

We smoked the pipe in silence. Kim was a bit of an outlaw, a dubious feature that attracted me to women.

"That didn't taste like Irish tobacco," I said.

"It's more Lebanese this week. Did you like it?"

"Yes, thanks. Where did you learn your appreciation for these imported herbs? Smoking them doesn't seem to be a common New Zealand custom."

"I traveled. First to England where I worked in advertising for three years. Then, I hitchhiked through France and Spain to North Africa, Marrakech. It was the in place to go."

"I've heard about it."

"I followed the hippie trail for two years, before I went to North America to make some money."

"It must have been quite an education."

"I learned what the saying 'you can't go home again' means. Although I was raised on a farm here I can't visualize myself being a stay-at-home, house spouse." She relit the pipe. "After the show we're moving to a farm eighty miles north. Felix is going to write a book, and I'll probably shrivel up. I'm not looking forward to it. Auckland has just barely enough life to keep me occupied. I miss the adventure of traveling. That's one thing that attracted me to you, your carefree, here today, gone tomorrow attitude." She finished her wine, "Could you get me some wine, please? And have a glance at Felix."

"It's really black out here," I said when I returned with our drinks, "I couldn't see you until I was very close."

She took her glass and I sat next to her.

"Did you notice Felix?"

"Yes. He's sitting on the couch talking to a couple of girls."

"He'll be busy for awhile. He loves the attention." She turned away and put her drink on the ground, then leaned back on me. I inhaled the scent from her hair, moved my face closer to her head and brushed my nose along her ear. She tilted her head forward and I kissed her neck.

Suddenly, she sat up and took my drink, setting it next to hers. "We don't want to get wet, do we?" she said with a giggle. She leaned back against me and allowed my hands to slide over her warm, satin covered curves. She arched her back and I stroked her from breasts to navel.

She reached behind her, found my crotch and gave it a squeeze, "Mmm, you don't take long to arouse."

"It's easy with you," I walked my fingers along her leg and began inching her skirt up until they were underneath and moving up her thighs. She parted her legs slightly, revealing a panty-free zone. "You're not exactly a slow burn, yourself."

"I've thought about being with you a few times last week."

"You were featured in a couple of dreams I had, as well."

"Tell me about them."

I made one up. She had a quick imagination and embellished her part, acting it out. Awhile later she sat on my lap, her back towards me, her pleated skirt covering the rocking motion going on beneath it. Over her shoulder, my half-closed eyes gazed dreamily across the yard to the rectangle of light in the back door. It seemed a mile away until a face peered out. Kim didn't drop a beat, then I saw that her eyes were closed.

"It's Felix," I whispered.

She opened her eyes and stared straight ahead at the face in the window, eighty feet away. Her bottom stopped rocking. Felix started to open the door when Sandra appeared in the window and held a glass of wine up to his lips. He turned towards her and they moved out of sight. The close call increased our ardor and urgency and a few minutes later we soared.

"I hate to kiss and run, but I'd better get back. Are you free Sunday? I'll have the car since Felix is going yachting with some friends and won't be back until late."

"I don't have any plans."

"Good. I'll pick you up at ten am. Is that all right?"

"That's perfect. I live in Ponsonby, at seven-eleven John Street."

"Yes, I know. I asked Robyn."

She asked Robyn? I stayed and smoked a cigarette after she left. I had my share of three-cornered affairs but didn't learn much from them except that they all had messy endings. Maybe I wasn't too good at them. Maybe I didn't have to be, maybe Kim was. Anyway, I couldn't turn down her offer. To spend a day with her would have been my first wish if I knew it had a chance of coming true. And besides, she's not really married to Felix.

Tension ran high in the dressing room on Saturday night. The male leads complained about everything and even threw a couple of barbs at each other. Then when they got into makeup and costume, they began perspiring. "Shit, it's hot!" Felix said. It was the after effects of last nights drinking tournament with Sandra. Kim and I didn't throw many kisses from the wings, when she wasn't meeting cues, she was blotting Felix's face. They went home right after the performance. I hoped he was well enough to go yachting tomorrow.

On a brilliant, Sunday morning we drove across the Harbor Bridge, the "Coathanger" with the "Nippon clip-on," two lanes added to the sides by a Japanese engineering company. Below us, dozens of sailboats and fizz boats flitted on the Waitemata Harbor.

"Will you continue yachting when you leave New Zealand?"

"I don't know. I haven't really thought about leaving here, yet. Fact is, I like the place. The cost of living is low. The weather reminds me of Southern California. The people helpful. The girls friendly and pretty. It's got a lot of features."

"Umm, but you've only just arrived, you might change your mind after a few months."

"Possibly, but the country's so big that it could take a year or two to become bored. Hawaii is so small that I ran into myself driving around the islands. Where are we going?"

"Devonport. There's a little cafe there that has the best cheesecake."

She turned off the bridge and drove along the harbor's north shore on a practically deserted street. Small, English style, wooden houses with tidy, fenced yards lined one side while moored small craft and the navy base took up the other. She pulled up at the ferry landing, dodging between passengers to a parking space.

"At last. People. I was beginning to think that we were in the middle of a nuclear attack drill."

We went into a bakeshop, sat at a window table and started our day with a strawberry cheesecake breakfast. We putted around the harbor rim for a few hours, then up to the top of One Tree Hill for the city view. She pulled up in front of my door that afternoon.

"Won't you come in for coffee?"

"Thanks. Is your housemate here?"

"No. He spends Sunday with his daughter."

I put the kettle on and showed her through the house, "This is my room."

"Why is your mattress on the floor. Have you no bedframe?"

"I like living on the floor. It gives me a lot of space to put my coffee cup, ashtray, books and it doesn't hurt if I fall out of bed."

"Oh," she said. Then she saw my stack of hats. "Do you make hats? Can I see them?"

I picked them up and was pointing out the painstaking craftsmanship when the kettle started whistling, "Here, have a look. I'll make coffee."

She was still in my room when I finished the coffee, I looked in, "Do you want your coffee at the table or in here?"

"In here's all right." She sat on the edge of the bed, flipping through one of my books. I sat next to her and wondered what came next.

"Have you sold any hats?"

"Not yet."

"Do you think there's a market for them?"

"I haven't a clue. I've never done it before in my life. But I have to do something soon. I'm running out of money."

"I have to do something soon, too. Look Max, I'm leaving for Sydney in a few weeks. Would you like to join me there?"

I heard the clatter of pencils dropping as the Committees in my mind gave her their full attention. "What about Felix?"

"He's not going. Nor does he know that I plan to. I'm leaving him. I've given it a lot of thought. I can't bear the idea of getting locked into farm life, even if I don't have to raise animals or vegetables. Sydney is perfect in summer and I know some people in advertising there. I'll find work. Maybe for you, too."

"I'll have to think it over for a little while. I don't know if I'll have enough money." I lit a candle and some incense, put some music on and sat beside her, "Let's put our lips together and see what we come up with."

Mmm, Sunday afternoon love. Later, my cautions dozed while my mouth said, "When do we go?"

She looked to see if I was kidding or not. I wasn't sure myself. "We can leave in a couple of weeks."

Now I wasn't sure if she was kidding. But I didn't ask. It was already too complicated.

"Think it over," she smiled, "we could have fun."

"I will. I had a great time today."

"Totally decadent," she laughed, "cheesecake for breakfast and a randy tart for tea time. I've got to go now. See you in the wings tomorrow night?"

I didn't answer but instead kissed her again and we fell into a lip and leg lock that joined us for another frolic on my ground level bed. After she left I relaxed, closed my eyes and let the mind movie roll. Thoughts of Australia always projected scenes of adventure, a last frontier mentality. 'Dream on. You can afford to do that. It's free,' said a cynical voice in my head. Then shut up and enjoy it, I thought back. I had a good day and I'm not ready for it to end. Come back tomorrow.

The Worry and Fret Committee sat on the edge of my consciousness until I woke up. After a piece of cake, two cups of coffee and a cigarette, I was ready for them. "Okay you guys," I thought, "don't nag me. I got to sell some hats today." I stuffed the hats into my daypack and headed for downtown Auckland which had several classy leather goods shops. I walked into them, hats in hand, and the third one bought all five. Suddenly I had seventy-five dollars in my back pocket from a ten dollar investment and a few days of crafting. I bought more hides and went into business. That night, between the acts, I told Kim of my hat sales.

"Looks like things are pointing towards Sydney for you."

"Yes, it does. But, perhaps not in two weeks. Now, I have to make hats."

"Let's hope, though."

That week I cut, stitched and glued leather during the day and after the show. In a few days, I had a dozen, leather truckin' hats.

The show's final weekend began with a tension filled green room. "The mayor is here!" Hubbub, hubbub. "I heard there was an Australian producer in the lobby, somebody I know recognized him." "Oh, God! Really?" Backstage rumours circle like a cyclone and always blew stronger when they got back to me. Then I heard, "Felix and Kim are arguing in the parking lot." I didn't start that one. He came in a few minutes later, sullen and seething. It'll take a different makeup base to cover his angry, red face. I eased out the door — irate actors use a lot of room — and stood nearby to overhear. But he was completely quiet. No usual gripes about costume, makeup or props. The other actors didn't pay him any attention, they were locked into their characters and Felix's real-life problems didn't matter for the next two hours. I walked through the open stage door into the parking lot and lit a cigarette. After a few seconds, I heard a whispered, "Max. Over here." I followed the sound and found Kim sitting in her car.

"What's the Light Lady doing out here in the dark?" I said as I walked up to the open window.

"Having a smoke. Care to join?" She handed me her glowing pipe. "Finish the bowl if you like."

"Is anything wrong?"

"Felix found out I'm leaving, I don't know how, and suspects I'm having an affair. I suppose he has a right. I've been caught before."

"What's going to happen?"

"He says he's going to help me pack."

We went to our places in the wings and shortly after the opening curtain, she looked over at me. I was just blowing her a kiss when Felix, who was not on stage yet, poked his head around her curtain and looked straight at me, then at Kim. I could almost hear the penny clinking it's way through his mind. Then he was gone. While he was on-stage, Kim mouthed the word "tomorrow" and pointed to herself then me. I took the hint and missed the cast party that night.

She knocked at my door the next morning. "Sorry to come so early but I had to talk to you."

I made some coffee and we went into my room. "How was the party?"

“Awful. It’s good you didn’t come. Felix got very drunk and we had a big scene. Now, the whole cast knows we’re breaking up. “The Yank” was mentioned, but he’s only suspicious since he caught you flirting with me. Can I stay here for a few hours?”

“You’re like a fox. You find little hideaways where you can watch from but not be seen.”

“You’re right. Lately, I’m always looking for a chance to look at my life from another perspective. Do you know what I mean?”

“I think so.”

“I mean, like I get caught up trying to figure out whether leaving Felix is right or wrong, selfish or sacrificial.”

“Yeah, I’ve been there. When my head and feelings are rationalizing my next move. I hate that state of mind. Keeps me awake. Now I try to get in touch with my real feelings and trust them. A friend who had been to some navel studying center in California taught me that method.”

“Can you do this?”

“If I don’t chicken out. It’s scary sometimes to really nail down how I feel about someone or a situation that I’m uncomfortable with, because then I have to face choices. If I no longer like my job or love my lady should I stay there for the retirement watch or so I won’t be lonely? If I do, I feel like a martyr one minute and a prostitute the next.”

“What do you do to sort it out?”

“I write out what’s on my mind. Unedited. At those times my head’s as noisy as an Irish parliament fighting a prohibition ruling. I write down every gripe, fear, hope, should and ought to that comes up. Sometimes I number them so they can’t repeat themselves. I let them pour out for awhile before I pose the question that’s bugging me. I put it in a way that can only be answered with yes or no. If the answer is ‘yes, but,’ or ‘no, but,’ I keep making the list. I ask myself the question until I get an answer without qualifiers. I sometimes get a gut feeling along with it, but there can’t be any mind games in it.”

“Does it really give you the right directions?”

“I don’t know. All the results aren’t in yet. But the writing down of my thoughts makes things clearer. My head can often cook up some cockeyed logic that sounds great until I see it on paper. If I can’t come up with an answer right then, I’ll reread the paperwork later and throw out the thought lines that aren’t part of the problem. Even if I don’t get an answer, the problem is a lot clearer.”

“Sounds interesting.”

“Well, you make yourself at home. Like some more coffee?”

I put the pot on, and started getting breakfast together. I took a cup of coffee into the bedroom for her. She sat in the center of my bed writing in a notebook. A while later I looked into the room and said, "Breakfast is ready." She was much calmer through the meal, and afterward did the dishes while I showered. The bathroom in this curious house was next to the kitchen and dining room and when I came out with a towel wrapped around me, Kim was standing there watching.

"Sexy," she said. Then she reached out and pulled my towel off. I made a show of being outraged and chased her into my room where we fell on the bed in a tangle. We tumbled, laughed and struggled, bucked and flew off into the mental universe for lovers. When she was leaving, I noticed the notebook in her bag, "Are we still going to Sydney?"

"Darling, I'll see you tonight. All right?"

"Sure thing." I kissed her lightly. I could take a hint — whether I liked it or not.

That evening when I arrived at the theater, I passed Felix at the stage door and gave him a nod and a half-smile. He did the same but his glance was about two-feet over my head and his smile was more of a smirk. We had never had a conversation, he only talked with actors, which was fine with me. I didn't want to know my lover's live-in. Not that I disliked him or thought of him as a rival, he's just a side of the triangle, like me. So why was he looking so smug? I went to my place in the wings and looked across at Kim who was busy testing lights with the curtain closed. Afterwards, she looked over at me and beamed a great smile. She was happy. With ten minutes until curtain, some loose ends began floating around in my head, 'If those two are pleased, that might not be good news for me.' The idea of going to Australia with Kim had moved up to the top of my fantasy hit-parade. After the final curtain, the cast hurried out of their costumes and makeup and raced to the cast's final party at Tony's. I caught a ride with Robyn who gave me the details of Felix and Kim's spat the night before. "They were really going at it last night," she said, "but I saw them leaving together tonight as though it never happened."

Some of my loose threads were joining up. At the party, I kept circulating until I saw Kim and Felix arrive, then I hovered in her sight, waiting for a sign. After awhile, Felix became engrossed in conversation with a young lady and Kim looked at me then towards the stairs. I casually made my way across the room and up to the rooftop sundeck. Kim followed a few minutes later.

"Hello, Light Lady."

"Hello, Soundman."

"This might be our last meeting on Tony's roof," I said.

She was quiet for a minute, then said, "This is our last meeting for awhile, Max."

"Why? Are you leaving for Sydney that soon?"

"No. I'm staying with Felix."

"That's an unexpected decision."

"Well, I did what you said. I wrote down what was on my mind and tried to look at my thoughts and feelings. Anyway, this is the decision that I've come up with. Believe me, the answer surprised me as well."

I almost asked if she wanted a second opinion but instead said, "I'm glad you're happy."

"I'm sorry if I led you on. I didn't mean to hurt or make you seem foolish. It's obvious how I feel about you or I wouldn't have followed your advice."

Me and my damned counsel. "No permanent harm done, I guess. We're still friends, aren't we?"

"Of course. Let's go downstairs now, there's someone I want you to meet."

I stayed for a few minutes after she left and wondered if we were living together, would she have taken my advice? That would have been a new type of relationship for me. As I came down the stairs I noticed Kim talking to an exotically beautiful Maori woman. She looked up and beckoned me to join them.

"Hello, Max," Kim said, "Kiri, this is Max, the ex-soundman of our show. In real life, he's a yacht sailor from Hawaii. Max, meet Kiri Marie. She's a model at our agency."

We shook hands and exchanged how do you dos.

"So, you're from the land of my Polynesian cousins," she asked, "were you born there?"

"No. It's my home for the past few years. I'm a California drop-off."

"Drop-off?"

"Americans always migrate to the west, so Californian gypsies naturally went to Alaska or Hawaii. For me, the choice wasn't hard."

She smiled, "So now, you're sort of migrating through here."

"Yes, I guess you could say that."

"Will you two excuse me?" Kim said, "I've got to find Felix."

The women talked a bit of agency business for a minute while I studied Kiri Marie. She was Maori, but her facial features showed signs of Caucasian blood, the nose and mouth perfectly defined. Her hair hung to her shoulders and she wore full bangs, giving her the look of a South Seas Cleopatra.

"Are you originally from Auckland?" I asked when Kim left.

"No, I was born in Matari Bay, near the Bay of Islands. Do you know it?"

"I'm sorry to say I haven't been out of the city." We stood and talked for awhile, then found a place on the floor to sit.

"Where are you staying?" she asked.

"I'm renting a room in Ponsonby."

"I live in Herne Bay. We're neighbors."

"Great! Can I come over and borrow a cup of sugar from you sometime? Or is your husband the jealous type?"

"I'm divorced, living alone, with my two sons. What about you?"

"Same boat, without the kids as crew."

"I never thought of them as crew," she laughed.

"Sure. Sign them up. I'll help you do it. I used to lie and brag for Uncle Sam's Navy, maybe I can sell them on how great it is to pick up clothes and wash dishes."

"If you can do that with my kids, you can move in."

We joked on for awhile, until a very drunk Felix started ranting accusations against Kim.

"I've had enough party," Kiri said, "can I give you a lift home?"

Chapter Six
A Polynesian Island Princess

As the summer holidays approached, hat sales picked up and by mid-December I was well ahead of the game and ready for a Friday night out when Kelly invited me to a nearby pub. Inside the Lion and Rose, Christmas decorations hung from the ceiling over a clientele of smartly dressed office workers and young professionals doing their holiday drinking early to avoid the last minute rush. Before long, Kelly's ex-wife showed up and sat at our table. We talked for awhile, but when they started rehashing their past Christmas fun times, I got up to watch the dart game.

On my way, I saw two attractive women sitting at a table along one wall. The one that looked like Cleopatra waved to me. Kiri! I hadn't seen her since the night she dropped me home after the party. She had given me her phone number and I called a few times, but no one answered, so I thought she had given me a bogus number and threw it away. I walked over to her table.

"Hello Kiri," I said, "Merry Christmas."

"Hello, Max. What a nice surprise to see you. Are you alone?"

"Yes. I came with a friend, but he got lucky and met his match."

"Well, then join us. Cecily, this is Max."

"Hello, Max."

I turned to Kiri, "How have you been, busy?"

"Yes, actually. Though not with work. I've been in Wellington on a private matter for the past three weeks. I just got back yesterday. This is my first night out in a while. How about you?"

I told her what little I had been up to for the past few weeks.

"Except for making money, your life has been as boring as mine," she laughed, "let's hope our luck changes. Cheers."

Mine has already, I thought. We nattered on for awhile before I asked, "Do you girls like to dance?"

"Love to," Kiri said, "come with us."

We left the pub and got into the front seat of Kiri's Holden, a sort of Australian Chevy and started off. "My mom says I should get a different car. 'Holdens are Maori cars,' she says. 'Mom,' I tell her, 'look at me,' " she laughed.

We went to a downtown disco where the music was continuous and the three of us danced together for a couple of hours. When we left, Kiri took Cecily home first, then drove towards Ponsonby.

"I called you a couple of times while you were gone," I said.

"Then we're even. I wanted to call you before I left to tell you I'd be away for a month but didn't have your number."

"I'll write it down for you when we stop."

"If you want to do that at my house we could have some coffee? Or are you too tired? My kids are away."

"I'm wide awake."

Her house sat on a hill side overlooking the harbor bridge and Westhaven Marina. In the living room were two, overstuffed chairs which faced the bay view front window. She put the coffee fixings on the telephone table between them and we sat down. "You can write your phone number in here," she handed me an address book and a ball pen. I did so and while she mixed her coffee, I glanced at her telephone and copied the number onto my wrist.

I put the book and pen on the table and picked up my cup of coffee.

"Do you need the light, anymore?" she asked.

"No, I guess not."

She got up, switched off the light and adjusted the door so that a beam glanced through from the hallway, then returned to her chair. "It's a relaxing view in the dark, isn't it?" she said. The lights from the harbor, the bridge and the cars crossing could be plainly seen through the window. "That was good fun dancing tonight. Thanks for asking me. I love to dance but most guys don't."

"It's good for your blood circulation."

"You don't drink, do you?" she asked.

"No."

"Any particular reason?"

"It's not good for my social circulation."

She laughed, "Anyway, I like it. It's fun to go out with someone who is not trying to pound drinks into me so they can get my knickers off. Why do men think they have to get a woman drunk before she'll go to bed with them? Are they insecure?"

"Beat's me, Kiri. I'm aware of the theory but haven't found the logic behind it." I didn't mention that it used to be part of my m.o.. "Maybe it came from the movie line that went, 'You got me drunk and took advantage of me.' It was never said by a man. You didn't drink much, tonight. Afraid I might try and take advantage of you?"

"I never have more than two. I like to be awake when I'm being taken advantage of. Besides, dancing makes me randier than drinking does. Come, let's look at the view." She walked over to the window and stood looking out.

I followed and as I came close she turned, put her arms around my neck and kissed me hard. I held tight for a few breathless seconds as we sunk onto the window settee. She was a hang-up free lover who enjoyed being teased and sat with her back to the window and one foot on the settee so that her dress fell to her lap. We kissed and I stroked her long thighs. After awhile she got up, took my hand and led me into her bedroom.

When I awoke the next morning, she was lying next to me, her eyes open, "Good morning," she said.

"Hello."

"I was watching you for a few minutes before you woke and noticed some numbers on your wrist. At first I imagined that you were an escaped something-or-other and became somewhat anxious. Then I felt sorry for you. Poor man. A fugitive. When you moved, I saw the entire series. It took me a few minutes before I realized it was my phone number. What on earth is it doing on your wrist?" She laughed.

I wasn't fully alert yet, "I had it tattooed there," was all I could manage.

"I don't believe you. Let me see your arm." She grabbed for me and we started wrestling, laughing all the time. In a few minutes the "tattoo" was forgotten as we began our day with a bang.

Reality returned with a phone call from her mother saying that she was bringing Kiri's kids home. I studied her while she talked on the phone. It was the first time I'd seen her in daylight. No tan lines on her body, she stayed Polynesian brown all year round and used no face makeup. I was in love.

"Call me in a couple of days," she said at the door, "my number's on your left wrist. And it better be there the next time I see you." She kissed me, patted me on the butt and sent me home.

A few days later she had me over for tea, the meal, and I met her kids, very active boys aged five and seven. But they minded Kiri and went to bed on time. Afterwards, we sat in the front room, talking over coffee. "My boys will spend New Year's week with their father," she said, "so I'm going to visit my grandmother's tribe in Matari Bay. Would you like to go with me? I could use some help driving and you can see how Maoris really live."

"That sounds fun, but I don't know how long I could stay."

"Stay as long as you like. There's nothing to do here in Auckland, all the businesses close up for the month of January."

"I'd love to." What was I stalling for?

"Kim and Felix live near Whangarei, we can stop and see them along the way."

Hat sales kept me punching holes in leather and Kiri had a full modeling schedule, but we found time for a dinner date in town a couple of days before Christmas. We met at The Steak and I, an intimate, second-floor restaurant near the ad agency. She sat at a corner table, lit only by a candle in a wine bottle. Our warm greetings were stifled in a few seconds by a kiss.

"Seems longer than a week since I've seen you," she said.

"I missed you, too."

We brought each other up to date during dinner. "This week has really been hectic," she said, "the agency is trying to get as much work done as possible before the country shuts down for the holidays."

"That matches my objective."

"Well, it'll all be done with on Christmas Eve. Then, on Christmas Day the boy's father will come over for dinner. We're not enemies, Max, and the boys need him."

"I understand."

"What are you going to do for Christmas?"

"Nothing special."

"I hope you won't be lonely."

"Actually, Christ's birthday doesn't mean any more to me than Buddha's or Mohammed's. I take them all off if I can."

"You're not Christian?"

"No, though I was drafted by them while still a baby and given rations of guilt through twelve years of parochial school."

"What happened?"

"I decided that there were some major issues I couldn't resolve and became disillusioned with religions that don't believe in life after birth."

"Are you an atheist?"

"No, but I keep my theology simple. There is a God and I'm not It."

"I thought you were going to say 'Him.' "

I laughed, "I know. I read your mind and chose the safe pronoun. What about you? What religion do you follow?"

"Why don't you read my mind?" she teased.

"I am, but there I'm getting mixed signals."

"Well, right or wrong, I play the Christmas game for my kids, but I don't really believe it. I follow the old Maori religion. Are you surprised?"

"No. I've met Hawaiians and Fijians who didn't really 'convert.' Hawaii has a fire goddess and Fiji has a kava God, both with a lot of followers."

"The Maori God is one of fertility, maybe I'll convert you when we go to Matari Bay. That's still on, isn't it?"

"You bet, I've already had my loin-cloths cleaned and pressed."

"Really? Let's go to your place and see them."

A week later, she picked me up in the morning and we headed north. Her Holden's tires hummed their way across the metal grating of the harbor bridge. Then she hummed as we drove through the north shore suburbs, singing a few words under her breath.

"There's a favorite singer in Hawaii whose name is 'Myrtle K. Hilo, The Singing Cab Driver.' She used to sing Hawaiian songs to her fares and then started cutting records."

"Along with knitting and crossword puzzles, singing is a cab drivers pastime. I did it all the time when I drove a taxi in Wellington."

"You drove a taxi?"

"Only for a year when I was first married. Do you like to sing?"

"Yes, especially while driving."

"What songs do you like?"

I thought for a few seconds, "Do you know 'Hey, There?' It's got some two-part harmony. 'Hey there, you with the stars in your eyes.' "

Clear, New Zealand days are postcard perfect. Sheep looked like golf balls on the mid-distance, green hills. Cattle stood motionless as paintings in the lower meadows. The biggest roadside activity went on at the fruit and veggie stands where we stocked up on peaches, oranges, nectarines. We stopped in a Whangarei pub for a meal and arrived at Matari Bay in the last minutes of the long, evening twilight. It was surrounded by low hills and after a few minutes of bending curves, Kiri pulled up in front of a small cabin.

"This is it, Max. Here's where you change from a *pakeha* into a Maori. Bring your loin cloth."

I unpacked the car while she opened the house. It was too dark to see anything except for a couple of flickering lights a mile or so in the distance and a thousand stars twinkling overhead.

The cabin, or *bach* pronounced batch, was a timber, single-wall box with a partition separating the kitchen from the bedroom. We made some coffee on the Primus stove and sat around the roughly hewn table in the low light of a hurricane lamp.

"I planned to get here late so we wouldn't have to meet the relatives until tomorrow. They would have insisted we stay up and party. I wanted you for myself, tonight. Besides, there'll be heaps of questions about my divorce settlement. I don't mind, it's just that I'll have better answers tomorrow."

"Oh," was all I could think of to say. We'd never talked about her marital status.

"That's what I went to Wellington for. He got the apartment in town and I ended up with the farm. It seemed a better place to bring up the boys. It's a nice little farm, with fruit trees, a veggie garden and space to raise animals."

"Have you ever farmed before?" I asked.

"Not a whole lot. We lived there for a few months when we bought it, raised some table vegetables, kept some chooks."

"What are 'chooks?' "

"Chickens. Haven't you ever done any farming?"

"Sure, on Maui for two years. I took care of a 50 acre ranch with twenty head of cattle, two pigs, four chickens, two dogs, and from five to fifteen cats, depending on the season."

"Really?"

"No joke. It was a sort of experiment to see if I could live off the land and an unemployment check, or dole as you call it."

"My place is only an hour from Wellington so I'll be able to take assignments there. Farming doesn't use all of one's time."

"That's true. It's an enjoyable life when your tractor payment is in the bank."

She laughed, "I don't think I'll get a tractor. Maybe just a new hoe."

The sun's rays probing through the windows at seven am woke me, so I got up and made a billy of tea and took it to the bedroom. Kiri awoke and we sat in bed, wordlessly drinking tea.

"Now, I'm ready for today," she said when she poured her second cup.

"I'm still a half tank low," I said.

"Come, let's go to my sister's for breakfast."

The cabin sat on a hillside a few hundred feet above the southern end of the small bay and the view stood out in stark relief in the bright sunlight. A mile away, the shoreline formed a crescent shaped beach where a dozen canoes rested on the sand near the mouth of a small stream. Spires of smoke poked through the trees behind the beach though I could see no houses in the thick foliage.

"My tribe has lived here forever," she told me as we drove down towards the village, "It's not like an American Indian reservation."

The road led through the trees to the edge of a collection of assorted, one-story houses. We got out and walked along a lane between modest timber homes and newer ones of cinder block, each with a small yard, garden and chooks pecking and scratching in the ground. Dogs were everywhere and several people were outside polishing cars, pulling weeds. One tall, elderly woman stood in a yard, hands tucked into the pockets of a long, wool coat, looking down and shaking her head so that the red tassel on her knit cap bobbled around.

"Hello, Queenie," Kiri called.

The woman looked up at us, "Hello, Kiri! I was wondering if I would see you this New Year."

We walked over to her, "Queenie, this is my friend, Max. He's from America."

"Do you know anything about washing machines, Max?" Queenie asked as she pointed to an old wringer washer sitting upside down on a blanket.

"Only that they work better when they are turned over," I said, feeling that Queenie knew a lot about them.

An old man came down the back steps of the house carrying a dish pan of steaming water. He set it near the half stripped machine and stuck the end of a hose into the water. After a few minutes of softening, he tried to push a fitting into it, but the hose didn't stretch.

"He won't get it on," Queenie laughed, "he's been at it all morning, ha ha."

The man looked up at us, and grinned with the embarrassment of a man having a hard time.

"Poor guy," I said to Kiri when we left.

"Yes, but her boyfriends are not the only ones she pecks on. About six months ago, she was out in her fishing canoe when a Japanese trawler came to close to suit her and she drove them off with shots from her twenty-two rifle. She's a no-nonsense woman."

"That's what queens are for, but by the time they reach her age they have cannons and ships, not rifles and fourteen-foot boats."

"This is her 'navy,' " Kiri said, "she goes out fishing every day and she's well past sixty."

We walked along the shore for a few minutes, the only humans in sight, though a couple of dogs trailed us. The loudest sound came from our footsteps in the sand.

"Man, this is really peaceful," I said.

"Yes it is, but then New Zealand has a heap of peaceful places, and lots of noisy ones too. Like the white house up on that hill. The one in the clearing."

"With all the cars parked in the yard?"

"That's my sister Cheryl's. She's the family hostess for New Years. Listen."

From the house came the deep voice of Maori singer John Rowles crooning his hit tune, "Cheryl Moana Marie."

"She ruins her stereo every New Years," Kiri said, "let's go help her."

We returned to the car and drove up the hillside to the modern, timber house. There, John belted out his song so loudly he raised a thin aura of dust over the roof and porch. Inside, voices shouted above the 200 watt volume. As we climbed the steps to the porch, the song ended but the voices hadn't noticed. Kiri opened the door and looked in, "Happy New Year," she yelled.

"Halloo, everyone! It's Kiri," someone roared, and she disappeared inside amid greetings and laughter. I timidly followed a few seconds later. She was the center of a hugging, kissing, greeting mob — as a clan member you get plenty of relatives. The gushing reunion would have gone on much longer but she looked around and saw me pretending to be invisible.

"Just a minute, everyone," she said, "I want to introduce you to my American friend, Max."

In quick succession, I met a Trevor, Cam, Robbie, Nigel, Florence, Rose, Tina and Cheryl.

"Happy New Year, Max," Cheryl said, "What'll you drink?"

"A glass of L&P if you've got it."

"What would you like in it?" she asked.

"Just some ice cubes for a start, thanks."

"Right," she left for the kitchen.

"Come over here, Max, I want you to meet my mother."

"Uh, sure thing." Sure thing?

"Mother, this is Max."

Meeting a girlfriend's mother is always risky business. Even when they're pleasant, you know you're being sized up. The usual man fears run through your mind. Is my fly open? Are my nails clean? Is my laugh a little high pitched casting doubts on my masculinity? If you grin too much, you're taken for an idiot. If you stay straight faced, she'll guess that you're a sourpuss, introvert or hungover. Take your pick. But Kiri's socially smooth mother made it easy.

"Hello, Max. Well, you've come a long way to meet my Kiri, haven't you?"

"Yes, ma'am."

"Well, sit here for awhile and tell me if it was worth it."

I sat next to her on the couch. Around us, the party got back on track as someone flipped the stack of records over and two couples started dancing. Kiri began talking with people and Cheryl brought me a drink. Mum began with the usual leader, "So, how does New

Zealand compare with America? A bit backward, I'd guess," she laughed.

"Except for being colder, it's a lot like Hawaii, that's my home state, now."

"Then you should be used to this sort of Polynesian bash."

"Yes, I am. But then, my mother's family used to have week-long, holiday parties with relatives coming from all over."

Her antenna went up, "Please, tell me about them."

"My mother's side is Spanish, originally from New Mexico, but the war shuffled everyone around and many ended up in California. My aunt's house in Los Angeles became the holiday gathering place. Probably since she had the largest family, six sons and two daughters."

She looked pleased by the numbers of my extended family and gently probed to find out more about me. Awhile later, Kiri rescued me, "C'mon Max, you must be hungry."

"Yes," said Mum, "You get something to eat. You'll need your energy to see the New Year in."

In the kitchen I anticipated Kiri's question, "Your mother seems very nice."

"She used to embarrass my dates with, 'when are you getting married,' " she laughed, "did she ask you?"

"No. If she does, what should I say?"

"That's your problem," she smiled.

"Well, what did the other dates say?"

"When Kiri says yes," she lifted the last word slightly, pleased with her little entrapment trick. Later, we drove back to the bach where we made soft, sensuous, afternoon love after which Kiri fell asleep with her arms around me. "It doesn't get much better than this," whispered a voice inside my head, "cruising around the country with an attractive, vibrant woman who says she likes you more than average. I better keep my feelings at bay for awhile. She's too easy to love."

We returned at eight to find the party's pace hadn't slowed down. A few of the afternoon players slept in chairs and on the couch but the slack was taken up by a new batch of replacements. The house shook under their energy when they danced to a whoop and holler tune called "Mexican Joe." Then suddenly it was the New Year and everyone seemed to double their efforts to have fun. Kiri took my hand and led me out the front door, "I want to show you something," she said.

She got a flashlight from her car and we walked down the road for about a quarter-mile where she turned onto a narrow path which led to a door at the base of what appeared to be a rounded mound of earth about twelve-feet high. Kiri opened it and we went into at bare, circular room about thirty-feet across. Pale moonlight drifting through narrow windows placed high along the wall all around illuminated the surroundings enough to push my senses back a century or so.

"This is the *pa*," she said, "it was the defense center in the old days but now it's the place where tribal decisions are made. Look at the roof beam." She played the flashlight along a wide rafter with a sweeping geometric design carved from end to end. "Every tribe has its own motif that holds its *mana*, or power. When you're underneath the beam, this power flows through you."

She turned off the flashlight and set it down, then slipped out of her shoes and walked to the center of the room where a thick, pandanus mat lay on the floor. I took my boots off and walked over to her, then looked up to make sure we were directly under the beam. I nuzzled her neck and shoulders. She leaned her head forward, "Unzip me, please." Whether it was because of the mana, the setting, or the brown, sensuous woman I was undressing, my hands fumbled with those little hooks and eyes. She stood still while her clothes fell to the floor, then stepped out of them and began unbuttoning my shirt. When she slid my pants down, my dick bounced around like a spring toy. "The power is going into you already," she said. It was powerful all right. We squirmed, lolled, laughed, humped, and tickled each other like pagans are reputed to do. At one point I said, "I love you, Kiri." I don't know what compelled me to say that. I hadn't been drinking. She looked into my face, "I love you too, Max."

On New Year's we went to Cheryl's for dinner. The party hadn't thinned out but it was quieter and hangover clouds hovered over a few heads, but not Mum's. "So, you two finally roused yourselves. This mob around here is bloody useless," she laughed. "Look at them. I've been up since seven."

It was my turn to size her up as a potential mother-in-law. Up at seven in a cajoling spirit, I thought, not a good sign unless she lives far away. But I had to give her a few points for tagging an honest chuckle onto most of her digs. Maori women are not wimps. Until the early 1900's, their favourite facial adornment was a "moko," an intricate, fine line tattoo which covered the entire chin, sometimes going into the cheeks. The one-color design was similar to the roof beam carvings. You can bet these ladies didn't get this done at Painless Nell's Tattoo Parlor. According to their old enemies, the British Army, Maori men are among the best fighters in the world. Their system of static defense with the pa and its outlying forts held the Redcoats back more than once. This toughness allowed them to cut an honourable peace treaty and avoid the genocidal fate of the American Indians or Australian aborigines. Yet for all the rude talk and tipsy roughhousing among themselves, none was directed at me. They acted as though they always have a token pakeha who drinks only L&P at their New Year's celebration.

The next morning we packed up, then drove to Cheryl's for breakfast. In the yard, a couple of her brothers worked on a car. Inside, Mum sat at the table while Cheryl cooked.

"So, you're going back to Auckland today, Kiri," Mum said.

"Not directly. We're going to stop and see some friends along the way for a day or so."

"When will you go to your place in Wellington?" Cheryl asked.

"About the middle of March, I think."

"Are you going, too, Max?" Mum asked.

"Oh, mother," Kiri rolled her eyes, "You'll find Mum is quite outspoken."

We left Matari Bay that morning and headed south, not talking much for a couple of hours. I closed my eyes and dozed while listening to the "Farm Issue" being debated in my head. It was really more like a soft sell since the logical side of the table agreed with the emotional on most of the points. The buzzwords were "Gentleman Farmer" and "Country Gentleman". Though I'd done a bit of farming on Maui, my friends and lifestyle there more resembled "The Gentleman Sharecroppers of Pakalolo Road," rustic as a *Whole Earth* catalog hanging in an outhouse. Gentleman Farmer was an American who owned several miles of Central California, employed hundreds of wetbacks to whom he was a kindly, but firm, father figure. His wife looked like Barbara Stanwyck or Nancy Reagan. He seems constantly faced with a moral dilemma, "Should I sell to the Navy for their missile range and retire to Monaco or keep the family spread and the tax-free, three million dollars a year subsidy?"

Country Gentleman, Esq. is the English version. He lives in a cold house with a wife who spends her considerable leisure time writing poetry and repairing cast-off clothes to give to their poor tenants. He's most often seen riding his horse or walking along the lanes. He wears a jaunty hat with a feather, a tweed coat with elbow patches and woolen trousers tucked into lace top boots. He does his brooding at home, so the public sees the Contented Squire, favourite pipe tucked into the corner of his smiling mouth, engraved shotgun tucked under his arm — the master of all he surveys.

The New Zealand version was not yet clear to me. So far it was a hatless man in a sleeveless singlet, short pants and knee length gumboots. He most often had a dog with him that he yelled directions at and constantly threatened to harm. Maybe being a Kiwi sheep-counter wouldn't be so bad. If I got a visa extension I could try it for a few months, that is if Kiri wanted me to move in with her.

"You're looking very serious," she said.

"I was just thinking it was time for lunch."

"We'll be in Whangarei soon. I know a great little pub by the marina."

Whangarei is a small, hilly city straddling a river which connects it to the sea, several miles west. Fishing boats and yachts easily navigate to the Town Basin, and a few dozen small craft were moored to pilings and anchored near a low bridge. From there, we drove west along the north bank road, hemmed by steep hills on one side and marine chandleries and repair shops on the other. Kiri pulled up at The Oar House, a two story house that had been converted into a trendy riverfront pub. There were more cars in the parking lot than I had seen in town. We sat at a window table and recapped our family visit during the meal. She explained some of the relationships to me.

"Did you enjoy yourself?" she asked.

"Yes, really. I felt easy all the time, except for sometimes with Mum."

"She likes to tease," Kiri smiled, "By the way, you didn't answer her."

"You like to tease, as well," I nimbly evaded.

"I'm my mother's daughter."

I looked absently out the window, trying to think of another tricky answer in case she repeated the question. I could see her out of the corner of my eye, her elbows on the table, chin resting on her knuckles, gaze locked onto my head trying to see inside. Then, through the window, I saw Mike walking past. I rapped on the window but he didn't hear and kept going. "Excuse me a minute, I've seen an old friend."

"Yoo-hoo, Mike," I called when I got outside.

His planter's hat made a 180 degree turn, "Hey, Max!"

We exchanged "I'll be darneds" then I said, "C'mon in for a drink."

I introduced Kiri to Mike when we sat down and then asked, "How long have you been here, Mike?"

"For a couple of months. Didn't you get my letter? I sent it to Poste Restante, Auckland."

"No, but then I haven't checked Poste Restante since I got a house address."

"Well, I sailed down with Pere about a month after you and have been hanging around here since."

"Did you get an apartment?"

"No, but I don't live on *Simba* anymore. I'm staying on a trimaran, the owner's name is Harold. Did you meet him in Fiji?"

I shook my head. We rapped for awhile and brought each other up to date, then I asked him, "What's your plan?"

"I'll hang around until April then sail with Harold to Fiji. And you?"

Kiri shifted her interested eyes to my face, "I'm not sure, yet."

"Where are you staying tonight?"

"We haven't decided," I said.

"We've got plenty of room on the boat, come on down and have a look."

We drove the short distance to Oram's Boatyard where Mike led us along the dock and onto a white trimaran. He showed us through the boat.

"You guys can sleep here, if you want," he said as we looked into the forward cabin.

Kiri indicated her disapproval with a quick flash of her eyes. I glanced up to see a man riding a small bicycle along the wooden dock towards us. His white bell-bottom pants flapped in the breeze, the brim of his canvas hat bent up in front like a Pony Express rider, a reddish blond, handlebar mustache completed the likeness. He parked the bike and came on board toting a small knapsack.

"Hi, Harold. This is Max and Kiri. He's a friend of mine from Fiji."

"Hello Max, Kiri, welcome aboard *Seabird*," we shook hands, "Excuse me a minute, I've got to put something on ice." He crossed the deck and went down the ladder into the aft cabin, quiet and nimble as a ship's cat. Not bad, I thought, for a guy who's age was hovering around the half-century mark. But then he was slim as a tire iron, the shape of most budget yachties after a few voyages on rice and canned goods. When he came on deck, we settled in the cockpit.

"Harold was delivering a boat to Whangarei when you were in Fiji," Mike said to me.

"How long did it take you," I asked.

"Thirty days," Harold said.

"Isn't that kind of long?"

"I suppose so, but some days were so pretty that I didn't raise a sail, just drifted. Days at sea are special to me, I milk all the pleasure I can out of them," he laughed, "though the owner got a little anxious."

"Did you get paid for that?"

"Six hundred dollars plus an air ticket back to Fiji. I had to return and sail my boat here. That voyage took nine days, there was a lot of wind."

"Harold's been cruising the Pacific for a long time," Mike said.

"About fourteen years," Harold added, "and no intention of living on the land again."

We touched on a few subjects and Harold must have liked the company since he went below and brought up a jug of chilled wine and a thermos of hot coffee to fuel the conversation. Like most yachties, he readily talked about his voyages which ranged from Panama to Australia on both sides of the Equator. He amazed me, not only his adventures — he had been shipwrecked twice, the second time on lonely Raoul Island where he lived for two months with the New Zealand crew manning the navigation station there — but also his attitude. "Sailing puts you into the now," he said, "it's life at its purest. When I first started I used to worry what I would do when I got to another port. Then I decided it was useless to sweat over the future when I still had to get there."

"The life seems to agree with you," Kiri said.

"It better," he said, "it's the only one I know."

His humourous storytelling filled my head with scenes of cruising adventure. I had practically forgotten about sailing over the past couple of months. We visited for a couple of hours then Kiri and I left to get a room at a hotel in town. I couldn't hold my newly raised enthusiasm down and at dinner that night, bored Kiri with more sea stories. She didn't think much of ocean living but listened politely. Later in bed, the most vulnerable time, she asked would I go cruising again if I had the chance. I didn't answer.

The next day we drove to Kim and Felix's farm, arriving in the early afternoon at their dirt driveway. The farmhouse nested among soft, rolling hills a quarter-mile from the road. As we pulled up, Kim came out on the porch. I half-way expected to see her dressed in coveralls and a flour-sack shirt, instead, she wore cream colored, linen slacks and a sheer, white, long sleeve blouse. She held a glass of wine in one hand, waving with the other, "Hello, you two! I'm so glad you could come." As we came up to her, she gave both of us a European, cheek-kiss and whispered, "Hello, Lover," when she delivered mine. "Come inside. We've been waiting lunch for you."

Inside, Felix greeted me cordially, which surprised me since we didn't speak at all, before. He wore his Landed Gentry lounge suit, baggy pants and a silk trimmed, smoking jacket, a paisley cravat covered his throat, a smooth, briar pipe filled his left hand. "Well, let's sit down to lunch," he said. Kiri kept the words flowing as she told them the details our holiday in Matari, briefly mentioning the stopover in Whangarei.

Kim served a large country meal of lamb, mashed potatoes, gravy, green vegetables, and home made cheesecake. "I bet you like cheesecake, don't you Max?" she said with a smile.

"How'd you know?"

"Have you tried Kiri's Pavlova, yet?"

"I might have, describe it to me."

"Don't you know what Pavlova is?"

"Sounds like the Russian scientist who experimented on his dog, but local words could mean anything. In Hawaii, hors d'oerves are called pupus."

The women laughed but Felix let it go by.

"Pavlova is a pastry, silly," Kim said, then started giggling again, "Is that really true about Hawaii?"

"Yes, but it's the only state with that usage. Don't ask for them in Texas."

"Oh, that's funny. We must go to Hawaii, Felix."

"Yes, well, first Max and I will go into the front room while you girls clean up."

In the living room he settled into an overstuffed chair and propped his feet on an ottoman. I sat on the matching sofa which nearly swallowed me up. Felix wore glasses all the time I'd been there, he never wore glasses at the theater. I wondered if they were a prop, like the pipe he held. It hadn't once been lit though it had been exchanged for a deep curved clay, one with a large bowl from the rack of pipes sitting next to a small, smoked-glass humidor.

"It must have been exciting to see your sailing friend again," he said.

"Yes, it was."

"I'm a sailor, myself, you know."

"No I didn't," I fibbed.

"Yes, I sometimes race on a friend's yacht. I learned to sail while attending university in Canada. I thought I could get more work in advertising and films if I knew how. I took an equestrian course for the same reason, as well. Do you ride?

"Yes, motorcycles," I answered.

"No, I mean horseback riding," he looked over at me as though he expected to see the word "equestrian" plastered on the wall about a foot over my head.

"I tried, and though I could kick-start a horse, I couldn't stop it when I wanted, so I decided to break my bones on a two-wheeler. Do you ride motorcycles?"

"No. The image wasn't exactly what I was after, besides, horseback riding is much more useful for rural life. I have even been toying with the idea of raising horses."

I had trouble picturing him in the saddle. He looked more like a crooning cowboy than a wrangler and I'd bet that behind the smug expression his Anglophilia created visions of him riding on a fox hunt in a brilliant red and white costume. Tally ho, old chap. The women joined us and we went for a tour of the farm. Kim showed us her garden plot and compulsively pulled a couple of weeds.

"You need some chooks to help keep your garden clean," I said.

"Listen to him, Kiri," she laughed, "two days in the country and he knows all about it."

"Well, he told me he punched-up cows, or something like that, in Hawaii. He might have hidden talents."

"Or it could be a lot of bull," Kim added. They laughed together at this repartee as only friends can.

"Tell the truth, Max."

"I'm not pushing your leg," I said, determined to get in on the humour.

"How can you manage cattle if you can't ride?," asked Felix The Unmasker.

"I ran them down Indian style, on foot. Actually, I trained them to come to the corral when I beat on a hubcap, that meant I was going to feed them grain. Pavlova's cows, you might say. Hawaiian scientific farming."

"He might be a good hand to have on your farm, Kiri," Kim said with a mischievous glance at me. Good shot Kim, you handed the question ball back to Kiri for me.

That evening I sat alone on the porch watching the sky's colors changing through a two-hour twilight. I had never lived this far from the Equator and thought about how it might be to live even further south, say in Wellington. I couldn't yet bring myself to precisely define my feelings toward Kiri. Why not? That's what confused me. There was no doubt I loved her, but how much?

Later, in bed, we lay relaxed in each other's arms, listening to the night sounds around the quiet house. The world hadn't stopped but it sure slowed down. Then her whisper cut the silence, "Would you like to move to Wellington with me? You don't need to answer now. Think it over."

"I've already thought it over. I'd love to."

We left for Auckland the next morning after breakfast, and avoided saying anything about the Big Decision until we were rolling along the highway.

"Did you mean what you said last night?" Kiri asked.

"I wouldn't kid you about a question like that."

"No, but you could have changed your mind."

"Kiri, you've been on my mind since I met you, I can't change it overnight. I want to stay with you, I just didn't feel it was my place to bring it up."

"I love you, Max," she reached over and squeezed my hand. "Here's my plans. I'm going to stay in Auckland until the middle of March, then move to Wellie. That's two and a half months from now. How does that sound to you?"

"I think that'll work. My second, three-month visa comes up next week, that will see me to April, then I'll try for another one. The Immigration Department seems pretty liberal with them." As we drove to the city, we projected our plans and imagined our life of wedded bliss without the bothersome vows.

Kiri thought it best to live separately in Auckland which fit my feelings since the city seemed more like a middle-class trap than the setting for a honeymoon fantasy. But we dated a lot and took her boys on weekend trips to Gray's boat and camping on the black sand beach on the western side of the Auckland isthmus. I brought a bag full of sand back and packed it into a small casting box I made in Kelly's back yard. Then I bought a slab of wax and made a sand candle, complete with driftwood and fern leaves. I gave it to Kiri as a gift and a few days later she had orders for more from her friends at work. I filled that order, made a dozen more and took them to the city's boutiques and sold them in a day. I put on my candlemaker's hat and went into production.

One morning a few weeks later, when I had sold to most of the shops and my shoulders ached from humping lumps of wax and sand around town, I watched a street peddler setting up his jewelry tray on Queen Street.

"Pardon me," I said, "can you tell me what the rules are for selling on the street, like you are?"

He looked at me while he decided that I wasn't a cop, not with an American accent and a backpack full of something heavy. "Well, you can't be right on the footpath. You've got to find a doorway or the coppers will move you."

"Thanks a lot."

"Sure thing," he smiled, "good luck."

At Whitcolls Stationery store nearby I bought a marking pen and poster board, then went outside to a blind doorway of the store and unpacked the candles. I arranged them and wrote "Sandtorches $10" on the poster. It was next to a busy bus stop and by the time the lunch rush ended at one I'd sold all the candles. Now I had a "corner" and showed up every day, set up my display box and sign, and turned $100.

I made friends with Phil, the guy who gave me the basic rule of street selling, and went for coffee to his "office" directly across from his corner in an old, ten story building with a light shaft in the center and the offices paned in glass from the waist up. He had hung oriental tapestries, and batiks over these windows and decorated the room randomly with Asian paintings, carvings, bronze castings and bells. On the floor, next to the pile of cushions, sat boxes full of colorful beads.

"Those are the beads I'm using now. I shipped them from Africa."

"You've really been around, haven't you?"

"I left New Zealand when I was eighteen and managed to stay away for five years. I've made a few trips to Asia since. It's really difficult for Kiwis to travel since the government won't let us take more than a couple of thousand dollars out of the country."

"How did you manage it, then?"

"By buying in one country and selling in another. Nothing illegal. I made as much money on legal imports without the risk of being murdered. Like these beads. I paid twenty dollars for the box full and have ten boxes. As handicrafts, they come in duty free. I'll make more than a thousand dollars from that box," he smiled, "and it's income tax-free."

I visited Phil several times and learned more about life on the road. His blonde, curly hair and smiling, baby face concealed a guy who studied karate in a Japanese prison, and dodged bullets in Nepal while cruising the hippie trail trading for beads, magic carpets and gemstones.

One afternoon, we sat talking in his office. "You ought to get into selling jewelry, Max. You can make as much with one handful as one pack full of candles."

"Maybe so, except there's lots of street guys peddling it, and only one candleman."

"Yes, but you've got to know what's going to be the next, big seller and have a lot of it on hand, like the puka shell necklace you're wearing. Did you get that in Fiji?"

"No, this was made on Maui."

"I had some from Fiji until last week, when I sold out. They cost seventy cents and I sell them for ten dollars, about twenty necklaces a day. The only place I found them was a small island named Motoriki. I brought one hundred back and the villagers sent me a couple hundred more. Then last month they started selling. If you're going back to Fiji, let me know."

But my course lay in the opposite direction and the date for the Wellington move drew near. A week before Kiri's departure we had dinner together at her house. Afterwards, when the kids were tucked in, we sat in the darkened living room and watched the harbor view. For her own reasons, Kiri wanted me to wait in Auckland for a couple of weeks after she left before following her to the farm. My not knowing why had opened a debate in my mind. Will she be saying good-bye to her old lovers? Or, even, hello? Was it to avoid snoopy neighbors or prying family? Perhaps her parental instinct said it would "be best for the kids." But the Relationship Committee in my head avoided the real question. Had she cooled on the idea?

"This time next week, I'll have to color you gone. I'm going to miss you."

"It won't be long, darling, only for a few weeks."

I could hear pencils scratching in my head as the Committee took notes. "Darling," she never called us that before. "A few weeks? I thought you said, two weeks."

"Look, darling, it's a big change for me. Let me get settled in for a week, then I'll call you, please." In other words, no more questions, please.

I had to admit that the prospect of wintering in Wellington had lost some luster. Friends told me of the cold, wet winds that sweep across the region for days at a time. The sun rises at nine and sets at four, when it comes out at all. "Farm life there is like living in a bowl of porridge," Kelly said, "mud underfoot and clouds overhead." I stayed with Kiri the night before she left and the next morning helped load her car and the rental trailer she towed. We'd expressed ourselves physically during the night leaving us nothing to say. When she started the car, I leaned in and kissed her, "Call me soon, lover."

"I will, darling, in one week."

She drove off and I walked home, feeling more confused than the day I arrived in the country.

Although my visa was good for a few more weeks, I went to the Immigration Department to see about getting another renewal.

"We can't issue another visa to you unless your work category fits in with the country's needs," the poker-faced clerk said to me, "What sort of work do you do?"

"I'm a candle maker."

"Sorry," she sniffed.

"And leather hat fabricator." She was doubly impressed. "Is there no way I can stay in the country, legally?"

"Yes. You can marry a Kiwi girl. NEXT!"

I pondered that solution for the rest of the week, going circular on the idea, hot, cold, tepid. Seems everything in life has a catch. Now, I had to question my love for Kiri, an emotion I hadn't been very good at analyzing in the past but I could no longer let my feelings pull me around by the short hairs. Life gets too messy that way. Then I worried about the phone call. What would she say when I told her about the visa condition? Maybe she'll expect me to propose. "Do you take this candleman to be your lawful wedded hat maker?" I'm sure she's had better offers.

By the time Kiri called me on Sunday night, my thoughts and feelings on the situation tumbled in my mind, tangled as long-sleeve shirts in a tumble dryer.

"Hello, Max, darling," that buzzword again.

"Hello, Lover. Good to hear you. How's everything going?"

"Perfectly. I've got the house in order and the children settled in. I had to do some painting and paperhanging but I've had help. I haven't been alone since I arrived."

"Oh?"

"Well, I mean some family and friends have stopped by to help me or I wouldn't have got this much done. How are things going with you?"

"I went to Immigration to see about another visa —," I stalled.

"And?"

"I either have to leave the country for six months before I can reapply, or I can marry you."

Her turn to stall, "You mean they won't give you one unless you're married to a New Zealander?" How easily she stepped out of the equation.

"That's right," I said.

"That's a major decision, Max, for either of us. I'll have to think it over for a while. You must understand. I'm sure you thought about it over the past few days. Please, give me some time."

The conversation dulled and ended with "I love yous" and a promise to write. I felt better afterwards, especially since she spared me the question, "What do you want to do?" She didn't omit that by accident, I thought, Kiri was a sensitive, caring woman. That's why I wanted to be with her. The mental spin dryer started up again.

Her letter arrived on Thursday. It delicately explained her feelings in a tone that implied that I had proposed to her. I could live with that. Then came her rejection, "...Max, Darling, I've just got my freedom and I'd like to experience it for awhile. This doesn't mean I love you less." Less than who? My ego and id took off on a run, joined by a blend of self pity, resentment and a couple of other unworthy characteristics. By the next morning, my bruised pride simply pouted. I recovered over the next few days, boosted by the gut feeling that the outcome was inevitable and soothed by memories of pleasure that easily outweighed the pain.

That weekend, Mike showed up at my house. He had hitchhiked down to Auckland to buy supplies for *Seabird* and spend a couple of days in town. On Saturday night, Mike, Kelly and I went to a pub.

"The last time I came here with Max," Kelly said, "he left with some gorgeous Maori sheila and I ended up with my ex-wife."

"Is that the one you came to Whangarei with?" Mike asked.

"Yeah. But I don't see her anymore. She had to move to Wellington and I have to leave New Zealand. My visa is finished in about three weeks."

"What are your plans?" Kelly asked.

"I haven't made any."

"Why don't you sail with Harold and me to Fiji?" Mike said.

I thought it over for about ten seconds, looked at him, smiled and said, "Where do I sign?"

Two days after Mike returned to Whangarei, he phoned to say that Harold had accepted me as crew and I should join the boat in a week. I felt like I'd been summoned to serve aboard the space shuttle and visited Phil at his office to tell him the news.

"Do you want to look for that treasure in puka shells while you're there?" he asked.

"Sure, I'm ready for anything."

He got a map of Fiji from a bookshelf and spread it on the floor, "Here's Ovalau island and nearby Motoriki islet. Do you know this area?"

"Yes, I've stayed at a village on Ovalau for two weeks."

"Well, you can get to Motoriki by canoe across this strait. There are three villages on its west side that have these shells. They get them from a sand cay a couple of miles offshore which is said to be nothing but puka shells. I'll front you some money if you'll send necklaces back to me. I'm desperate for them."

He must have been to trust someone he didn't know very well, but I assured him that he would get my best shot. After all, he turned me onto a cache of puka shells, which sold for $25 a necklace in Honolulu. I made plans to buy a few hundred strands for myself then return to Hawaii and make heaps of dough. On the first Sunday in April, I tossed my battered suitcase and newly-made leather backpack into a Whangarei bound motor coach and rode through an end-of-summer day. Clouds piled up a mile high, pierced by shafts of sunlight which spotlighted valleys, houses and the road ahead. It was late afternoon when I arrived in town so I took a room at the hotel where Kiri and I stayed. Tomorrow I would move into a cramped wooden tube.

Chapter Seven
Return to The Coconut Inn

When the year's first wave of Antarctic air arrived Sunday's towering clouds caught up with Monday morning. I walked the mile from the hotel to Oram's boatyard, boosted by gusts of wind that bowled their way over the hilltops and through the narrow, river valley. A cold drizzle washed away any lingering resentments I had against the Immigration Department for their visa refusal, but carrying my impractical suitcase gave me a new gripe.

Seabird was a 35 foot, center cockpit trimaran, with a berth cabin and camping toilet in the forward end of the main hull, and two berths and the galley aft. A dock awning covered the center and as I approached, I could see Mike and Harold sitting beneath it in the cockpit. Steam from the mugs that sat on the table between them rose to mix with the cigarette smoke.

"Good morning, mateys," I said.

"Har, me bucko," Harold said with a Long John Silver twist, "sure 'n it's the long lost mate," he wheezed, "Welcome aboard!"

Mike helped carry my gear down to the spacious, forward cabin, "It's all yours," he said, "we bunk aft."

In the cockpit, Harold said, "Har, and what be the second mate's pleasure? Coffee or tea?"

"Coffee, thanks, Cap'n," I answered in a gruff voice. Next to sailing, I like acting best.

He poured me a cup from a thermos, "Will you be wanting anything in it, sahr?" He opened his eyes wide and the corner of his mouth pulled up.

"Milk and sugar, thanks. I like my coffee like my women, hot, blonde and sweet." Harold laughed and said, in his unaffected voice, "I never heard it that way. Is it the same for tea?"

"I don't know. I just made it up. It's pirate talk."

"I'm glad you're joining us. Mike's seen my act so much he refuses to take a part anymore."

"Well, I'll give you a go. I've seen 'Treasure Island.' "

"Sure, we'll bounce it around again. Now I suppose you want to know our plans. I think we can leave in one week, by then this cold front will have passed. Do you have everything you need?"

"All I have to do is buy a seabag."

"Yeah," Harold laughed, "when I saw your suitcase I thought you were a paying passenger for a minute."

"I'll take you to the sailmaker," Mike said, "he can make you one."

"I like your leather backpack," Harold said, "Where'd you get it?"

"I made it."

"If I buy the leather will you make me one just like it?"

"Sure."

"Good. Then I'll take you to Fiji for free. You'll still have to pay your third of the groceries."

Over the next few stormy days we worked on the boat's "TO DO" list — fix the stove, repair the oarlock, grease the bicycle, polish the sail track, paint this, epoxy that, sew this, rivet that. A boat's service and repair list seems endless. You discover later that it really is. Harold split *Seabird's* demands into two priorities, things that must be done in port and things which can be done while underway. Practically everything could be done at sea since the most exotic piece of equipment was the kerosene fired Primus stove. Small, brass bottomed, hurricane lamps provided the lighting, while a Zenith, Trans-Oceanic receiver made up the communications center. No motor, no power generator.

The skies cleared on Friday and I picked up my new, white canvas seabag.

"Well, Max, I see you've got your duffel," Harold said when he came on board, "Good, 'cause we're leaving Monday. I was just talking with the guys on the fishing boats. The weather's breaking up and there's nothing more in sight."

Later, Poor Richard, a farmer friend of Harold's, pulled up in his battered VW and sold us some of his latest crop of hay. With our senses tuned, attitudes adjusted and appetites refined we headed for the San Pedro Pizza Parlor in Whangarei.

The yachtics had made the restaurant their hangout since it didn't have a liquor license and was too small for the fishermen who preferred the Oar House pub.

"Hello, Harold," the man behind the counter called as we walked in.

"Hey, Nick. How's my paisano?" Harold answered as we sat at the round table in the middle of the room.

Nick came over to our table, "I hear you're leaving, soon."

"Yep, on Monday," Harold said.

"I wish I was going with you."

"Well, hell. Fold up this popcorn stand and let's go. But first, bring us a couple of pizzas and some glasses, we're gonna party."

We settled on pizza ingredients and I ordered a cup of coffee. Harold took a bottle of Mateus wine out of his shoulder bag and Mike pulled out a bottle of beer. When the glasses and coffee arrived, Harold proposed a cheer, "To *Seabird* and her crew." We clinked cup and tumblers and drank.

"I've never been in a toast with a cup of coffee before," Harold said with a grin towards me.

"I haven't been in too many, myself," I said.

"You don't drink?" he asked.

"I did, but I don't bother with it anymore. I don't like the way I feel afterwards."

He nodded like 'I know what you mean' and looked around the room. Guys don't usually prod each other for health records or reasons why they choose to do or not do something. Most men have problems of their own and Harold had seen enough of me to know that I wasn't a crusader of any sort. That's more than I knew about him. Other than his occasional lapses into the Long John Silver persona — which appeared to be controlled, not schizoid — he seemed to be a standard issue, Sea Gypsy, one each, who scuttled around the South Pacific for a living. That night, our table became party central since everyone knew Harold and Mike were leaving and people stopped by for awhile, among them, two lovely lady friends of Mike's.

"What are you going to do in Fiji?" one of them asked me.

"I'm going to make a fortune in puka shell necklaces."

"Is that right?" Harold said.

"Does it sound like a dumb idea?"

"Not if you have the market. A friend of mine did very well in shell jewelry from New Guinea."

"What are your plans for Fiji, Harold?" I asked.

"I don't have any. I'll get there first."

"Maybe you'd like to go to my treasure island. It takes a boat to get there."

"I might."

The next day he brought out the chart of the Fijian Islands and found the location of the sand cay that was reputedly made of puka shells. The description of the area given in the Admiralty *Sailing Directions* read, "the direction and force of the currents here are unpredictable, reaching their peak activity four hours after the moon's transit overhead."

"Har, Matey!" Harold crowed, "It's a regular old beach landing like I used to make with Kidd. Except, this time I'll be taking treasure out rather than burying it and stranding the crew. How about you, Mike? Are you in?"

"Sure," Mike said as he looked over the chart, "why not?"

The puka shell craze swept the crew for about five minutes, a sort of primeval gold fever. “Hey! Seashells with holes in them? That’s like money in the bank!” We even knitted the logic of happenstance to indicate that the treasure hunt was our reason for going to Fiji. Oh well, a dreamy motive for life can’t hurt, especially if it helped ease the decision of what to do next.

Harold spent that night at his girlfriend’s house, Mike went to the riverfront pub to get drunk and sleep in a bed for the last time and I had the boat to myself for the first time. I sat at the galley table drinking cocoa, reading navigation books and listening to the short wave band, trying to tune in WWV, the time-tick station. It was time to get in tune with the wooden tube I called home, to single-up my mental mooring lines.

Monday morning, we cast off and headed down the river toward the sea. A crisp offshore breeze pushed the tri over the water like a three-bladed ice skate and a couple of hours later we cleared the heads and set our course due north. Harold adjusted sails for an hour and coaxed the boat up to eight knots in the clear offshore air. This boat cooks! We could be there in a week, I thought. We set watches, four on, eight off, and by the end of my first 1600 to 2000 watch all thoughts of land had slipped away, replaced by those of food and sleep.

Harold had the 12 to 4s and woke me for my morning watch by thumping on the deck over my head. I wore jeans, a pullover sweater, socks and gumboots, for although the night was dry the sea wind had a cold edge to it. Topside, the clear skies gave me plenty of stars to sail by. I took the helm and Harold went aft to note the mileage on the taffrail log, then went below to the dimly lit galley and made entries into the logbook. Awhile later, he came up to the cockpit with two cups of cocoa. I concentrated on sensing the trimaran’s motions. They were quicker since the boat rode on top of the waves. From where I stood in the low, center cockpit, the deck spread out like a huge table and I couldn’t see the tips of the hulls. It took some imagination to remember that this was a boat and not a space platform. Harold had his head tuned onto another channel.

“Do you see the Coke bottle constellation?” he pointed into the sky.

I pretended to look, but instead thought about how a carrier captain must feel sometimes, ‘Will someone look over the edge of the deck and find the pointy end of the boat?’

“Nah, that’s the Corona beer bottle,” I said.

“Look, over there, the Mercedes-Benz star.

“Right, and there’s the MGM Lion constellation.”

He went below after a few more giggles, and I settled in to watch the light show from the clouds piled in the west, their undersides strobe-flashed by lightning while the eastern horizon took on its first faint glow of morning twilight. For years the profound feeling of watching a new day dawn had escaped me. Then, just before I left Hawaii I went to the top of Haleakala volcano on Maui to watch the sunrise over the crater. At the 10,000-foot summit, tourists shivered inside the dark, glass sided, viewing gazebo, waiting for the sun. Everyone lined the windows when a smudge of light gray appeared low in the east. Murmurs of "here it comes" circulated. A woman in her pear-shaped forties, with Buddy and Sis in tow, moved next to me. "Go get dad out of the car," she told Buddy, "it's coming." He returned from the parking lot a few minutes later, "Dad says he seen enough of 'em in the Navy." "Well, I haven't," Mom said, "look kids! See how the sky changes colors! Oh, my God!" The first, direct rays catalyzed her into a pillar of cholesterol and cellulite. She stared, speechless, directly into the fire as it rose above the clouds. Without moving a muscle, she said, "It's just like a sunset in reverse! Take some pictures of it, Sis!" Sis put her anyone-can-operate camera to her eye and took four, flash photos of the sun through a thick, plate glass window, "Got it, Mom." From that incident I gained a whole new perspective on sunrises, and people.

The next day, Harold showed me a method of finding the boat's longitude by calculating the time of sunrise. I later found out that other than the ship's clock, compass, mileage log and a pencil he used no instruments to determine his position. He had the nav books, sextant, chronometer watch and let me use them all I wanted. But each noon, he simply calculated the dead reckoning position, entered the leeway factor and put his dot on the chart.

"The soul of navigation is dead reckoning, Max. And the most important element is drift. You know you're going sideways a little, all the time, but which direction and how fast? You gotta learn to read the boat's wake. No matter which way a boat is pointing, the line of the wake is the direction of travel. Trimarans, especially, will fool the hell out of you."

Harold spent his off-watch hours making a rope hammock on deck, while Mike read paperbacks in the galley. He had gone book swapping with the other yachties before we left and devoured two a day, subject matter irrelevant. I studied navigation with a 1000 page volume of Bowditch *American Practical Navigator*. For the first 500 miles, a steady west wind pushed us at an average 150 miles a day. Then it turned fitful for a day and quit altogether. The trimaran stopped dead. Not even moved by current. Harold threw paper balls into the water; they sat only twenty yards away a day later. We rigged the awning and lived as though we lay snugly moored in a marina. On the second day of the calm, we sat around the cockpit talking about the puka shell venture.

"I've been thinking it over, Max," Harold said, "It might be a month or so before the weather is steady enough to take my boat to Motoriki. It's wide open to the tradewinds and seas. I don't know if you'll want to wait that long."

"I hadn't thought of that. We'll figure it out when we get to Suva."

I didn't want to wait any longer than I had to. Fantasies of making $300 a day selling shells on the streets of Honolulu danced through my head. Collecting them would be easy, with or without Harold. Maybe it's better to go solo on this and not be restricted by someone else's timetable. If this pans out, I could return to Fiji by September with a lump of cash, ready for some serious travel without worrying about money. Funny how when I was broke, I only wanted enough money, now that I had enough, having a lot became important.

For the next two days of calm, I traced the area of chart around the Motoriki sand cay and studied the volume of *Sailing Directions* for the islands. Then the southeast tradewinds found us. They blew gently at first but in twelve hours they built up to 15 knots and stayed there. Three days later we passed the Cape Washington light on Kandavu and entered the Fijian Islands. The following morning, we anchored at the quarantine buoy while the port authorities cleared *Seabird*. Then we moved to the yacht club anchorage. An hour later, while we celebrated in the Y.C. bar, the rains began.

By the fourth day of continuous rain, the inside of the boat smelled like a mushroom cellar. Mildew sprouted on everything. The boat sent roots to the bottom and Harold seemed content to watch them grow. But the boredom got to me. I moved to the Coconut Inn where I had a room to myself since it was the rainy season and only six other hostelers stayed there. I met them the first day, not formally, but in a passing, "Hi, my name's Max," manner. It felt good to be off the boat and back into the shoreside hustle. The city had several places to get out of the rain and I spent my time studying about Fiji at the Carnegie Library and the Suva Museum. One evening I arrived at the library just as one of the hostelers came out.

"Hello, Joan."

"Oh, hello Max."

We stopped to talk, seems both of us had time on our hands. "Great library, isn't it?" I had to start somewhere.

"Yes. I love it. I used to come here when I was a child."

This caught me. She was in her mid-twenties, with brown hair, blue eyes and spoke with a clear, British accent. “Did you live here, then?”

“Yes, for seven years, until I was fourteen. My father served in the Foreign Office.”

“Where do you live, now?”

“I’m on my way to England. I’ve just finished working a two year contract with an oil company in Brunei.”

“Oh,” what an interesting lady, “Have you had dinner, yet? Would you like to share a pizza?”

She thought it over for a few seconds, then smiled, “Yes, that would be nice.”

We walked to Punjab Pizza, Suva’s newest restaurant, and over dinner she told me what it was like to grow up in Suva.

“...We lived near the flying boat base and it was the event of the week when the Sunderland would land. Almost as big as steamer day.”

“It sounds like you enjoyed living here.”

“I loved it and cried when we left. I finished my schooling in England then got a job in Brunei, Borneo. I hate living in England. It’s so different from the tropics, and not only the weather but also the people, pace of life. Everything.”

“How do you feel about Fiji, now? A lot must have changed.”

“I’m not sure, yet. It’s been ten years. Anyway, I’m booked for a job in England in one month’s time, I’ll know by then. What about you? Indulging your wanderlust are you?”

“I’m on a treasure hunt,” I told her a little of my background and puka shell plans, “...so I’m going to Motoriki, an islet near Ovalau island, do you know it?”

“I know Ovalau. I used to go there with my father to the old capital of Levuka. There’s a guest house on the hill with an incredible view where we always stayed. The owner, Bill, was a remittance man from one of England’s finest families.”

“What’s a remittance man?”

“The ‘black sheep’ of the family, you might say. He’s paid a remittance so long as he stays out of England and doesn’t embarrass the family. Bill’s sin was that while he was stationed here, he married a dusky island woman from Rotuma,” she laughed, “It must have been love, I recall that they had several children.”

We returned to the Coconut Inn, made some cocoa and kept the conversation going strong. “What kind of work were you doing in Brunei? I don’t know anything about the place.”

"Well, Brunei is a small country on the coast of Borneo that's incredibly oil-rich. British oil companies have a big interest there and I work for a bank which keeps track of the money owed to the Sultan. I was posted there because I had lived in the tropics. Most British banking personnel couldn't take the weather," she laughed, "not enough fog. My job's boring; let's talk about your treasure hunt."

I showed her the chart tracing of the islands. "I'm not sure how to get to Motoriki but I know a friendly village on Ovalau that would be able to help me," I said, "I'll stop there first."

"It sounds like fun."

"It could be if the rain ever stops."

"Well, I'm off to bed now. I have the apartment upstairs."

"I didn't know there was one."

"Yes, the back stairs lead up to it. It's quite large. You'll have to see it sometime. Oh, by the way, I'm going to visit some of my old haunts tomorrow, would you like to come with me?"

"Love to."

The next morning's cloud blanket had gaping holes in it for a change and strong sunlight angled through every fissure. Joan still remembered the bus routes and we hopped from one to another as we toured the city. Along the way, she small-talked with Fijians and Indians — the weather, their babies, the price of food — without the slightest hint of reserve or condescension often shown by Whites towards Browns.

"You've got a lot of friends," I said as we rode along.

"I don't know them. I just like talking to people when it's so easy. I rarely had a chance to speak with the natives in Brunei, and in England if you talk to someone without being introduced, they'll probably snub you."

"Fijians are the most openly friendly people I've met."

"Yes, that's why I miss this place."

We got back to the hostel just ahead of an afternoon rain shower and she invited me up to her flat. The apartment had a bathroom, kitchen, and a bedroom at the end of the building, complete with a tea table, chairs and a real bed.

"How did you score this place?" I asked.

"Ken is an old friend of my father's. Make yourself comfortable. I'll get us some coffee."

I sat by the bedroom window and watched cloud masses collide with each other over the city. Huge raindrops began splattering on the hot pavement and roof tops raising small columns of steam. Then came the dark-gray curtain of a tropical downpour which replaced the steam with spray as solid rain pounded the street, the trees, the buildings. It beat on the roof like a drummer at hyper-speed and gurgled down the drainpipe to splash like cymbals on the ground. My mental Committees sat around in my head, playing poker. They had been getting along for the past month, but then there was little to disagree about. I had enough cash to stay in Fiji for a few months, at the present level of living.

'So, why the big rush to gather seashells?' a member asked.

'So we can live better than this,' another answered.

'How could it be better than this?' said a third, 'We've got a roof, food, cash-in-hand, an attractive companion. What's wrong, is the decor not suitable? Deal the cards.'

Another one threw his hand on the table, 'Naw, I want to hear more about this. I think it's important to be united if we want to better ourselves. Let's air the disagreements.'

'There's that word 'better,' again. I don't think anyone here knows what it means.'

'Oh, yeah?'

The voice-over came on, 'Be sure to tune in tomorrow to another episode of Meet The Mess.'

Joan came in, put the cups of coffee on the table and sat next to me.

"I love warm rain," she said, "I used to spend afternoons like this reading Somerset Maugham stories, pretending I was the romantic heroine, the lonely planter's wife. Silly, isn't it?"

"Not really. Fantasizing is what fiction is for. Life is for fulfilling the fantasies."

"This rain reminds me of his story about the preacher and harlot who were confined to the same hotel in Pago Pago. The woman entertains men at all hours until the preacher goes to convert her from her 'evil ways.' But she ends up seducing him."

"Lucky preacher."

"Yes, but then he committed suicide. Men are sometimes so unnecessarily serious, so complicated."

"I agree. They are."

"You do? What about you?"

"Me? I've never once thought of killing myself because I was seduced."

"Oh?" she said with a grin, tilting her head to look at me better.

I looked into her face, "It's the truth." I leaned over and kissed her gently on the mouth. "Was that kiss serious or fun?" I asked.

She laughed, "That was fun. And very direct, not at all complex."

We liked each other. We trusted each other. We enjoyed each other. That afternoon, we had her squeaky bed springs screeching like a demented string section playing Stravinsky's "Rites of Spring" with a thunder shower carrying the counterpoint. After that, we sort of knew that we would be partners for awhile, a few days, weeks. And though neither of us said, "I love you," that didn't deny the feelings. There's no way to disguise the sappy looks on new lovers' faces, and ours beamed like Raggedy Ann and Andy dolls over pizza that night. During a lull in the conversation, I said, "Do you want to go treasure hunting with me?"

She looked across the table at me, "I'd love to. When?"

"When the rain has stopped for two days in a row."

For the rest of the evening we made plans and lists for the adventure. I felt a renewal of excitement about the puka shell scam and though it rained for the next two days, my mood buoyed above it as we shopped for *sevu-sevu*, gifts for the villagers. Then, one day the sun blazed clear and my laundry began steaming on the clothesline. A second, sunny day finally dried my jeans. I was ready for the road again, and the road, after two days of drying, might be ready for me.

Chapter Eight
The Fijian Treasure Expedition

A third day dawned clear when we boarded the bus behind the post office and headed north on the King's Road to Nausori town where the pavement ended. Though not as "smooth" as the Queen's Road which belted the dry side of the island, the potholer made up for it with incredible scenery. The highway passed through dense jungle, climbed mountain ridges and angled into steep ravines, then forded streams where the hulks of discarded bamboo rafts littered the banks. What's more, the verge crumbled beneath the tires and afforded an awesome cliff-edge view at the same time, all at top speed. Sure, I felt anxious when the bus slipped like a dog on a waxed floor as it squirmed around curves, and careering on downgrades, unstoppable, out of control, held my attention but I didn't want to lose face by over reacting. Besides, the Indian driver seemed confident enough, singing at the top of his lungs. And, unlike Mexicans in a similar situation, none of the silent passengers had crossed themselves or clutched worry beads. But then, I knew very little about religions and nothing at all of the fearlessness of those who believe in reincarnation. I played back-seat driver once and yelled out, "Slow down! Slow down!" But even Joan, sitting next to me, barely heard me over the din of Indian music mixed with the screeches, rattles, creaks, and groans of the old, wooden bus.

Around noon, the driver stopped at the mountain town of Korovau for lunch. The passengers piled off the bus and headed toward the open-sided restaurant or the bamboo sided outhouse and peddlers emerged from the town's woodwork and circulated through the no-frills, Indian curry shop hawking their goods. But these weren't the usual curio and chewing gum sellers. One woman offered me six, live crabs strung together but another traveler beat me to them. I settled for a pair of coconuts and some bananas. From there, a one-lane, soggy track branched off the King's Road and headed to the coast. For an hour the bus flew down the curvy shelf cut into the sides of mountain ridges. When we reached the flat coastal plain the passengers broke into a friendship frenzy like all survivors. They laughed, introduced themselves, shared food, tobacco, anecdotes and showed family pix. Nothing like a little terror to zap a person into living the moment.

An hour's drive along the coast and the road ended at the Natovi pier. The bus went right to the end where a boat waited and the forty or so passengers carried their bags and boxes onto the vessel and sat wherever there was room. This bare-bones people mover had a cabin structure where the passengers shared the shade with an oil spitting, heat emitting, Gardner diesel. Joan and I sat atop the wheelhouse. It was cooler and the view infinitely better. The boat cast off and chugged into the seas of Central Fiji.

More than three hundred islands scattered over thousands of square miles of ocean make up the nation. The largest island, Viti Levu, has the same land area as the Big Island of Hawaii, but there the resemblance between them ends. For, while Hawaii is still being born, Fiji is a great-grandfather with erosion wrinkled mountains timeworn down to four-thousand feet, carpeted with thick jungle and streaming white mists like wispy hair. The immense, coral beard fringing the islands also showed Fiji's ancient age and the captain had to con the boat through a maze of sparkling, parti-colored living coral before reaching relatively deep water where coral heads stood like sentries, twenty feet below the keel. They'll cut the surface in a few more eons — time is one thing there's plenty of in Fiji.

Due west, 20 miles, Ovalau's mountainous spine stood up like a green, silhouette cutout on a reflective table. The cloud caps floating on the peaks looked just as phony. Three hours later, the boat closed the shore near Arovundi village and followed the coast for another hour to the tiny port of Levuka. Here, the British established the nation's first capital in 1875. The warehouses and store fronts had their last face lift fifty years later when copra was money. Since then, gravity sagged the buildings and time gave them the texture of eczema. The pier marked the center of waterfront street, from there the edge of town lay only a few hundred yards in any direction. The center of this main drag was lined by dingy restaurants, a pool hall, hardware stores and Chinese shops selling radios, cassette tapes, combs, hair oil, clothing, knives, playing cards, dice, and under-the-counter girly magazines — just about anything a lonely oriental fisherman would desire.

The port's main business was provisioning and repairing the Japanese fishing boats which based there and a couple of low-rent doss houses provided the crews a place to sleep off their hangovers. Behind the town, the rugby pitch lay at the base of a mountain ridge and a long, single story barracks, the Overlook Guesthouse, perched high on the flanks. When I visited here the year before, I walked straight out of town and hitched rides until a village invited me to stay. This time I headed up the path to the guesthouse.

The wartime leftover had porches sticking out from both ends and sash windows with cyclone shutters lining the seaward side. Inside, double bunks filled the undivided room, a mattress neatly rolled atop each one. Otherwise, it was empty. We checked the view from the windows and snooped around the room. It was in good shape. The paint still covered the wood and the floor had a dull shine. We wandered into the kitchen where the waxed linoleum and gleaming stainless steel sinks proved the existence of a maid, but no one was around. I looked out the windows into the back yard where a small wooden house sat. A man stood to one side, chopping away at bushes with a cane knife.

"There's someone over here," I said.

She looked outside, "That's him," she went out the back door, "Hello, Bill."

He stopped cutting and looked over at her.

"Do you remember me?"

"Yes, that is, I think I do," he glanced at me on the porch then walked over to Joan, "Ah, it's Little Joan! Yes, that's who! How wonderful to see you after so long."

They nattered excitedly for a few minutes, then she motioned me over, "This is my friend, Max. Max, this is Bill."

We shook hands and looked each other over. I half expected a "remittance man" to be a disheveled, rum-soaked beachcomber who had a covey of native girls living with him. On two of these points, Bill let me down. He dressed as neatly as a model in a seed catalog and his clean shaven cheeks showed no trace of grog blossoms or erupting blood vessels. He must send his head to a Chinese laundry to press out the wrinkles, I thought, it looked fifteen years younger than his neck.

Bill was civil, not over friendly to either of us. He led us back into the dormitory and said, "Take your pick of the bunks, you're the only ones here tonight. Dinner is at seven o'clock. See you then."

We unrolled a couple of mattresses, threw our bags on top and headed down the hill to nosy around, then followed the waterfront road out of town. It curved along the shore, crossed a small stream and passed a Christian girls school just as it was letting out. A group of chattering teenage girls caught up with us.

"Bula," one said to us, "Where are you going?"

"Just for a little walk," I said, "where are you going?"

"To my village," she smiled and played her eyes. Fiji girls are natural flirts, even in school uniforms. "Where are you from?"

"I'm American, from Hawaii."

Joan seemed stumped for an answer, "I'm English," she said finally.

"Are you married," another smiling maiden asked. Our "no" answers tumbled over each other.

"Is he your boyfriend?" a third teaser asked.

Joan stalled and looked at me with an embarrassed grin, "Yes, in a manner of speaking."

"And what about you, mister, is she your sweetheart?" the first girl asked.

I looked around, squirming for an answer while the girls, giggled and Joan smiled with a look that said, "Well?" I hooked an arm around her waist, gave a little squeeze and said, "She sure is! Isn't she pretty?"

The students shifted their attention to Joan, "Yes," said one, "she's so lucky to have English hair." The others agreed and crowded around her, "and gray eyes," said another. They gushed over her straight, brown hair, the top item on many a Fijian girl's wish list, and ignored her reddening cheeks. A few of them tested their comely smiles and flashing eyes on me, to see if they could get a rise. I smiled back, wondering how I looked since I felt somewhat salacious. We bantered as we walked up the road to where it crested a mountain ridge near the school. Here, at two hundred feet, the sea lay below us like a crazy quilt of brilliant coral colors with deep-water channels separating the reef clusters like swaths of indigo velvet. Fringes of wave foam seamed them together like piping. Islands filled the vista from the mid distance to the horizon and the girls named them off, M'batiki, Wakaya, Koro, Makongai. They invited us to stay in their village and I gave a vague promise to visit them tomorrow, then they left us there. Joan and I rested against the road bank as the sounds of girls' laughter and chatter died away, replaced by the sound of trade winds mushing through the trees. I had rested at this lookout the year before on my first visit. From here, the road climbed over six more ridges before it arrived at Arovundi village.

I found out about Ovalau from a truck driver I met while hitchhiking on Viti Levu. It was his home island and he raved on about its natural beauty and friendly people.

"...And the bus-boat ticket costs less than five dollars," he said.

"Do you think I could stay in a village?"

"Oh yes. Just walk along the road and someone will ask you into their home."

And that's how it happened. Arovundi lies between the beach and the road, with a ridge at one end and a stream at the other. It was customary for bored young people to sit at the intersection of the road and stream under a huge breadfruit tree and hope for something to pass by. I happened on the scene in the late afternoon.

"Bula, bula, where are you going," some boys called the usual greeting.

"Just for a walk," my stock answer.

"Would you like to stay in our village tonight?"

I thought you would never ask. I met Barney and Bo there that night. They were headed for the next village and when they left the next day I asked Josese, my host, if I could stay longer. "Stay as long as you like," he said. A week passed with a continuous parade of impressions and events — tin-roofed houses of straw, wood or stones, hissing gas lamps and voice twisted, short-wave radio reception, low-talking men, chattering children and gossiping women weaving mats, kava sessions and jamming with the village combo of tea chest bass, tin pan drums, gas guitar and assorted chorus.

Besides road watching, bath-watching was a village activity that drew a crowd. Within thirty minutes of meeting, my host family asked if I wanted a bath. Josese led me upstream, through the jungle to a small pool, and along the way we collected a following of fifteen males aged from six to thirty, I was apparently the only dirty one since the others just watched. I lathered as thick as a sports jock doing a deodorant soap ad and tried to pretend all those guys weren't checking me out. When I came out of the water, Josese handed me a wrap around sulu, a mirror and a comb. At the house, *bure*, I completed the bathing routine with a coat of homemade, scented coconut oil. The bath routine was the same everyday, my watchers falling in behind as I walked through the village wearing a sulu, a towel in one hand, a hand mirror and comb in the other. I thought of it as a sort-of, afternoon "soap opera." What people watched before they had TV.

That evening we sat at the guesthouse dining table with Bill. He treated us like regular guests and we paid $3.50 for the night which included dinner. Three, teenage island girls with long, wavy hair served us lamb chops, sweet potatoes and rice, then went to the kitchen.

"Those girls don't look Fijian," I said.

"They are my daughters," Bill said, "Their mother is Rotuman, from the Polynesian island of Rotuma, way to the north of Fiji." His voice carried the icy tone that didn't invite more questions. The smidgen of social warmth he showed to Joan that afternoon had chilled and he shoveled food into his mouth like a man who didn't want to talk.

"I remember her, Makareta," Joan said after a while, "Where is she now?"

He turned his head slowly towards her, and though his upper lip remained stiff, the lower twitched, "She's gone."

"Oh, I'm sorry."

"That's all right," he firmed the quivering one, "you couldn't have known what everyone in the islands knows. She ran off last year without a word. I thought something had happened to her and notified the police. They found her in Suva, living with the crew from one of the Korean fishing boats. It was quite embarrassing, but I'm over it now."

Maybe his intellect was but his emotions weren't. They twisted and stressed his face into a brooding scowl. Joan changed the subject and for the rest of the meal she rambled on about her life in England. After dinner, the girls put on grass skirts and danced a few Rotuman hulas accompanied by a tape recording.

"They have been performing these dances every night since they were children," Bill said, "whether anyone is here or not. Their mother taught them so that they 'would not forget they were Rotuman,' she said," he smiled cynically. "My daily, heritage reminder is the BBC news on short-wave at six pm. I haven't been home in fifteen years, but I'm still British. What about you, Joan?" he tilted his head and looked at her in a smug, deprecating way, "Do you subscribe to *Pacific Islands Monthly* when you're in the UK and tune into the BBC when you're away?"

She stumbled for an answer.

"That's all right, I understand. Well, time for bed. Will I see you in the morning?"

He sounded like a hermit who hoped for a "no" answer. I obliged him, "I don't think so. We're leaving early for Arovundi."

"Good. Well, give my best to your father, won't you Joan."

They trooped out the kitchen door to their house in back, Joan went to get ready for bed and I unrolled our sleeping bags on adjacent, lower bunks then went out to the porch for a smoke. I sat on the railing, looked down over Levuka town and began counting the streetlights.

Bill's aura of futility and loneliness hung on him like a hair shirt and it made my mental Committees itch with argument. Over the past year, they loved to split hairs over the meanings of the words "alone" and "lonely."

'Alone means by yourself,' said one side of the table.

The other side countered with, 'Oh, yeah? Then why do I feel alone in a crowd?'

'You're lonely because you don't know anyone in the crowd.'

'Maybe, but I feel that way sometimes when I'm with a lover, and especially when I'm by myself.'

'That's because you don't know you.'

'Assuming you're right, how do I get to know me?'

'By being alone.'

'But, that's lonely.'

I went back inside. The lights were off in the dorm but enough moonglow bounced in through the windows to see my way. I stretched out on my rack. The springs squeaked and chirped on the bed frame with every move I made to get comfortable. Finally, I lay on my back, looking up through the wire net of the top bunk, the lyrics of a song tripping through my head, "wide my world, narrow my bed," trying to determine whether I felt alone or lonely.

A few minutes later, Joan called softly from her bunk, "Max, are you awake?"

"Yeah," the debaters stopped and listened.

"Do you feel like talking?"

"Sure."

"Bill said something that I didn't think anyone knew about me."

"What's that?"

"That I subscribe to *Pacific Islands Monthly* magazine."

"Just a lucky guess,"

"Perhaps, but it's spot-on. I've missed Fiji a lot over the past few years and kept track of what happened to it, like a boyfriend in the navy. I didn't really know that I was coming here again, but I wanted to. I took the job in Borneo because it was closer to Fiji than the UK. I even turned down a secure marriage with a broker from Somesuchwich, complete with promise of 2.6 kids, a suburban house, and a Jaguar sedan for old age."

"Ooh," I said quietly, the safe, all-purpose word.

"I was never sure if I did the right thing, and after hearing how Bill's life turned out, I'm really confused."

"Poor guy," I said, "gave up his England friends to live here, and now, his friends here are either laughing at him or pitying him. He'll likely be a loner when his daughters leave." Older men don't make many new friends.

"And there's no point going back to the UK," she said, "most of the people he knew would have moved on, some would have passed on."

"It's almost the same for you."

After a few seconds, she said, "That's true. It's a lonely experience."

"Traveling is a lonely experience, sometimes. I'll bet Marco Polo felt the lonelies while surrounded by the hoards of Asia."

She laughed, "Yes, he probably did."

I sang a few bars of "Are You Lonesome Tonight?" with a crooning-cowboy twang.

"You can come here and serenade me if you want."

"Hmm, these narrow bunks are meant for one, but we could put our mattresses on the floor."

We arranged a bed in the center of the room, in a space lit by a rectangle of moonlight coming in through the window. When we were settled, we discovered that we knew the lyrics of a few songs, and did some low-key singing. We kissed between the tunes. She was long and languorous with the sheet draped across her hips and I wondered if the silvery light was kind to me. After awhile, we made love.

The next morning we shouldered our packs and walked to the marketplace at the edge of Levuka town. Here we waited for a couple of hours for a "carrier," a pickup truck with bench seats in the bed that went to the villages. This South Pacific stage coach chuffed its way over mountain ridges and stopped at the villages in the valleys and a half-hour later we hopped off at Arovundi. No one loafed around the roadside tree. In fact, there was neither sight nor sound of the villagers though it was early in the afternoon, a time when leisure activity is heaviest. We walked down the deserted lane towards the bure where I stayed last time. Though Arovundi was more than two hundred years old, it didn't look a day over a century as grass shacks shared the shade with tin-roofed, wood or stone houses, like the abodes of the Three Little Pigs, except here, the Wolf is the big, bad cyclone. And while the community boasted a water supply system from a conduit which tapped the stream, power cables, phone lines and TV antennas were non-existent, somewhat like the villagers that day.

We found them seated on the grass facing a new footbridge which spanned the twenty-foot wide, seven-foot deep stream bed, and connected the pig farmers on the downwind side with the main village. A dedication ceremony was being held for the bridge and the village elders sat with four Peace Corps Volunteers on folding chairs at one end of the span. One by one they gave speeches predicting great progress now that this concrete wonder spanned the chasm, allowing man and animal to visit each other so easily. Urban renewal had come to Arovundi. The PCVs and the village elders each drank a ceremonial cup of kava, then the informal party began. The kava cup made the rounds, cigarettes were lighted, people relaxed and turned to talk to their neighbors. Some recognized me and waved. Then Josese saw me and came over, followed by a mob of kids.

"Bula, Max. I am happy to see you," we shook hands.

"It's good to be here again, too. This is my friend, Joan."

"Bula, Joan. Welcome to my village."

"Bula, Josese. Vinaka vaka levu."

Joe smiled, "You speak Fijian very easily."

"I spent some childhood years in Suva."

He tilted his head politely but his interested eyes never left her face, "Is this your first visit to Ovalau?"

"No, I'd visited Levuka twice before with my father, but it's my first visit to a village."

"Then, I'm especially glad Max brought you here. Come, we'll go see Neumbi."

He sent one boy off with a message to the old man, and directed two others to take our packs. After a round of saying hello to people I'd met last year and introducing Joan, we walked along the stream bank to Neumbi's bure.

Joe, a quiet, twenty-five year old bachelor, lived with his father Neumbi, mother Lavinia, three brothers, two sisters and six other youngsters whose relationship was not clear to me. It added up to an average of fourteen people sitting around the dinner cloth at night. Their forty by twenty foot house sat along the bank of the stream directly across from the old, whitewashed church which stood at the end of the village green.

At the house, I leaned against the door jamb while I took off my boots. Across the room, Neumbi sat in the back doorway looking upstream towards the bridge, his silver, teased-out hair backlighted by the lowering sun, radiated like a halo. He turned as we came into the room.

"Bula, Neumbi," I said.

It took him a few seconds to recognize me, then he smiled widely, "Bula, Max, Bula."

Neumbi raised up from the doorway and with the aid of a cane, walked to his place at the head of the room and sat on the floor, indicating that we should sit beside him. His small, slender frame creaked and ached from more than seventy years of village life, but his puckish, toothless, smiling face would never let you know.

When we sat down, I introduced him to Joan, "She lived for several years in Suva," I added.

"Suva," he laughed, "I haven't been there in almost forty years."

"What was the occasion then?" I asked, "Were you running away from home?"

"No. I was in a dance troupe," he gestured with his arms and grinned.

"He danced the meke," Joe said, "the traditional Fijian dance. It's done while sitting down. He's showing it to you."

Neumbi went on with his sit-down hula for a few more seconds. He enjoyed himself. His hands flitted like birds, while his body swayed and bounced to an inner rhythm. Then he stopped, clapped his hands three times and laughed.

His wife came in from the pantry carrying a tea tray. When she set it down in front of us, I said "Bula, Lavinia. This is my friend Joan," I turned to Joan "she doesn't know much English."

"Bula, Lavinia," Joan said, then spoke to her in Fijian.

Lavinia answered in Fijian and they passed a few more sentences. She smiled as she poured the tea and glanced shyly at this pale woman who spoke Fijian so well. Neumbi withdrew his smile, and except for the questioning eyes he kept a poker face while he studied Joan. He probably thought she was a missionary.

"Miss Joan lived in Suva when she was a child, Father," Joe said.

The explanation had time to sink in while we drank tea, and the old man asked Joan some gentle questions and soon his smile returned.

"I am glad you came with Max," he said, "he is the only white man to return to our village, and he makes me laugh."

After awhile, Lavinia returned with towels, sulus, a mirror and a comb. She handed them to Joe who looked at us and said, "Would you like a bath?" I hadn't told Joan anything about the bathing routine here, she hadn't asked. She looked at me and I said, "Let's go." We collected every loose kid in the village as they saw us heading for the baths. When we crossed the road, the girls told Joan to follow them and they went ahead of us. "The ladies pool is further up the stream," Joe said. The guys sat around the pool as usual, pretending not to notice me and I did the same, though I heard some tittering in the bushes from girls who would rather watch me than Joan.

Afterwards, the girls came downstream and I met up with Joan walking down the jungle trail to the village.

"Do they always watch you?" she asked.

"Yeah."

"It's pretty unnerving."

"You'll get used to it."

"I'm afraid to ask about the toilet."

"Ah, glad you asked. The plumbing-free W.C. is behind the house, next to the stream. It looks like a bush since the walls, which are made of tree branches, have begun sprouting leaves and roots."

"Where can I wash some clothes?"

"There's a cement pad near the house with a standpipe, you'll see the women washing there. I'll arrange for someone to do your laundry."

That afternoon, Joe, Joan and I wandered through the village, stopping to watch the volleyball game, have a look inside the church, and walk along the shore. The sea lay still as a reflecting pond streaked with the colors of sunburned clouds. Joan and Joe did most of the talking, she with questions about the village, he with answers and explanations.

At sundown, Lavinia lit the pressure lamp and unrolled a dark green cloth, ten feet long and two feet wide. The boys set ten plates on it then sat down for dinner. The house had a pantry where Lavinia made snacks and hot water for tea, but she cooked the evening meal in a separate hut and girls brought in bowls of steaming n'dalo and tapioca roots, m'bele leaves and daniva, a tiny reef fish, cooked in coconut milk. This night, we also had boiled rice and tinned herring from the groceries that Joan and I had given to Lavinia as a sevu-sevu, a house gift. Mom, dad, sons, daughters, grandkids and guests sat around the green cloth, heads bowed while Neumbi offered thanks for his food. He prayed in Fijian, eyes closed, for a few minutes, then we feasted.

"Rest" was the only word Neumbi said after dinner as he stretched out and listened to the battery powered radio. The floor had been comfortably padded over the years with woven mats so I lay down and watched the kids doing their homework in the lantern light. I closed my eyes and lost my sense of time. It was easy to do. I didn't own a watch and had no place to go. No one in the village wore a watch. What for? Villagers know what needs to be done and when, and their uncluttered lives give them freedom from the tyranny of time. When the dishes were washed, the homework completed and Neumbi rested, the family gathered for evening prayers. He prayed in Fijian, but to which deity wasn't clear. The old Fijian ones? The newer Christian one? Maybe both, since the prayer session lasted a long time.

Afterwards, the kids ran out to play in the moonlight. Joe, his brothers, Joan and I sat in a loose circle on the floor, talking. Neumbi fussed with his radio, searching for a static-free station. Lavinia and two girls sat next to a pile of dried pandanus leaves, weaving a mat. Suddenly, everyone in the house became attentive. Talk stopped, the radio was turned off. Outside, the children's yelps and laughter had been replaced by a booming voice from the village green. It had the same strident tone as the one in the Suva nightclub.

"What did he say," I asked Joe.

"He told us what to do tomorrow, our work assignments."

"Who needs a telephone?" Joan said.

Almost unnoticed, men began arriving at the house singly and in pairs. They entered the softly lit room, greeting each other with a low "Bula" as they decided where to sit. Before long, a dozen had joined us on the floor; some leaned against the wall, their eyes just above the light spread by the hissing pressure lantern placed in the center of the room. Occasionally, someone would light their foot-long, rope tobacco and magazine paper cigarettes from the lamp, then slip back into the shadows.

Joe unhooked a wooden bowl from the wall. It was eighteen inches in diameter and carved from a single piece of vesi wood into the unlikeness of a five legged turtle with a concave carapace six inches deep. The head of the "turtle" had a white cowry shell attached to it by a short piece of sennit. Joe dusted the tanoa, as it's called, and set it next to the lantern, pointing towards Neumbi. From outside, I heard what sounded like church bells and looked out to see a group of youngsters grinding kava root in a homemade steel mortar using an axle shaft as a pestle. Within minutes, a mound of kava mulch was brought in and set on a cloth next to the tanoa. Joe was the brewmaster but before he began, Neumbi and several other men offered the kava to the old Fijian Gods with a series of chants, replies and hand claps. Then he tied the cloth like a bag and held it over the bowl while a young boy poured a gallon of water into the tanoa. Joe kneaded the bag of pulp through several re-pours and when he was satisfied that the potion had been squeezed out, he scooped up some in a bilo, a polished half-coconut shell, and handed it to his assistant who knelt as he offered it to Neumbi from outstretched hands. The old chief followed his role in the ceremony and accepted the cup on his fingertips, his face reflected the solemnity of this kava invocation, one of Fiji's oldest customs. He raised the bilo to head level, announced "bula", drank it in one gulp, then spun it on the floor with a flick of the wrist. "Toomba," it is empty, he proclaimed. He turned to me and said in a low voice, "nga-nga," which meant, "it tasted awful."

He was right, it tasted like river water and no one said, "Mmm, good" as the bilo made the rounds. For centuries, "Fiji Grog" has been the all-purpose, social lubricant present at any of life's celebrations occurring between birth and burial, like wine in France or Italy. But other than traumatizing my taste buds and making my lips tingle, I couldn't define any other effects the jungle drug had on me. Joe said the best kava grew on Kandavu island, though he couldn't explain how it was best. The kava mystique is like jazz, if it's gotta be explained to you, you don't have it. Joan didn't like it either and was thankful we weren't pressed to drink too much. Kava isn't guzzled like beer, it's tossed back like whiskey, a couple of ounces at a time, two or three times an hour. In between times, cigarettes are rolled up and smoked, someone picks tunes on a guitar, polite questions are asked of us and we told our stories.

Later, we unrolled our sleeping bags on the floor, under the table, while the low-key party continued. It was the first time in hours we could speak alone.

"I really love this place, do you think they'll let us stay for awhile?" Joan asked.

"Probably, but I'd like to get going to Motoriki in a day or so, before the rains start again."

"Oh, yes. Motoriki. I'd forgotten."

The next morning, Joe, his brothers, Joan and I gathered around the green cloth to share a breakfast of tea, rice pudding, and crackers smeared with treacle. The kids were off to school. Neumbi sat dozing in the back doorway. Bright sunlight splashed into the room.

"After breakfast," Joe said, "we're going up to work on the plantation."

"Can we go with you?" Joan asked.

He looked at her, his face a question mark, "It's up the mountain," he said.

"That's all right, I've done some hiking before."

Joe glanced at me, "Sure, I'll go," I said.

Three more guys joined us as we passed through the village. We followed the jungle path upstream past the bathing ponds, the women's bath had a ten foot waterfall feeding it. Why is it that women always get the best bathrooms? From there, the trail scaled the steep sides of a ridge to emerge into a clearing on the crest. I could see the village a mile away and a few hundred feet below us, spiked with spires of cooking smoke rising in the still air. The wake of the morning ferry boat scratched a "V" on the glassy sea as it chugged its way to Viti Levu. Nearby islands stood out clearly in the slanting sunlight, their underwater, coral skirts glowing like polished turquoise. The plantation had a few dozen tapioca plants which needed weeding and when the men were finished we collected some of the roots and went back to the stream where we had left the cook. He had brought only a couple of pots, a can of fish and a coconut with him, but along the way he had collected m'bele, Fijian spinach, breadfruit and other wild edibles, and we sat down to a satisfying lunch.

"Did you have enough to eat, Joan," Joe asked.

"Yes, thank you, Joe. That was really quite delicious."

"How are you? Are you tired?" he asked her.

"Not at all, actually."

"You are a pretty good hiker," I said, "Where did you learn to hike?"

"In England. I used to go for weekend hikes in the country. The freedom was exactly opposite of working in a bank. I'd really like to do more of this."

That afternoon we loafed by the big tree on the road to see if anything went by. Two boys from Rukuruku walked past. They didn't stop but talked to the village boys as they went and told us their village was having a Saturday night dance.

"Let's go to it," Joan said.

I thought for a few seconds, that's only two days away. We can leave for Motoriki on Monday. "Okay," I said.

Except for a few new faces at the kava session, that evening was a repeat of the one before. While the next morning was unlike any I'd ever had, hangovers included. I woke up with sweats and chills, fever and headache, my skin burned and bones hurt. To top it off, it rained heavily all day. I stayed in my sleeping bag for two days and had improved by Saturday night but not nearly enough to go to the dance, so Joan went with Joe and his brothers.

Over Saturday night, my fever broke and I finally got some real sleep. I didn't wake up until mid-morning, just as the family left for church. Outside sparkled with sunlight and I no longer felt I would have to get better to die. I sat in the back doorway looking upstream towards the bridge, worrying about a relapse. Joe said I had "mosquito fever" and that sometime the effects lasted for weeks. My Central Planning Committee clucked over this news when they returned to my head space. I don't know where they went when the fever and headache moved in, but they were glad to be back.

'Well, that fever didn't last for weeks,' one member said.

'Good thing, too. We don't have that much time to just lay around,' said another.

'We've been here too long already. We should be leaving tomorrow.'

'What will we do if it rains?' asked Mr. Gloom.

'We'll go anyway,' said The Willful One, 'What's a little water? You're a sailor, aren't you? You won't melt.'

'Besides, we need the money! We always need the money!' The Accountant ranted a little loudly. The sudden fall from health jacked him into hyper-thinking.

'What about Joan?' asked the Head of the Relationship Committee. 'What's the story there? What if she doesn't want to go when you do?'

"I don't know," I said aloud.

'You mean you're waiting to hear what she wants to do before you make up your mind? She didn't wait for you to get well to take off to the dance with Joe.'

"We're not exactly chained together," I mumbled. Still, if Joan was a guy, I could have said, "have a good time," and meant it. Why is that? What brings on that dichotomy of emotion? Because I care for her? I had men friends I cared for just as much without sleeping with them. It's probably a person's non-logical sexuality since it didn't make sense to feel hurt about Joan going to an all-night dance while I was sick, she wasn't my keeper. Still there was no denying the tinge of jealousy and stabs of hurt pride. They teamed up with the self pity and money fear and started cranking out the propaganda in my head. "When sick, a person should never think about anything except their state of health at that moment. No memories, no projections." I don't remember who told me that, but I forgot it when I needed it, besides, a rational idea like that wouldn't have stood a chance at that time.

Joan's cheery voice tinkled through my thoughts, "Hello, Max. We're back."

I looked to the front doorway where she stood, taking off her shoes. Joe stood behind her, grinning.

"How are you, Max? I hated to leave you." She came over to me and sat on the floor.

"I think I'm practically over it. Did you have a good time?"

"Yes. Once Joe convinced me that with Lavinia taking care of you, there would be nothing I could do."

I looked over at Joe by the door and gave him my best "Thanks a lot" look. And as for you, woman! What if I died, how would you feel then? But my face masked this emotion masterfully.

"Is something wrong?" she asked.

"No, what makes you think that?"

"You had a troubled look on your face. Is it your headache?"

"Yeah. That's it."

"I'll get you some tea."

"I'm bringing some," Joe called from the pantry. He came out with the tea set and sea biscuits and we moved to the center of the room.

"Tell me about the dance."

"Oh, it was heaps of fun, Max. Some boys on guitars played the music and there were drummers on anything that would pound."

"The wild, primitive rhythms, huh?"

"Max, I fancy classical music, some jazz, absolutely no rock. But the beat last night was compelling. Like it was from the soul of the people."

"Maybe it was the kava you drank," I said without a smile.

"You're in a great humour," she said, looking through my mask, "Yes, we enjoyed ourselves. The dancing was wild. Wish you were there."

She picked up her cup. Joe sensed my direction before I did, "We had to stay overnight. It was too late to come home."

"I understand," I said. But why did it take until noon, I thought as the church bells signaled midday and the end of the morning service.

A few minutes later the family returned from services, the kids peeling off their Sunday clothes as they came through the door. Lavinia, too, changed out of her bright floral dress into her work sulu. On her way through the room, she looked at me smiled broadly, opened her eyes wide and nodded. "Are you all right?" the expression asked. I smiled and nodded back. This day, she seemed uplifted by the chance to wear something pretty for awhile.

Neumbi, too, was in his Sunday best and in no hurry to take it off. A dark brown, long sleeved silky shirt and a royal blue sulu. He took his place and we changed our positions to face him. Lavinia brought him a cup for tea, then asked Joan if she wanted a bath. Joan said yes and they left together. Joe said he had something to do and took off, leaving Neumbi and I alone. We never had a problem finding things to talk about, and after awhile I asked if he knew anything about Motoriki island.

"I haven't been there in a long time, but I don't think anything has changed on Motoriki in a hundred years," he laughed, "Do you want to go there?"

"Yes, I'd like to see it."

The old man didn't ask why I wanted to go, he probably figured that any reason qualified for traveling.

"Get my glasses from the table, will you Max? And that tin box."

I brought them to him, then got my map and journal. He adjusted his glasses and studied the map. Motoriki was separated from Ovalau by a shallow channel about a quarter-mile wide.

"First, you must go to Levuka and take a carrier to here," he pointed to a place on the south coast of Ovalau, "N'gelemdamudamu. There you will find canoes that go to Motoriki." It took a couple of minutes for me to get the spelling right. "The canoe lands here, at the largest village, just across the channel. There are only nine villages on Motoriki."

"How do I get around the island? Are there carriers?"

"No carriers," he laughed, "No road. But the villages are on the shore and a path connects them. You could visit them all in a day." He studied the map closely, "I have a friend in a village on this side. He comes to Levuka once a year for our church gathering."

That's convenient, I thought, Nasautombu, the shell-money islet, is just offshore from his friend's village. Neumbi pried the lid off his stash box, an old shortbread cookie tin, took out a worn address book and thumbed through it while I peeked at his stuff. There was a square-face watch, a few people snapshots and letters, a bronze medal and a *tambua*, a sperm whale tooth. Only six inches long, Fijians consider it to be a tower of power and practically no request can be refused when accompanied by a tambua. It could be a bride price or a peace offering. I wanted to ask.

"Here is my friend's name. Write it down."

I took the book and copied the information, then handed it back to him. He put it into the box and started to put the lid on.

"That's a tambua, isn't it?" I asked. He hesitated, looked me right in the eyes and nodded, then he clamped the lid down.

I slept well that night but still didn't feel like traveling on Monday, so I stayed another day in Arovundi. In the evening, the Peace Corps presented a birth control movie. They erected a screen on the village green, fired up a generator carried in the back of their Land Rover, and entertained the villagers for an hour. Even Blind Tom was there, laughing like mad, his mind making pictures for the words. For although it was not intended, the script was hilarious. The plot centered around an Indian caneworker's family. Mom and dad were about thirty and had seven children under ten years of age. It opened with a concerned friend telling pregnant mom that intercourse causes babies. The Arovundians were still laughing about it at the kava parties where they agreed that birth control for Indians was a good idea.

"But, Max, why do they show this film to us?" Neumbi asked, "There are no Indians on Ovalau."

"Probably brought the wrong film," I said and imagined a sugar worker's camp solemnly agreeing with their film showing the need for Fijian birth control. Lack of privacy plays a big part in Fijian birth control. It's practically impossible to be alone. Someone always goes with you, walking alongside or following a hundred yards behind. Joan and I were never unobserved. But that night at the kava party I made eye contact with her and indicated the door with a slight head tilt. A few minutes later she went out. I sidled out the other door and we met in the yard.

"Hello," she said, "we haven't had a chance to talk today."

"Sshh, follow me." I led her along the huts to the tree line on the beach where we sat on the sand leaning back on a coconut log.

"I hope we got away unnoticed."

We lay quiet for a few minutes, listening to the soft, shuush of tiny waves splashing.

"How are you feeling?" she asked.

"Well enough to travel. I'd like to leave tomorrow morning. Are you ready?" I couldn't see her reaction in the dark but the long pause sent signals loud and clear.

"I'm not going with you. I'm going to stay here for awhile."

Even though something told me that was going to be her answer I still had no ready reply, "Maybe I'll come through here on my way back," was the best I could manage. We quickly ran out of things to say and got up to go back to the house. Sure enough, not a stone's throw away sat two tittering, teenage girls watching us.

Chapter Nine
Win Some, Lose Some

The next day, I took carriers around the island to the wide spot in the road named N'gelemdamodamo. From here, I studied Motoriki's cloud topped, green mantled mountain for a couple of hours until an outboard-powered canoe showed up and took me across the narrow straits. The boatman beached at the main village and pointed in the direction of Uluimbau, the village I wanted. I sloshed though knee-deep water along the edge of a mangrove swamp which, I was sure, teemed with banded sea snakes. I continued along the beach past a couple of villages where I picked up some followers, then through a tunnel in the mangroves for a mile to emerge at Uluimbau village.

I arrived escorted by a throng of chattering children who led me past the huts sited in the trees behind the small, crescent shaped beach. Nicco's timber and tin house sat in one corner where the beach and jungle came together, a low mountain ridge rose just behind it. A well built, middle aged man stood on the porch as I came up and introduced myself.

"You are a friend of Neumbi," he said, "is he well?"

"Yes, and he sends his regards. He thought perhaps you could help me with something."

"I wondered why you came," he laughed, "We don't get many visitors here."

"I'm not surprised, your village is not exactly on the main road."

"We are not even near a minor one. Come, let's have a cup of tea." Nicco's house was also the village store and people came to buy things and have a nosy while we talked. Nicco's wife Mariah or Aquila, his ten-year-old son, waited on them.

"I want to buy shell necklaces like the one I'm wearing. I heard they came from this island."

He looked at it, "Yes, those are the little shells from Nasautombu. The fishermen bring them sometimes and the children string them. I'll see what I can do for you. It will take a couple of days, won't you stay with us while you wait?"

"I'd appreciate that very much." We sat on his porch and small talked until dusk. From there, I could see the tan, thin outline of Nasautombu and a couple of other desert islets smearing the horizon a half-dozen miles away.

Since I could see Treasure Islet from Nicco's house, my urgency diminished rapidly and I kicked back into village time. The afternoons were spent on Nicco's porch watching rain squalls range across the sea. Each night was a kava gathering where I retold my story, every time someone new joined us. "You see, Max," Nicco said, "many of us have only been as far as Ovalau and at our ages it is unlikely we will go any farther, so we like to hear stories of other places and people." In the meantime, Nicco organized the villagers into puka shell stringers and the chokers were starting to come in. After a few more days, I had collected 300 necklaces for my New Zealand partner and bought 25 for myself when the supply dried up. "They have run out of shells," Nicco said, "The fishing boats haven't been to Nasautombu in a long time because of the weather. They only anchor there when it's calm."

A neighboring village operated the fishing boats, twenty-foot long, open dories with outboard motors. I had passed through and seen several outrigger canoes on the beach.

"How about the canoes, could I rent one of them to take me out and back?"

"You could ask. But what's the hurry? You already have hundreds and a boat will be able to stop there in the next two weeks."

"I guess you're right." I didn't want to go through the explanation that I wanted to get to Honolulu for the summer. Besides, only two dozen of the strands were mine, unless I wrote and told my Auckland friend that due to blah, blah, blah I am unable to comply with the terms of our deal. Just a thought. I'll take these to Levuka tomorrow and mail them off to New Zealand, then come back and get my stash together. I felt feverish the next morning, but threw on my leather backpack, told Nicco I would return in a few days for more shells and backtracked through the mangrove tunnel. The kids were in school so I walked alone. It was mid morning when I emerged at the fishing village. I slowed down to light a cigarette while a couple of teenage boys walked over to ask where I was going.

"Levuka," I looked at them for a few moments, "but I'd really like to go to that island out there." I pointed.

"Nasautombu?" one said, "whatever for?"

I told them about the puka shells.

"Oh, you are the one buying the shells. We've heard about you."

"Do you think you could get me out to that island and back in a canoe for twenty dollars?"

It was a challenge they couldn't refuse, they looked at each other, "We'll get two other boys as well," one said and they took off. I split my cash, putting $100 in my pack, and the rest in a plastic bag in my back pocket, keeping out $20 for the boys. They had returned to the beach with two others and were dragging a dugout canoe to the water. One of them took my pack to a house while the others collected bailing buckets and rice sacks. I felt uneasy about the venture when I saw the canoe up close but my Finance Committee prodded, 'We have only to nip over to this islet, fill a few bags with man's oldest coinage, string them together and we're in the money.'

The canoe floated like a topless submarine and before long, I had to bail water out. The boat clipped along towards the desert island glowing white in the overhead sun, surrounded by a blue sea which sprouted little cauliflower shaped whitecaps. Since there was little wind, I figured it was caused by tide meeting an undersea stream. I stopped thinking about it when we landed on the islet. It turned out to be everything I envisioned, a heap of marine skeletons in the middle of the South Pacific Ocean, totally incapable of sustaining life. A curious sense of vulnerability came over me. I shook it off and started scooping up shells from the beach, more than 50 percent of each handful was usable for necklaces. We had three bags full in a few minutes and loaded them into the canoe. Though we laughed like buccaneers when we landed, no one spoke afterwards. The dismal thought of being stuck there kept me in sight of the canoe and I didn't relax until we had shoved off, then I lit a cigarette and started whistling a tune.

"Don't whistle, please," one boy said. I looked to see if he was kidding. His face said "serious," while his mouth said, "There is a spirit in these waters. We don't want to offend it."

"Okay," I said. I could go along with anything. I had shells. Mission accomplished. I even stubbed my cigarette and put it back in the package, no litter.

We didn't talk. The boys concentrated on paddling, for while the breeze barely ruffled the surface of the water, waves shaped like miniature volcanoes began popping up all around us and the going got harder. Within minutes, the cones grew a foot high and slopped water into the canoe. I started bailing and at first kept up with the inflow. But the water's action increased so that the paddlers often had to hang on to the bouncing canoe and we lost speed. The waves seemed alive, animated. They rose alongside and leaned over to dump their top half into the canoe. Though I bailed with a bucket in each hand, I couldn't keep up. The level in the bottom rose above the top of the shell bags. I knew the canoe wouldn't sink, but it could easily turn into a log with five bits of shark bait hanging onto it. I glanced ahead. We still had a couple of miles to go and there was no telling how long this crazy wave action would continue since I didn't know what caused it. I'd never seen anything like it and judging by the tense expressions of the boys, this was not an everyday event in their life either.

The bags of shells lay in the center, right in the way for efficient bailing. They weighed about 60 pounds each and shifting them around caused an imbalance, allowing even more water to pour in. I was moving one when a boy looked at me with a "Please throw it over the side," expression. His fear got through to me and without a second thought, I heaved it into the sea. The bailing became easier but continual and the rhythmic splashing sounds from paddles, bailing buckets and waves filled the air. I looked up to see if we were gaining on the island. The clear sky and gentle breeze showed no trace of the drama which unfolded in my head. In any vessel with higher freeboard than a canoe, this situation would not be particularly life threatening, but we were nearly swamped. If we foundered and were not found by nightfall our chances for survival would drop drastically. I threw another bag over the side and bailed furiously. This brought an unexpected laugh from a couple of the boys, a sign that their spirits weren't flagging. The crisis had joined my Committees into a single voice, 'What do we do now?' For once they were firmly locked into the present moment. No time for whining over past mistakes or looking for future failures. We bail! The level had risen higher than ever. I reached into it and pulled the third sack up, just as I raised it a voice in my head yelled, 'NO! Maybe you can just dump half of it.' I hesitated, looked around at our situation hoping to find a break, then tossed it out. 'You dumb turkey,' the voice jeered. His tune changed when it took another long spell of constant bailing just to break even. Then, just as subtly as it had grown, the condition subsided and we rested a little while.

That afternoon we beached at the village where I paid the boys. I then got my bag, pulled out some dry clothes and changed in a hut. My Committees were exuberant, 'What an adventure! Dear Diary, Guess what happened today?' They were having a great party until I picked up my wet jeans and saw that the back pocket was torn and remembered that I had put money in there. Even before I checked the pocket, a memory flashed through my mind of some plastic I threw out with a bucket of water at the height of the battle. My head went silent except for a small voice, 'Go on, check it.' It was gone. That trip cost me $100. My Committees called me everything but bright as I walked through the jungle to the main village. The Collective Conscience asked, 'Why did you split your cash? Why did you go to the island instead of waiting?' Because it seemed like a good idea at the time was my only defense.

The water taxis were busy bringing students home and I didn't have to wait for one to Ovalau. There, a carrier had just pulled up with more kids and I hopped on for the return trip to Levuka. At dusk, I arrived at the Overlook Guesthouse and went to see Bill about a bed. I even made it in time for dinner, though I could barely stay awake during the hula show. I had the large room to myself and slept until late the next morning.

I had no choice but to stay another day in Levuka, the daily boat to Viti Levu had gone, besides, my body felt too beat to travel. On top of it all, my head ached, possibly from the murmurs of self accusation, and gloomy forecasts being tossed around inside, probably because I was a quart low on coffee.

'Hey! Why don't we stop moping about what we lost and count what we have left?' said one of the Positive Energy Committee.

'That won't take long,' the Cynic answered.

'Good. We still have one hundred bucks on us, one hundred at the Coconut Inn and the air ticket to Honolulu. We have enough for today. Everybody happy? Now let's go to town, drink some coffee and make a plan.'

I liked that guy. I rolled up my sleeping bag, tied it onto my backpack and humped down the hill to Levuka town. I stopped at a Chinese restaurant near the pier where, after a couple of cups, my direction became clear. Leave on tomorrow morning's boat to Viti Levu and catch the bus to Suva. Make another decision there. The lunchtime crowd rolled in so I gave up my table, there were only four, and walked down the pier. The *Adi Moapa*, an old, inter-island trader lay moored alongside with stevedores hauling crates of beer, sacks of rice and kava, and cartons of groceries out of the hold. The Fijian captain stood in the wheelhouse door.

"Bula, captain," I said, "where's your next port?"

"Koro, then Vanua Levu. Do you want to go?"

"No, thanks. I'm going to Suva."

"We'll be returning there in a couple of days."

"I'll think about it. What time do you leave?"

He glanced at his watch, "In about half an hour."

We small talked for awhile then I ambled back up the pier, past the customs shed and stopped at the post office to read the notice board outside. Suddenly Joan came out the door.

"Hello, Joan," I said.

She looked over, "Hello Max!" She smiled tentatively, "You're back."

"Yeah. More or less in one piece. How are you?"

"Fine. Fine. Everything's just fine."

The next line took a long time coming. We had more to say the first time we met. "What are you doing in town?" I asked.

"Just some shopping."

"Are you still staying in Arovundi?"

"Yes. I'm planning to stay for a few months."

"Do you have time to talk? There's a place nearby."

"Uh, yes. Yes I do."

The restaurant was still packed, so we went into the gloomy pool hall which had a few beverage tables. The only customer sat at a dark, corner table. He watched us as we walked in. On a hunch, I went to a table well away from him. I'd worked as a bartender in the past and learned to follow my instincts. Two guys played pool in the back. The Chinese bartender came over and I ordered a couple of Cokes.

"How did your treasure hunt go?" she asked.

"Fair enough. I bought a few hundred necklaces."

"What are your plans, now? Are you coming to the village?"

"No. I'm going to Suva tomorrow, then to Hawaii."

"For good?"

"Until I can get out again. What's happening with you?"

"Joe's asked me to live with him. I'm going to try it. I just sent notices to concerned people in the UK. They'll be surprised. God knows, this is all a surprise to me. Until I met you, I had my future planned. Now I'm living without a clock or calendar. I've never felt so free."

"I wish you and Joe the best of luck." I meant it, after all, they were my friends. I didn't feel possessive towards Joan because we'd slept together. After all, people have to sleep with their friends, their enemies won't let them.

"The carrier is leaving shortly, why don't you come out to the village and catch the morning boat when it passes by?"

"I'm still sick and don't feel much like moving around."

"To be honest, you don't look too well."

Except for the click of pool balls, our voices were the only sound in the room, and apparently carried very well.

"He needs a drink," the solitary man said. He had been watching us from the start, his dark face casting smiles and hoping for one in return.

I ignored him. "I don't think I've lost all of that fever, yet," I said in a lower tone.

"Wong," the man called, "give my friends a bottle of beer."

A couple of minutes later, the Chinaman showed up at our table with the beer and indicated the lone drinker. I looked over at him, put on my best refusal smile and said, "Thanks, but no."

"What do you mean you don't drink? You look like a drinking man to me."

"Probably so. It's the result of a misspent youth."

"Well, then spend some more and have a drink with me."

"Sorry. We've got to catch the carrier. Some other time."

"Let's go," I said to Joan. I put my pack on and turned to see Mr. Friendly an arm's length behind me. He was stocky, about my height, smelled like fish, had bad teeth and an attitude to match. He looked like a mixed islander.

"I am a fisherman. I sail across the sea to bring you tuna and you don't have the decency to drink with me."

"Look, even though I didn't order the tuna, I'll have a drink with you." I picked up my Coke bottle and said, "Cheers."

"I mean beer," he said staring into my face.

"Read my lips. I said, 'no.' " I had two options, beaning him with the Coke bottle was one.

He moved closer, "I mean beer," he tapped me on the chest with the glass he held in his hand, slopping beer on my shirt. My knee came up fast, smashing his balls and bringing a falsetto squeak from his throat. He dropped his glass, and fell to his knees, gasping for air. Joan and I headed out the door. "Let's go to Arovundi," I said, "Where's the carrier?"

"It stops in front of the post office."

We crossed the street and stood under the building overhang. I kept an eye on the doorway of the pool hall and wasn't surprised to see the lone drinker stagger out followed by two guys carrying pool cues. At first, I thought they were escorting him out, but then he saw me and shouted, "There he is!"

They started towards me. "I'll catch up with you later," I said to Joan as I took off down the pier. I immediately regretted my dead-end avenue of escape since only a few people lined the edges, not enough to get lost in. Some of them saw what was coming down and turned to watch the showdown forming before them.

The pool shooters had no trouble tracking me and ran down the quay, yelling to each other. Up ahead, the *Adi Moapa* sounded one long blast from the ship's whistle and started to move away from the pier. Without thinking, I sprinted for it and jumped over eight feet of water to land on the mooring lines heaped on the fantail. The three men ran up to the edge of the pier, yelling threats and cursing. A couple of crew members saw the scene and laughed. It was probably a common way to board an inter-island trader. I waved bye-bye, then went below into the cabin.

The *Adi Moapa* was an uncomplicated vessel, an old, 80-foot schooner with her masts cut down and a deck house built from the plans of Noah's Ark. Rectangle ports set high in the sides lit the interior as brightly as an opium den. The bunks, fastened in three tiers to the ships sides, completed the effect. In the center, a huge, yellow, Caterpillar diesel roared and fumed. The half dozen passengers, sat or reclined on their bunks, apparently overcome by the ambiance. I found an empty berth near the door to the foredeck, threw my backpack on it and went outside.

From the bow, I looked back at Levuka and wondered if Joan was feeling bad because I had to leave or glad that I couldn't stay. I wasn't sure, myself. I heard a rapping at the wheelhouse window and looked up to see the captain beckon me with his hand. I walked around to the side door of the wheelhouse, its deck was at my eye level.

"Good afternoon, Captain. I changed my mind and decided to go with you."

"Fine, come on up."

I climbed the ladder into the wheelhouse, "Nice view," I said as I looked out the windows.

"Yes, I was looking out these rear windows for a signal from my deckhand that we were clear to leave, when I saw you running towards us. I'm sorry I made you jump so far, but if I held it any closer, those misfits would have made it on board as well. Would you like a cup of tea?" He sent a deckhand off to the galley, and I offered him a smoke. "Pall Mall," he said, "New Zealand cigarettes."

"Yes. I was there for awhile. I sailed to Fiji a few weeks ago."

"Oh, you're a sailor?"

I struck our common chord. It was easy to play and gave us something to talk about over tea and biscuits. He showed me his charts and course lines. Koro lay dead ahead, a few hours away.

"We will stay there tonight," he said as he traced the course with his finger, "Tomorrow we will sail for Savusavu, the capitol of Vanua Levu island. These are the seas that Captain Bligh sailed when he was cast adrift. He was chased by the people of Vanua Levu and nearly ended up on the chief's table. Ha, ha, ha."

"I hope they've changed their ways."

"Yes, of course they have. Though some tribes on Taveuni island still hold onto ancient customs and beliefs."

"Really? Where is it located?"

"Here, just east of Vanua Levu. It's one of Fiji's prettiest islands. I was born there."

I looked at the chart and became aware that the 180th meridian, the geographic, International Dateline passes through the island putting the eastern section into yesterday. Interesting concept.

Adi Moapa anchored in a Koro lagoon that afternoon. The ship's boat was lowered and loaded with bottles and cans of food and drink, a couple of live piglets and a few passengers and then went ashore, returning with sacks of copra bound for Suva. The captain and engineer stayed on the island that night while I stayed on board playing cards and drinking kava with the crew.

The yellow Caterpillar fired up at dawn the next day and was soon joined by the clatter of the anchor chain being hauled in. I got up and went to the wheelhouse.

"Morning, Captain."

"Bula, Max. Would you like some tea?"

"Thank you, Captain, that would be nice. Would you like a cigarette?"

"In a while, thank you. Once we are clear of the reef and I can enjoy it."

He could probably have sailed out of the lagoon blindfolded, by feeling the wave action on the boat, but he's old. There are bold captains and old captains, but there are no old, bold captains. Especially around reefs.

Outside the reef, he set the boat on course and invited me to steer. I thought he would never ask, but tried to hide my excitement behind a mask of 'Ho, hum. Just another job of steering an island trader through the fabled South Pacific.' As usual on a boat I don't know, I oversteered for a few minutes but the captain didn't seem to mind. He sat on a stool nearby and had his tea break with a cigarette while reading a week-old newspaper. For him, just another day in Paradise. When he finished his tea he said, "Can you manage for awhile on your own?"

"Sure thing, Cap'n."

"I'm going to freshen up, then."

He climbed down the ladder and headed aft, leaving me alone in the wheelhouse. Up here, the engine noise was merely a vague thrumming, more felt than heard. It was often muted by the sound of splashing water from small wavelets which smacked the side of the hull. Ahead, the sea darkened to the royal blue of a deep-water channel. Its surface dotted with brilliant whitecaps marking the wind line. On the horizon, Vanua Levu stretched like an enormous, ridge-backed sea monster basking on the surface. The bow of the boat became an arrowhead flying toward the island. I sat on top, holding on to this fantastical ride.

After staring at the vista for awhile, I imagined Captain Bligh crossing ahead, rowing like mad while pursued by cannibals in canoes, *takias*. And it wasn't just a quick sprint for life, but went on for several windless days. Contrary to popular Hollywood mythology, Captain Bligh was not a wimp. His mutinous crew set him adrift in the mid-Pacific on an open boat adventure that has never been equaled. He not only survived, but went on to see the mutineers hanged and later was appointed Governor of New South Wales, a prison colony. Did he ever stop in his career and say, "What am I doing this for? I don't even like this job! I wanted to be a doctor, but no, my dad said to join the navy." While he and his crew rowed for their lives, did he think, "Why am I here? I should be back in London doing some career climbing, going to parties, playing some golf." Did he have a Committee of Shoulds & Ought Tos like mine, whining in the background, 'We probably shouldn't be here in the first place, but it's certain that we shouldn't be enjoying it so much. We ought to be doing something gainful with our life.'

"Man, it's getting hard to find a perfect day," I said out loud, looking around to see if anyone had heard.

'Yeah,' said a silent voice from the Just For Today Gang, 'can't we have a little fun for a few hours without arguing about it?'

'I'm not trying to start an argument,' said the Shoulds & Ought Tos Committeeman, 'I'm just pointing out that we do have some old values to apply to our life's situations.'

'Well it's time to plug in some new ones,' said the Just For Today Guy, 'and the first one is to learn how to take life as it comes — the good right along with the bad. Cheer up, it can't be all bad.'

'Even so, while we're out here driving a boat around the South Pacific, there's probably other things we should be doing right now.'

'Like what? At this moment, pointing this arrowhead is all we're capable of doing.'

'Well, you shouldn't be enjoying it so much.'

'Would it be better if we viewed the experience as a penance? Is this like adultery in Ireland where it's not a sin if you don't enjoy it?'

An hour later, the captain came back and took the wheel.

"It's a beautiful day, isn't it captain?"

"They're all beautiful, Max, some are just prettier than others."

"I think you're right." I stayed in the wheelhouse and talked about Taveuni while we sailed across the channel. Once out of the lee of Koro island the tradewinds were free to build up some bulky seas and the steeper ones slapped the bow, exploding into instant rainbows, but the deep-keeled trader kept her course and soon crossed into the wind shadow of Vanua Levu where Savusavu Bay lay like a pond, rippled only by the vee of our wake. As we drew close to the island, I went up to the topmost deck, sat in a chair under an awning and studied the shore. Mountain ridges descended to the narrow skirt of flat land which fringed the beach. Small valleys lay squeezed between the ridges and a few spikes of smoke poked through the jungle covering the lowlands. A carrier raised a tail of dust as it drove along the shoreside road towards the town of Somosomo, which twinkled up ahead from the sun reflecting off the tin roofs of the waterside buildings and the windows of the Holiday Inn perched on a hillside nearby. This two-street transportation hub of the island is located at the head of a small river and the end of the cross-island roads. *Adi Moapa* was the only vessel that docked there that afternoon.

After talking with the captain about Taveuni, I decided to try and go there. Following his directions, I went to the Mom & Pop Chinese store to see about the bus to Loa, a village on the other side of Vanua Levu where I could take a boat to Taveuni. The owner told me the bus had already left. "Tomollow. Twerve o'crock," he said.

"Is there a hotel in town?"

"Horiday Inn."

I went to the Holiday Inn. "How much for a room?" I asked the clerk.

"One hundred dollars."

"How much is a cup of coffee?" I had a few cups of coffee, American style where I paid only for the first one, and thought about my next move. Might as well get into the street, for sure the clerk isn't going to come down to ten dollars, my hotel budget. I investigated the entire town in ten minutes, including five minutes of wandering through the residential section — a collection of assorted bures near the docks. I ran into a couple of the *Adi Moapa* crew who invited me for dinner and said I could sleep on the boat until they sailed. With my needs covered and three hours of daylight left, I took a walkabout down the shore road I'd seen from the boat. On one side, the flat bay stretched to the horizon. The land side was thick with coconut trees through which houses could sometimes be seen. An offshore breeze tumbled down from the ridges and blew with the steadiness of a gentle air conditioner. The smoke columns from the hillside village fires now leaned seaward. I had gone a couple of miles in solitude when I saw a man standing in the middle of the road a little ways ahead. He wore shorts and a singlet and held a cane knife in his right hand. He looked at me for a few seconds then went into the bushes on the mountain side of the road. I became wary but not alarmed, since cane knives, bush knives and machetes are essentially tools. Just as I got to the place where he stood, he popped out of the bushes with a mile-wide, gap-tooth grin, a coconut in his left hand and a raised cane knife in his right. He got my attention.

"Would you like a drink?" he asked.

While I tried to make sense out of his request, he lopped the top off the coconut with four chops of the knife and handed it to me, "Bula." he said.

"Bula. Vinaka vaka levu," I thanked him as I accepted the coconut and checked him over. A slightly built, coffee colored man. Somewhere over fifty with frizzy graying hair.

"My name is Harry. Half-breed Harry," he said as he tucked the knife under his arm and extended his hand.

"Hi, Harry. I'm Max." I shook his hand.

"Where are you going?"

"Just for a walk. I just got in on the *Adi Moapa*."

"Yes. I know that boat. I work on her sometimes. I am a shipwright at the boatyard in Savusavu. Harry the Boatbuilder. What do you do, Max?"

"I'm —" it was tough to put an answer into one sentence "— a sailor. On holiday right now."

This started a stream of questions from Harry. What kind of boats? Where did you sail to? How long did it take? We walked down to the beach and drew boat shapes in the sand to explain specific points of their rig, shape or construction. Harry climbed a forty-foot palm tree and chopped some coconuts down. "What are your plans," he asked as he opened a coconut.

"I'm going to Loa, tomorrow. Then to Taveuni."

"Where will you stay tonight?"

"On the *Adi Moapa*."

"You will have to be off the boat very early, before she sails. If you wish, you could stay with me. If you leave with me in the morning, you'll be in plenty of time for the bus to Loa."

I thought about it, took a drink of coconut milk, then said, "Thanks, Harry. I appreciate that offer. Vinaka vaka levu."

We crossed the road and entered a narrow valley filled with coconut trees and walled by steep mountain ridges. After ten minutes of slipping and sliding through mud, the path began climbing the side of the ridge and passed several wooden bures randomly clustered on bits of flat ground. Harry walked up to a box frame cabin, "This is my house." I followed him up the three steps to the porch, took off my boots and stepped inside. From the outside, Harry's house could be described as Tin Roof Rustic. Inside it was what you would expect from an artistic shipwright who enjoyed home improvement projects. A polished hatch cover served as a low table in the center of the room with an open book and this morning's teacup still on top. Signs of a bachelor's life. A cabinet "hutch" of Early American design, stood along one wall. Its tall sides intricately carved with the geometric designs seen on Fijian tapa cloth, its open shelves crammed with a mixture of books and magazines. A model of a two-masted schooner sat on a shelf. In one corner, Harry installed a set of bookshelves designed like the ones on boats. They even had the turned "fiddles" to keep books from tumbling out in rough seas. Here again, carvings decorated the sides of the highly polished wood. Other well crafted shelves, stools, chairs and tables filled the house. "You make beautiful furniture," I said, "Where did you get the design for the cabinet?"

"From a book," he went to the bookshelf and pulled out a battered magazine, "This one." He handed me a wartime issue of *Popular Mechanics*. "I'll make some tea. Have a rest." I sat on the floor near the table and he went to another part of the undivided room to brew tea. I leafed through the book, checking out the ads of the era. General Motors apologized for not being able to supply Buicks for Americans, "...But right now, tanks come first!" The patriotic rhetoric throughout the magazine called for Americans to sacrifice. "Bonds Buy Bullets. Buy War Bonds!" A do-it-yourself article, "Build this New England Hutch For Democracy."

"Where did you get this book, Harry?" I asked when he returned with the tea billy and cups.

"From the Americans I met during the war."

"Were you in the war?"

"Yes. I was a sergeant in a Fijian combat battalion that was sent to the Solomon Islands with the Marines." He sat down and poured the tea.

"I've read a lot about that campaign. World War Two history is my hobby."

"You weren't in it, were you?"

"No. But I had a lot of relatives who were. One landed at Tulagi, in the Solomons. What are the natives like, there? I've read about the invading armies, but nothing about the residents. Are they like Fijians?"

"Oh, no. They are very primitive. They are not Christians. They still practice magic, worship sharks, collect heads and use shell money."

"Shell money? What does it look like? What do they buy with it?"

He told me of the Solomon islanders as he remembered them and talked openly about his wartime exploits. For awhile, he was a young man passing through the rites to become a warrior.

"Oh, I forgot to open the window," he said as he went to a low window on the wall facing me and opened the wooden shutters. The view overlooked the valley, down onto the hundreds of palm fronds twisting in the breeze. A thin, beige line marked the beach bordering the turquoise waters of the bay. Low, cumulous clouds piled up like laundry on the horizon under a blue sky just getting its first touch of gold from the afternoon sun. "You've got a million dollar view, Harry. How much is the rent?"

He laughed, "You don't have to pay rent to live like this in Fiji. Who would rent it? A Fijian just builds his own bure."

Besides myself, I knew of several past associates who are working their butts off so they can live in a place like this when they retire. By then they won't be able to make the climb up here and will settle for a mobile home in a desert, retirement community. "I guess you're right. Have you always lived here, Harry?"

"Oh no. I've only been here for ten years, since I lost my boat," he motioned towards the model of the schooner.

"That's a trim little trader," I said.

"She could go anywhere. I used her for trading between Tonga and Fiji mostly. Though I did go to New Zealand once for a load of trade goods."

"What happened to her?"

"She was driven ashore in a cyclone, on the point at the end of the road here. I was aboard with my crew, and we got off safely but my ship was a total loss — except for the timber I salvaged to make this house and furniture." He paused in his story while he poured some tea. "I had no insurance or money. I was bust. So I found this site, cleared it, and built my house. I got a job as a chippie at the boatyard and have been here ever since."

"As simple as that, huh?"

"Life becomes very simple when you don't have much left."

You got that right, I thought. "Will you be going back to sea?"

"No. I've had my travel adventure and am too old to start another. I am happy to settle down, repair boats, make furniture for people. But I would have kept right on sailing if I hadn't been shipwrecked. It's easier to keep traveling than it is to get started."

That's true, unless you're motivated by expiring visas. I would probably still be in New Zealand if I could've stayed. Just because it offered a bit of "security." It's curious how easily my groove in life can slip into a rut that feels so secure that I want to furnish it. We talked for hours. He told me of his English father who taught him boat building and left Harry the schooner when he died. He questioned me about my life and experiences. I was used to giving monologues of my story and embellished it freely. It was talk-story time. Though we had no watch or clock, I could tell that it was past midnight and yawned a couple of times. Harry caught the hint. "You must be tired," he said, "You can lay your sleeping bag here," he indicated a stack of mats.

"Have you been to Taveuni?" I asked.

"Once. Several years ago. But only to the port. It's a different island from the rest of Fiji. It was invaded by Tongans a long time ago and some people say there are groups of them still remaining."

Chapter Ten
Close Encounters with Local Maids

The next morning, after a breakfast of boiled rice, tea, and sea biscuits coated with margarine and treacle, Harry and I started down the path to the beach road. The valley lay in the shadow of the mountain leaving patches of mist hovering in the coconut groves while the beach and bay sparkled in the sunlight. We didn't say much as we negotiated the slippery trail but once on the road, the going was easier and our conversation picked up.

"Thanks for the hospitality, Harry. I enjoyed the evening very much."

"So did I. You started me thinking about sailing again. It was a good life and I miss it. Do you think I'm too old?"

"Harry, any guy who can scale a thirty-foot palm tree is automatically approved for sea duties."

He grinned at me, probably guessing that I couldn't climb one without extensive training. "I'm going to think about how to get another boat. I've got some money saved and could probably get partners if I needed them. The islands need another trading boat. The *Adi Moapa* is the only one which calls here and is always booked with cargo. Did you see the stacks of beer bottles at the pier when you came in?" I nodded. "They have been there for more than a year, waiting for a boat to Suva." He talked all the way to town.

In Savusavu, we went to Harry's boatyard where he introduced me around and I had a cup of tea and a smoke with his workmates. Then I left to catch the bus, promising to visit him on my return from Taveuni. I waited in front of the Mom & Pop store near the main intersection of cross-island roads and studied the town's activity center where two cars arriving from different directions caused a temporary traffic jam — "You go first." "No, you go first." The bus arrived causing a minor bustle as the Chinese storekeeper and the bus driver loaded grocery deliveries onto the roof and a half-dozen passengers boarded the bus.

The locally made bus resembled an elongated, motorized stage coach, the design probably taken from a John Wayne film, made almost entirely out of wood. It twisted, squeaked and groaned through every bend in the road. Dust continuously fell from the slats of the overhead luggage racks only to be recycled by the windstream inside the bus. The fifteen other passengers and I bounced off the hardwood seats in unison when the coach hit a pothole. The road crested a ridge a few miles east of Savusavu then headed down to the coast and a smoother road. We stopped next to an idyllic tropic lagoon while the driver replaced a flat tire. During the day, people got off at various coconut plantations and clearings in the jungle. No one got on.

In the late afternoon, the bus began climbing a steep mountain ridge when the fan belt broke. The driver made it to the crest in short hops, stopping often to let the motor cool. There, a panorama opened that stretched eastward from the shadowed valley below to the shoreline and the Somosomo Strait with the hazy outline of Taveuni Island beyond. The sun was setting as the bus twisted down to the valley floor where it chugged along the level road. Finally, the driver pulled up to a stop, turned in his seat and said, "Loa. End of the line." A young Fijian woman and I, the only passengers remaining, got off and the driver pulled away leaving us in total darkness.

I could barely see the outline of the woman only a few feet away, "Do you know where the village of Loa is located?" I asked her.

"No, I don't. I'm not from around here. I'm going to Taveuni but I missed the boat since the bus was so late, and now, I don't know what to do. What about you?"

"I have exactly the same problem."

Neither one of us had a flashlight, and even so wouldn't have known which direction to go since thick bushes lined both sides of the road. I lit a cigarette. I didn't offer her one. Fijian men don't smoke much as a rule and Fijian women, almost never.

"There will be a boat leaving in the morning. But first, we must find someone to help us. We can't stay on the road all night. It will probably rain."

Suddenly I heard a deep, resonant voice behind me, "Bula, bula. Where are you going?"

The hair on the back of my head snapped to attention.

"Bula," said the woman, "we are taking tomorrow's boat to Taveuni."

A man moved closer to us and I could see a white singlet, "Then you will need a place to stay, follow me."

Although the T-shirt didn't exactly glow in the dark we managed to follow it down the road and then onto a muddy trail cut through the bushes. After a few minutes, we emerged into a clearing where the man led us to a house. I went up the steps to the porch, took off my boots and followed the others inside.

A hurricane lamp glowed in the center of the floor, giving enough light to see the man. Besides the singlet, he wore army camouflage pants and a frizzy hair style that doubled the size of his head. But he didn't look top heavy since the rest of his frame was muscled with a jailhouse build you could bounce baseballs off of. He woke a young boy who had been sleeping on a mat near the lamp. He spoke to the boy in Fijian and the boy left. I had followed the woman's lead and sat on the floor. He turned to us, "Would you like some tea?" He fired up a Primus stove and put a billy of water on it.

"I must admit, you gave me quite a start out there on the road," he said, "I was just coming back from a church meeting and didn't expect anyone to be on the road at that time of night."

We told him of our bus trip. The woman did most of the talking. "I am visiting my village on Taveuni," she said, "I live in Suva."

"Then it was God who sent me to you," he said. As if on cue, raindrops started tapping on the tin roof. Deity or coincidence, I was glad to be inside. "I am Ratu Nemia. Welcome to Loa."

"My name is Seini," the woman said.

"I'm Max. Pleased to meet you, Ratu Nemia." Ratu means chief, so I relaxed knowing I was with a God fearing, village headman.

The boy returned to the house and talked with Nemia in Fijian. "You go with this boy," he said to the woman. She thanked him, said good night, and left. "There is a house with women where she can stay. I live alone here with my son." He brought a tray with cups, tea bags and jars of Milo and Nescafe, then filled the cups from the billy of hot water. "Please, help yourself," he said as he sat on the floor across from me. I went for the Nescafe while Ratu Nemia mixed a cup of Milo.

"Thank you."

"Where are you from, Max?"

"Most recently, Hawaii. Before that, Los Angeles."

"You are an American. I met some of your countrymen when I served with the UN peacekeeping forces," he gestured towards the fatigues he wore. "So now you are traveling around Fiji."

"I like it. This is my second time here."

"Oh? Where else have you visited?"

It was talk-story time so I settled in and reviewed my wanderings for the past year and brought the Ratu up to date. I talked without interruption while he rolled up a foot-long cigarette from a shred of rope tobacco and magazine paper. When I finished, he offered the cigarette to me. I declined, saying that I was trying to quit. It must have been about nine o'clock. The bong, bong, bong of the kava grinders could be heard outside. I started to mix another cup of coffee.

"I don't have any kava. I don't like it very much. But, if you want, I'll get you some. Do you like it?"

"Not a whole lot. Sometimes it tastes a little nga-nga."

"Do you have kava in Hawaii?"

"No. The Hawaiians did drink it at one time, they called it 'ava, but the missionaries made them stop."

"I don't think that could happen here. The kava ceremony is one of our oldest customs. Kava is a spiritual connection with our old beliefs and our Gods."

"Oh, I see." I wondered which of his Gods led him to find us on the road, the Christian one or the Fijian one? It didn't matter to me if both of them were in on it, I'm not choosy about the divine assistance which gets me out of sleeping in the rain.

"The old Fijian faith has many Gods, or spirits as the missionaries call them. Many people have seen and heard them, usually at night, so it is very difficult to deny their existence. When I heard your voices on the road tonight I thought it was my turn to see one."

"A lot of Hawaiians still believe in their old Gods as well. Madam Pele, the Fire Goddess is the most popular. I've had friends whose judgment I trusted, tell me that they had encountered her while driving on some dark road."

"Maybe you'll see one when you go to Taveuni, tomorrow. The Somosomo Strait is the domain of a shark spirit named Ndakuwangga which has the power over ships. It has consumed several and it would be a good idea to offer some food into the water on your way across."

We talked for awhile then turned in. I lay in my sleeping bag puzzling over the ease with which Pagan and Christian Gods lived together in the Fijians' mind. I had been led to believe that their integration was not an option.

In the morning mist, Loa turned out to be only marginally bigger than its dot on the map. Ratu Nemia led me past a cluster of huts perched on poles and through a shoe-sucking mangrove swamp to the boat. The vessel resembled a thirty foot version of the *Adi Moapa* with an economy crew of a captain, engineer and deckie in one Indian man. A couple of dozen people with their jute sack and beer crate baggage filled the hull. I caught a glimpse of Seini in the crowd, then climbed onto the cabin top and set my pack down among the sprinkling of passengers up there.

"See me when you return from Taveuni," Nemia called as the boat backed off the mudbank. I sat on my sleeping bag and chatted with my neighbors who politely interrogated me with the standard where are you going, where are you coming from, who are you and are you married questions. Everyone in Fiji, from kids to oldies, men and women, asked "Are you married?" When I said "no", the line of questioning went into the "why not?" phase. I said "yes" a couple of times and opened up an area of my life that I wasn't ready to look at. The few backward glances I took set my Mental Committees off on a spree of night-long debate, though the past year of hustling a living left little time for deep reflection and allowed the emotions to cool. But the question remained. Was I evading responsibilities or seeking my destiny? It's a tough call. One that's easier to make on someone else. 'You ought to be good at it. This makes two marriages and a live-in, all with five-year life spans. Didn't even marry the last one,' the Morality Committee Chairman whispered into my ear. The Rationale Attorney countered, 'Besides, it's immaterial.'

'Is that so? Well look where your love them and leave them policy has gotten you. If you had followed the directions of your generation you would have a very stable life right now.'

'Oh? Who told you that? God? My generation's direction was simply to get a car, a wife, some kids, a house, a job, a medical and retirement plan, a cabin in the woods, a boat on a trailer and a mobile home in the desert. My generation was the one number-crunchers used to figure out all the insurance statistics. How long a man could be expected to make car, house, insurance, credit card interest and tax payments. It determined how long a person was expected to work and how many years they could expect to tick off on retirement watches. I took my turn in that middle-class churn and found out it wasn't for me. I tried to make it happen. Bought cars. Got married no kids. Had credit cards and insurance. Worked hard and partied harder. Been there, done that. I no longer want to be a part of anyone's numbering system. But, even as a dropout from the system, I'm still counted in the final tally.'

'You count as nothing,' whispered the Chairman.

'Wait a minute. Some of the vehicles crack-up in the human race. Some break down. Many are simply spectators parked around the trackside like a stock car derby in Texas. Maybe that's how it got the name Human Race. I think I'm driving around looking for my pit crew.'

A school of flying fish skimmed the wave tops for a few minutes. The Fijians yelling "Ika vuka," flying fish! Nothing excites a Fijian more than the sight of fish breaking the surface and the event had everyone chattering out fish stories for the remainder of the two-hour trip across the Somosomo Strait.

We pulled up to a short, concrete pier. The passengers from the lower deck hopped out and into the shade of the dilapidated shed which stood on the end. Then the top deck passengers got off. Seini came up to me as I walked into the shed. "Hello. Where are you going?" she asked in a singsong lilt.

"Hello, Seini. Well, I'm not sure. I'd really like a cup of coffee. Do you know where I could get one?"

"Yes. At the Holiday Inn Hotel. Just turn left at the road. You can't miss it."

"Thank you. Where are you going? Will you join me for coffee?"

She smiled, "Yes, I can do that."

We walked along the main street past a string of one story wood shops baking in the afternoon sun. A couple of loiterers sitting on the edge of the shaded porch in front of a Mom & Pop store were the only people in sight. The passengers had dispersed and faded out of sight. I don't know where they went, there were no vehicles around.

"Do you live here, in town, Seini?"

"No. My village is on the north side of the island. I will take the bus tomorrow. The boat was late and today's bus has already gone."

"I guess I'll have to wait for tomorrow's bus, as well."

"Does it bother you?"

"No. I mean, what can I do? The bus is either there or it isn't. Tell me about your village. What do you do there?"

"Oh, I don't live there anymore. I've been staying in Suva for the past three years. I'm just coming for a visit." As we walked, she described her village, then the Holiday Inn came into sight.

Inside, the hotel coffee shop swamped my head with memories of Hawaii. Its ambiance was a clone of the Americana Tropicale design so popular in Honolulu. It was great. Unlimited cups of coffee for one price. We got a booth and ordered breakfast.

"Will you stay here tonight," she asked me.

"I hadn't planned on it. Is there another choice in town?"

"There are some rooms behind the Chinese store. They are not very modern, but they are reasonable. Which way are you going?"

"I wanted to go along the north coast. Nowhere really special."

I didn't want to tell her of my quest to straddle the 180th meridian. It might sound immature to a person who probably crossed it every day as a child on her way to school.

"Why don't we travel together tomorrow and you can stay in my village?"

I paused a discreet, five seconds before saying, "That's a great idea."

She smiled and offered her hand for a handshake. I reached over the table and shook her hand. Her grip was loose, allowing her index finger to curl and softly scratch my palm. The message was plain but

I hadn't seen that signal since junior high school. When Fijian girls fancy you, you're the first one to know it.

After breakfast, we went to the Mom & Pop store where the owner showed me his two-room hotel, actually a small cabin behind the shophouse, divided in half with a partition. Both rooms were empty, so I took the one closest to the outdoor toilet. I threw my bag on the floor then did some shopping with Seini in the store. We bought rice, tins of milk, margarine, treacle, fish, meat, loaves of bread, bars of soap and a couple of bottles of beer. The usual shopping list of things which can't be made in the village. I bought a couple of small flashlights and gave one to Seini.

"Just in case we get stuck on the road like we did last night."

She smiled, "I don't carry a flashlight when I'm in Suva, but I'm sure I can use this while I'm here."

We carried the goods to my room, but she stood outside the cabin while I put them away. I understood her discretion. If she stepped inside for only one minute, the Bamboo Wireless would spread the gossip island wide in only a few hours. The old, Chinese shopkeeper is lurking in the gloom of his store, fifty feet away. Who needs a telephone? We went back into the store, bought a couple of bottles of Coke and sat on a small bench in front.

"Where are you staying tonight?"

"With an old couple from my village who live in town. Are you married?"

"Uh, no."

"Why did you hesitate?" she teased me with a smile.

"I guess I'm just not used to the question," I lied, "How about you?"

"I've never been married. I left my village when I was seventeen to attend college in Suva. After that, I got a job in an office and haven't found it necessary to get married."

"Why do Fijians ask if I'm married?"

"Just curiosity, I guess. I must be going now, the bus will leave from this store at eight-thirty," Seini said, "I'll meet you here, all right?"

"That's a deal."

"Well, I'll be going now. I'll see you tomorrow."

I watched her walk away. Medium height, slim, and crowned with shiny-black, crinkly hair that covered her head like an aura. I hadn't done any socializing with the Fijian ladies. In the villages, someone watched me all the time, just out of curiosity. In Suva, contact with Fijian women usually took place in pricey discos.

I slept that afternoon and went out around dusk to the noodle shop for dinner. Then returned to my room and read till the lights were turned off at ten pm. I drifted off to sleep and woke up to a gentle shaking and a flashlight beam in my eyes.

"Sshh. It's Seini." Without a further word, she straddled me, squirmed around while she hiked her sulu up to her hips and introduced me to pagan love.

Sometime during the night, she slipped out of the cabin and I grabbed a few hours sleep. In the morning, I carried my pack to the porch of the store, had a Coke and a small cake for breakfast then waited for eight-thirty. I didn't know what time it was but neither the bus nor Seini was there. Awhile later, she came strolling down the street in a colorful, wide skirt and a peasant style blouse. No shoes.

"Hello Max, you look tired, did you sleep well?"

I love cheeky women, "A mosquito kept me awake part of the night. Did you have a pleasant evening? You look very refreshed and cheerful."

"Yes. It's very peaceful at the old couple's bure. They go to bed early and sleep like logs."

Her eyes shifted from me to the doorway of the store where the owner stood in the shadow. I glanced over just in time to see him shuffle out of sight. Seini sat beside me and laughed, "He's a nosy old man. But then I don't blame him, it's a boring old town. I'll be glad to get back to Suva."

"Is this your first visit back to the village?"

"Oh, no. I come here once a year. I love to see my family and friends but I get so restless after a week that I can't wait to leave. Maybe with you around it will be different."

A silent alarm went off in my head, I ignored it and went on lapping up the words of this cheerful woman.

"Near to my village are fresh water ponds at the edge of the sea to bathe in. And there will be a feast. That's why I come at this time of year. It will be fun to show you around the village."

"Is it near the International Date Line?"

"Oh, you know about that? Yes, there is a sign on the road only a short ways from my village. I'll take you there."

The alarm was muffled by the purple clouds of fantasy drifting through my mind, which was replaced by the brown clouds of dust stirred up as the bus pulled up in front of the store. All of the out-island busses are made to one set of plans, those of a long, wooden stage coach mated to a truck chassis and engine. It had a windshield and a rear window but the sides had no glass, just a tarp to lower when it rained.

The bus passed the Holiday Inn hotel and my mind tripped out on thoughts of coffee in the restaurant. No, better yet, room service.

Yeah, that's the ticket. Air-conditioning for the afternoon siesta. A couple of novels. A dip in the pool. Western food. A wham-bam breakfast with hotcakes, sausage and eggs and an unlimited supply of coffee. For once, all the Committees chimed in agreement.

'Yeah, a soft bed. That would be nice,' said a member.

'Can we have hot water?' asked another.

'Sure. The room might even have a bathtub!'

'Why not treat ourselves? This isn't a crusade is it?'

'Believe me, guys,' the Accountant said, 'if puka shells were pennies we'd be in there like a shot. At least for one night.'

The road skirted the edge of the island, rising to cross steep ridges then diving to the valleys between. Jungle in the highlands, coconut plantations below. A couple of hours from Waiyevu we got off the bus at Seini's village, a string of unpainted, wooden and thatch bures tucked in the trees along the base of a craggy ridge. Two, teenage boys ran towards us.

"Seini! Seini! We heard the bus stop and thought it was you!"

They hugged each other and Seini turned to me, "These are my brothers, Moses and Ben."

They took our bags and talked as we walked into the village, passing houses which perched on piles that looked like they had been planted a few generations ago, and with siding to match. This old village must be cyclone-proof to last this long. Kids of all sizes gathered around us as we walked and adults poked their heads out of doorways and waved. I smiled and waved back.

"This is my family's house," she said, and led me up the steps to the porch, "Leave your boots here."

I followed her into the room and waited as she greeted her father, a slender man who sat cross-legged on the floor. Then, in a loud voice, "Father, this is Max. He is traveling in the islands. He comes from America." She turned to me and said in a lower voice, "This is my father, Jonas. He is hard of hearing."

We said "Bula, bula" to each other, smiled and shook hands, then he motioned for me to sit next to him on the floor. It was talk-story time. Our bags sat near the door and Seini sorted out the foods we brought and carried them off to another part of the house.

Jonas and I talked. Non-stop questions from him, improvised answers from me. After awhile, I gave him a couple of plugs of rope tobacco I brought. He thanked me and commenced the twenty minute operation to roll a thin cigarette in a foot-long strip of magazine paper. Peeling a leaf of tobacco from the rope, spreading it out and shredding it took time. This was not a tobacco for chain smokers. He wore a purple satin sulu and a faded, blue T-shirt with a grinning Mickey Mouse printed on the front.

"I like your shirt, Jonas."

"Peace Corps give me," he said, "I like yours." Mine had a surfer and "Hawaii" silk-screened on it.

Then he switched into sign language and got across that he would like to trade shirts. I had read that trading shirts was a custom with the Fijians, but didn't give it much thought. A couple of minutes later, the deal was made and we wore each other's shirts. Seini returned carrying a tray loaded with cups, tea pot, sweetened condensed milk, sea biscuits and orange marmalade.

"Father learned English in the mission school but never had a chance to use it much."

Though she said it in a normal tone, old Jonas nodded slightly as though he heard every word. I had a hunch he faked his deafness as a convenience, like an uncle of mine did.

"He gets along very well in sign language," I pointed to our shirts.

"He'll like you for that," Seini said.

We told Jonas how we met and described the boat trip, including the flying fish event. Seini described the Holiday Inn in Waiyevu. "He hasn't been to Waiyevu in seven years," she said to me. I mulled that fact over while they talked.

"Does he visit any other villages?" I asked.

"Not very often."

Polynesian Paralysis to the maximum. For a lot of people, it's just what a doctor used to prescribe. "Take an ocean voyage." "Lay back at the Club Med Tahiti for awhile." "Leave your wallet and watch where you can't get to them easily." "Stop running for awhile and re-examine your goal." All those good things you're going to do for yourself when you get the money.

Seini interrupted my thoughts, "Would you like some more tea?"

"Thank you." I looked at Jonas. He smiled at me and pointed to his new shirt. "Vinaka vaka levu," he said, then followed it up with a stream of Fijian.

"He thanks you for the shirt and invites you to stay in his house as long as you wish," Seini said.

"I appreciate your hospitality and hope I won't be an inconvenience to you."

Seini translated for him and he shook his head, "No bother. No bother."

Moses and Ben were sitting along the wall. Seini called them over, "Take Max to the pools. Go with them. You can have a bath. Jonas nodded and smiled at me like he thought it was a good idea, so I left with the boys.

We walked through the village and collected the usual retinue of kids, all boys. They knew we headed for a bath since I carried a towel, Moses carried a bar of soap and Ben had a hand mirror which he played at reflecting a sunbeam into the houses we passed. The party followed the road as it climbed the steep ridge which backed the village. A wind-proof wall 200 feet high. Tall grass covered the slopes on the other side of the ridge and small gullies lined with trees traced the routes of streams which converged in the narrow, jungle filled valley below then flowed to the nearby seashore. The valley showed no signs of habitation. It looked like a picture postcard from the beginning of time. My mini-guides told me a line of facts and fantasies about the area.

"No one lives in this valley," said one kid.

"And no one stays overnight," said another.

"Why not?" I asked.

"Because it is spirit land and they will carry you away."

"But we can use the bath in the daytime."

They smiled as they told me this, but then Fijian kids smile a lot and I was never sure when they were having me on. Ben and Moses led the way down the road onto the valley floor and turned off into a single-file trail through the trees then onto a beach at a small cove. A little further on, where the jungle met the sand, we came to two, stream fed pools formed in the natural depressions of a rocky outcrop. A dam made of smaller stones separated them, the pool closest to the beach filled by the overflow from the pool behind and above it about a foot. Trees covered three sides framing the view of the shore, the reef, sea and sky.

"Use the lower pool to bathe in," Moses told me, "Then you can rest in the other one."

I wore a sulu while I washed, even so, the audience still found a lot to giggle at. Then I slid into the resting pool which was deeper and wider. I faced the ocean, stretched my arms out along the brim and floated. My body rising with each intake of breath, sinking with each exhale. After awhile the kids got bored of watching me and ran down the beach to play. Moses and Ben drifted off into the bush and I was alone. The brilliance of the sky, the subtle pastels of the reef looked like a scrim for a Hollywood production of *Lost In Paradise*. The surfaces of the sea and pools lay still as painted foreground. Quiet on the set!

'Hey! This is pretty nice,' a voice in my head commented.

'Yeah, we know a few guys who would give their left one to live like this,' said another.

'Maybe this is the trade-off for not having much money. If we had money, we would be in beautiful downtown Waiyevu at the Holiday Inn.'

'That's life. If you have enough money, you take the easy way out and can direct your motions, somewhat. When you're on the cheap, you take what comes down the pike.'

'But if you work for the money to do the things you want to do, you don't have time to do the things.'

'Look at all the guys who have boats, golf clubs, swimming pools and never use them because they have to work to keep up the payments. You had most of those toys.'

'That's true. Maybe we should consider our past, financial bath as a blessing?'

'You're not hungry. Made a pile of warm friends over the past year, and today's not shabby.'

Everyone had something to say, and not a negative voice in the crowd. They all pointed out how easy life could be if I stopped trying to make it so complex, so planned. No, not planned, projected. Not the way it might be but the way it was going to be as I foresaw it. I tried to remember the last time I foretold what was going to happen in my life and had it come to pass. I couldn't. I couldn't even remember the first time, or any time. Sure, I had dreamed of coming to the South Seas but not as a middle-aged dropout pounding the hippie trail. I thought I'd own a long white schooner and wear a captain's hat an unbuttoned shirt and white duck pants like the guy in the *Adventures In Paradise* TV series. A gentle debate went on in my mind for awhile about the pros and cons of boat ownership. The committees reached the conclusion that owning a boat would not enhance that moment, and might even detract from the sense of freedom and serenity that I felt.

Moses and Ben came out of the bush, each carrying large breadfruits in their hands. "We must return, soon," Ben said. I got dressed and we started off down the beach where the kids were playing with Fijian Racers, foot-long sections from the stem of a palm frond, fashioned with a machete into a model racer on skids. A notch was cut into the top of the racer where the "driver" put the end of a three-foot stick. Then the driver pushed the stick and the race was on. Some experts could keep the stick in place throughout a full-speed, running turn. Adults enjoyed this pastime as well, and I once watched two, middle-aged women strolling along the road, shopping baskets balanced on their heads, leisurely driving their Fijian Racers. One of the kids loaned me his and I drove it back to the village.

"How was your bath?" Seini asked when I entered the bure.

"Great! That's a very special place, isn't it?"

"Yes, it is. The people have several superstitions about the pools."

"The kids told me a couple of them."

"The ones the adults have are different than the children's," she said with a smile.

"Tell me one."

"Sshh. Later." She glanced at Jonas, asleep, or pretending to be on a mat nearby. "You rest, now. I have work to do."

She left and I stretched out on the floor, tossed and turned for two or three seconds, then dozed off. I awoke to the sound of the pressure lantern being pumped up. Jonas lay on his mat, his head propped on one arm, watching Moses prepare the lantern. I went outside and watched the last bit of dusk fade out. It was around six o'clock. Tropic days don't vary much in length, the sun rising and setting about twelve hours apart every day. The village outlines disappeared, replaced by rectangles of soft light from nearby doorways and windows. Inside the bures, men relaxed, listening to the BBC on battery-powered radios, rolling cigarettes for kava time.

I returned inside the bure where the two boys placed settings on a dinner cloth which lay spread out on the floor. Then a stout, Fijian woman came in carrying a large pot of n'dalo, taro root. Seini followed her with a pot of steaming tapioca root. She introduced me to her mother, we exchanged "bulas" and though she smiled a lot, that's all she said for the rest of the meal.

After dinner, the kids rushed outside, the women left to clean up the dishes and cook house and the men lay down for another rest period. I couldn't sleep with the shrieks of children at play outside mixed with the jibble-jabble from the short wave radio inside. "This is the BBC World News. Russia and America are..." filtered into my mind and I imagined the scenes being described by the commentator. When the time ticks from Greenwich signaled 8 am International Coordinated Time, it was 8 pm M'bouma village time, a half a world apart, geographically. Immeasurably distant in practically every other aspect. On one hand, there's London, a centuries old, world capital. On the other, there's M'bouma, a centuries old, collection of bures clustered in a site on a dead-end road at the edge of the sea.

The kava grinders started up soon after that. Bong, bong, bong. Moses set the kava bowl in the center of the room and Ben brought him a bag of mashed up kava root and they began mixing the brew. The end of the kava bonging seemed like a signal for people to begin visiting hours and men began arriving at the bure. They nodded, smiled and found a place on the floor to sit. A half-dozen guys joined us by the time the kava was ready. After the kava invocation, the men settled down to a serious meeting. They spoke in Fijian, though I understood enough to figure out they discussed the upcoming village feast. One guy kept minutes in a wire bound notebook while another fellow jotted figures into a hardbound ledger. I had a couple of bilos of kava, acted suitably interested, then excused myself by indicating the outhouse. The men nodded, smiled, then went back to their business.

I went out on to the back porch and sat on the steps. My eyes had just gotten used to the dark when a voice whispered behind me, "Max." I looked over my shoulder to the porch. "Down here." I looked under the porch and saw the dim outlines of Seini. She came closer. "A mosquito might wake you tonight. Don't try to swat it." She giggled and disappeared under the house.

Her message was clear and set me to thinking about the sleeping arrangements. Somewhere on the floor, no doubt. Maybe near a doorway, closer to the mosquitoes. The bure's back entrance faced the outhouse, the jungle and the nearby ridgeline. The mosquito will probably come from those dark shadows.

I went back inside and listened in on the last hour of the meeting. Everyone's face relaxed when it ended, and the kava and questions flowed freely until after midnight when the last guest left. Jonas turned the lamp down to a low glow, then stretched out on his mat near the front door. Moses and Ben lay around the lantern like it was a campfire and I unrolled my sleeping bag along the wall near the back doorway. In the gloom, I could just make out the breezy movements of the cloth which covered it. I lay awake in the dark, trying to figure out if anyone was still awake. Jonas snored loudly. He was definitely out. The boys finally stopped giggling about Jonas' two-toned concerto, and seemed to be asleep. A silent mosquito brushed my face and I made a lazy motion to bush it away. It landed on my cheek and flitted to my lips, nose and eyelids without a sound. I grabbed for it and caught a slender piece of grass which tugged against my pull, then went limp. I waited for a few minutes, then got up quietly, retied my sulu and crept out the back door. Moonlight made it brighter outside than in the bure and I easily followed the tree covered path to the privy, about 60 feet from the house. Before I got there, I heard a "buzz- buzz" from a nearby tree. I followed the sound and found Seini in the shadows.

"You have good hearing," she whispered, "You heard the mosquito buzz." She put her fingertips to my lips before I had a chance to answer. "Go open the door to the loo, just enough to make the hinge squeak once then close it. But don't slam it. If anyone is awake, they'll think you went in there."

I did as she directed. She seemed to have this drill down pretty good, probably through practice.

When I returned, she smiled and whispered, "follow me." She headed off through the trees, away from the trail and after a few minutes we arrived at a rock outcropping where she led me to a niche obviously prepared for the occasion with a carpet of fresh, palm leaves. It was about eight feet long but only two feet high. She stopped and looked at me for approval of the site, "There are no mosquitoes, here," she said.

"Looks like a good spot to me," was all I could think of to say. She smiled, unwrapped her sulu, held it out like wings and faced me, "See? No mosquitoes on me. But I'll bet there's one in your sulu." She walked closer, then suddenly reached out and jerked my sulu off. "Oh, my goodness! Look at that stinger!" She giggled, grabbed my stinger and led me to the niche where she spread the cloths on the palm leaves and wriggled onto the nest. While Seini's lovemaking in the cabin behind the Mom & Pop store in Waiyevu the night before had been as quiet as a shadow for fear that the Chinaman might be spying. This night she had no inhibitions and we soon left the confines of the niche to find interesting positions among the boulders. The overhead moon lighted the scene, complete with fade-outs caused by moonshadows from passing clouds. Judging by the angle of the moon, it was between two and three am when she led me back to the trail and I returned to the bure.

I crept up the back steps, my legs still a little shaky from the stress of stand-up sex, and sneaked back into my sleeping bag. No one stirred. I listened intently while my eyes got used to the dimly lit room. The boys' breathing sounded like sleepers, but Jonas was not snoring. So? Maybe he doesn't snore all night. I narrowed my eyes to a slit and watched the area where his head would be resting. When you stare into the dark for a long time, all kinds of apparitions can be imagined but I'm sure I saw glints of light from Jonas' eyes.

I got up with Jonas and the boys shortly after dawn and had a breakfast of tapioca pudding, toast and tea. Jonas smiled a lot in a seemingly genuine manner. This put me at ease. If he was awake when I returned, he probably believed I had only gone to relieve myself. Right? Using a mixture of English and Fijian he told me about the feast that would begin that night and continue for a few days through the full moon period. He didn't give an exact reason for the event, it seemed to be simply a celebration of the village. A statement like, "Here we are, more than 200 years old and still going strong."

We left the house and walked through a grove of cocoa trees to a grassy area where the feast would take place. Here, a large crew of villagers were working, some carrying poles and palm fronds, others digging postholes. We joined in and by lunchtime, the corner posts and roof framework were lashed together and erected. The men sat in groups of six or so, talking and laughing as they ate. We napped for an hour after lunch, then put the palm leaf roof on the structure. By three in the afternoon, the feast house, a roof thirty feet long supported by poles, was finished when several village women showed up with mats, cloths, and an assortment of bowls, plates and glasses. Seini was among them. I kept busy tidying up around the site and worked my way close to Seini who was setting up the table.

"Good afternoon," I said somewhat formally since there was another woman nearby. "I hope it doesn't rain, tonight." The weather was always a safe subject.

"You shouldn't talk about the weather," the other woman scolded, "That will make it turn on you."

Seini looked up at me with a smile, "Good afternoon. I don't think it will rain. The moon is too strong tonight."

"What does the moon have to do with it?" asked the other woman.

"It's just what I believe," said Seini. The other woman turned away from us and Seini mouthed the words "See you tonight." Or at least that's what I thought she said. I gave her a slight wink and a grin and wandered off towards the village and a shower.

Like most villages, M'bouma had water piped in from a nearby stream to spigots and shower heads fixed on cement pads. It served as the meeting place for women washing kids, clothes and dishes, and for the men who showered after work. Adults always bathed with their sulus on. Arranging it as needed to lather up and rinse off. The men bantered with me, a sign I had been accepted, more or less, for working with them.

"Tonight, we are having pig," said one guy, "Do you like dead pig? Ha, ha, ha."

"I just love dead pig! I haven't had any dead pig since I left Hawaii."

"Really?" He appeared to be about 20 years old and looked like he didn't know if I was having him on or not. "How do you cook it in Hawaii?"

One time in my career, I tended bar in a restaurant on Maui which gave a Hawaiian luau every weekend and I explained to the guy and a few other men who listened in, how Hawaiians cooked in an *imu*, underground oven. They nodded their understanding of the process, probably comparing it with their own roasting techniques, then smiled at me with an intimacy of one back yard chef to another.

After the shower, I went inside the bure and stretched out on my sleeping bag against the wall. Jonas sat cross-legged, near the center of the floor, rolling a cigarette. I propped up my head and watched him. We were alone in the bure.

"Are you tired, Max?" he asked quietly.

"A little."

"Yes. You worked hard today. And you seemed not to sleep to well last night. You were gone for awhile." He tamped the cigarette with a matchstick, then lighted it. The magazine paper flared until the tobacco caught on and glowed steady after a couple of puffs.

I used the time to think. "My stomach was not well. It kept me up for a few hours."

He looked at me and smiled. I suspected he knew it wasn't my stomach that had bothered me. But he couldn't be sure. Could he? No one had followed me from the house last night and we were far enough from the village so that the sounds of our lovemaking couldn't have been heard. I lay on my back and thought of possibilities. Maybe he watched me leave. Maybe he woke up right after I left and stayed awake while I was gone. Maybe he was just fishing, checking out a vague hunch. But would he know that Seini, who slept at her aunt's bure, had been gone from her bed a few hours last night? He could probably find out. There are no secrets in the village, it's just a matter of whether or not they are told. I didn't know who or how many women stayed with Seini in her aunt's bure, but one of them will know that Seini was out of the house for a couple of hours last night. I nodded off before my suspicions became paranoia.

Chapter Eleven
Max, the Modern Farmer

I awoke at sundown to the sound of Jonas and Ben talking as they fussed with the lantern. It got up to brightness in a few minutes and then Moses came in with a tea tray. He set it on the floor and the four of us gathered around for a cuppa.

"You rest good?" Jonas asked me.

"Yes, thanks. I slept well."

"Good. Now we stay up all night. Ha, ha, ha."

"Great." I feigned a smile, not sure where this was leading. We finished our tea, then Jonas muttered something to his sons, picked up the lantern and headed out the door. The boys and I fell in behind him and walked to the feast house. We moved through the bushes in a silent, single file giving my mind time to conjure up scenario after scenario of what might happen if Jonas found out that Seini and I were lovers. In the best case, nothing would happen. In the worst case, 'You could be beat up,' said a member of the Survival Committee. 'You could be killed,' said another. 'You could be forced under threat of these two options to get married!'

The sound of tightly harmonized singing drifted through the air and flickers of light from the feast house filtered through the leaves and then we entered the clearing. Packs of children chased each other, leaping and yelping in the moonlight. The adults sat in the feast house around a table cloth thirty feet long. Lanterns were placed every few feet and a few hung from the support. The table was only about one-third full.

"We sit here," Jonas said to me, "We are early. More people, will come." Ben and Moses had noticed a group of their peers standing outside, at the edge of the light, and they slid off to join them. Jonas motioned to a young girl and she came over, "Please bring us some tea," he asked her. She left and he turned to me, "Have you been to a Fijian feast, before?"

"No, I haven't."

"This one is an old tradition with my village. We have each year. Three other villages join us and it is a time when the young people of each village can meet each other."

"That sounds like an honourable custom," I said.

"It is a way of keeping peace between the villages when they marry with each other. Are you married?"

"Uh, no."

"But have you been married?"

"Uh, no. I've always lived alone." I don't know why I lied.

"You are no longer young. When do you take a wife?"

"Not for a while, Jonas, I don't have much to offer one right now."

"Seini told me you are a sailor."

"Yes, that's right."

"Then you have no home."

The girl returned with cups of tea for us and Jonas turned his attention to the other people seated around the table cloth. There was probably some social order which assigned seats around the cloth but I didn't probe my hosts for in-depth explanations of their customs but just did as I was gently told to do. Like a house pet. Short cloths were laid out and the kids began sitting around them. The women brought bowls of steaming food and set them on the cloths, then returned to the nearby cookhouse for more. Seini set a bowl of boiled tapioca in front of Jonas and I and smiled at us. I smiled back, then self consciously shifted my eyes right to see if Jonas was watching. He was smiling fondly at Seini. He liked his daughter.

When all the groups had been served, the women sat down at the end of the long table, though a few sat with the kids. Everyone sat with their head bowed while a bass voiced man at the end of the table recited a lengthy prayer. Then he said something in Fijian to the effect of "Let the feast begin" and the diners dug into the bowls of taro, tapioca, wild spinach and fish cooked in coconut milk. After the meal, the women and children cleared the table and took the dishes away. The men relaxed in place, a few rolled magazine paper cigarettes. They talked in low tones, eyelids at half mast. Everyone gets dozy after a Fijian meal. I think it's the taro root, n'dalo, that does it. It's a solid lump, about four times denser than an Irish potato, and possibly that much more nutritious. The Fijians eat it all the time and they are very fit people, overall. But it was like swallowing a handful of bullets.

The women returned with billys of tea, hot water, and jars of instant coffee and chocolate. A few men roused from their lethargy to sit up while they mixed the beverage of their choice. Their conversations gradually picked up in volume and included more people. The women filtered back and sat silently in groups behind the men. Across from me sat a smiling guy with a perfectly teased and trimmed, Fijian-Afro hair style which added another six inches around his head. He bent over to talk with someone and I saw Seini sitting behind him, looking at me. After a few seconds, she shifted her gaze around the room, reminding me that it was not a good idea to stare at someone. Anyway, the bushy haired guy sat up straight and blocked the view. This action went on all night. The kava bongers began their grinding operation and bowls of kava were brewed, consecrated to the Pagan Gods and distributed among the people. Some had brought their own bilos, coconut shell cups polished smooth from years of use.

A group of guys began singing in mission school harmony. They did a couple of tunes. Next, a female quartet sang a number. Then, another group of guys performed a song. Another group of girls. I had no idea what they sang about, but after awhile everyone seemed a lot friendlier. When people from different villages mixed socially, a little, warm-up music loosened their attitudes. The kava flowed freely and the guys and girls bantered and teased each other. Asides to their friends. Nudges. Winks. The flirtation game. But the glances I had of Scini told me that she wasn't playing. She stayed out of the front lines and occasionally flicked her head in my direction. The party thinned out after a couple of hours, the women and children left for the bures and the men stayed behind to drink kava, smoke cigarettes and talk around the lanterns. I stayed with them for awhile longer, then got up to relieve myself.

"You want to go to bure?" asked Jonas.

"Yes, thank you," I answered quickly, "I am very tired, now."

He signaled at Ben to go with me to the bure and we left the party. At the bure Ben lit a kerosene lamp, lowered the wick to a low glow, put it on a plate in the middle of the room and curled up around it. He fell asleep in seconds. I sat on my sleeping bag, leaning against the wall, watching the steady flame of the lamp. That small fire was the nightlight for the house. The little reminder that you are not totally out of power. There were probably only a few days during the history of this old village when it didn't have a flame going somewhere. It looked as if it would be that way for the next few decades, as well. This idyllic collection of huts isn't likely to suddenly make enough money to support a generator.

'Welcome to Simple Living,' said a voice-over in my mind, 'Remember, you asked for it.'

'I didn't hear anyone complain,' said another voice.

Others chimed in, 'Hey, great feast!' 'Good fun.' 'Right out of a Melville novel.' 'Except, in those days, the kava was ground up by the maidens chewing the root.'

The good old days before the invention of axle shaft pestles and welded steel mortars. The days when everything was made out of wood. Wooden digging sticks and spears made up the tool and weapon inventory. Houses were made out of saxophone reeds and coconut coir, and ass-grass was the uniform of the day. Modern M'bouma seemed only a couple of notches upscale from its beginnings. Besides the cocoa grove it was dependent on the coconut plantations for income, and when the price of copra fell, the men didn't work. You won't strike it rich, here. But you can live an easy life.

'If you don't mind sleeping on hard floors.'

'So, we can buy a mattress.'

'Sure! We'll just take two weeks off, go to Suva and hump a mattress back here on the bus and boat combo.'

'Well, maybe an air mattress will do. Or a water bed.'

I woke at daybreak, pulled on a sulu and sat on the back porch, daydreaming, when I saw a flash of color go behind one of the trees along the outhouse trail. I watched the spot and a few seconds later, Seini's head peeked around the tree. She signaled me to follow her and disappeared. I went down the path and saw her about thirty feet ahead. She didn't look back so I kept the distance between us. Near the road, she stopped and I came up to her.

"Go to the pools. I'll meet you there," she said.

I did as I was told, walked up the road and over the ridge then took the path through the bush to the beach. The sun had not yet cleared the mountain when I arrived at the pools. I sat on a rock and looked around. In their dim, tree covered niche, they had lost the sparkling, waters-of-youth image I saw the first time. The atmosphere felt gently haunted. No birds chirped, not even a splash from the pools broke the silence. How many people are injured or killed by ghosts each year? I have never known anyone who was physically abused by a spirit. Not to say that it couldn't happen, but it's not a common occurrence. More than likely, spirits of any kind would go for the mind. Once there, they could be guardian angels, or spiritual guides, or devils. Maybe they are the source of intuitive thinking. Maybe it's only will power which selects the one to listen to. Maybe that's the mob that's in my head. If so, I won't worry about any more spirits entering my mind, it's already jam-packed with advisors. Take a number and get in line. Fill out an application and leave it with the secretary.

"Max," a voice whispered behind me.

The hair on the back of my head raised up and my skin stood at attention like a plucked chicken's. I turned to see Seini standing by the pool. "Good morning," I said.

She smiled her greeting, "Would you like to take a shower? These baths are not pleasant in the morning."

"Sure." They're outright spooky.

I followed her along a faint path which bordered the stream. It crossed the road and headed up the narrow valley shaded by a canopy of candlenut and breadfruit trees, then twisted through bamboo groves whose tops softly clattered like wind chimes in the light breeze. It stopped at a waterfall spilling from a twelve-foot ledge into a large pool. The water fell in a thin, continuous curtain and made a soft hissing sound as it entered the pool. Seini stopped at a cluster of boulders resembling the humps on a sea dragon's back and sat on the lowest one.

"So, this is the shower," I said.

"Yes. Do you like it?"

"It's beautiful."

"Then let's go in," she said. She removed her sulu and waded into the water.

I dropped my sulu and followed her. The cool water almost took my breath away. Swimming in tropical pools always seems cold and thick compared with the warm and buoyant ocean. But I soon got used to it and after a couple of laps I treaded water and Seini swam over to me.

"I'm glad you were awake this morning," she said, "If we waited too long, the rest of the village would be up. I'm sure we got away unnoticed."

"But how will I explain my absence?" I knew I'd be questioned when I got back.

"Just say you went for a walk. Come over to the waterfall."

We swam to the sheet of water, passed under it and into a niche carved out by the water. We hung onto rocks and looked at each other for a few minutes then she moved closer and kissed me, then broke away, splashed water at me, laughed and swam off. I took after her but she beat me out of the water, grabbed her sulu and scrambled up the pile of boulders. I bypassed my sulu and followed her wet footprints through the rocks. Hide and seek? I could play the game. I climbed the boulders and hopped from top to top looking down into the crevices. I found Seini hiding in one of them, her back toward me, looking the way she had come. I worked my way into a crevice behind her and crept up. "You're mine," I whispered.

We made love against the warm, smooth boulders. Played tag. Made love in the pool. Enjoyed each other without inhibitions. We frolicked like kids ditching school. Judging by the shadows, it was about noon when Seini said we should leave so we headed back to the road. We talked easily, and asked about each others views on life, in general.

"What do you think of Fiji, Max?"

"In what way? I like it overall, more than I ever imagined."

"Do you think you could live here?"

"I've wondered what it would be like to live for a year or so on an outside island. But I don't have enough money or visa to do that."

"If you had your own bure, you could live very cheaply, and with your skills you could earn money from odd jobs at the plantations."

I glanced at her as we walked down the path. She smiled most of the way to the road. "I'll leave you here," she said, "I've got to go to another village on an errand. That's my reason for leaving early." She held her hand out for a handshake and tickled my palm with her index finger, "I like you, Max."

"I like you, too, Seini. Thanks for the lovely morning."

On the way back to the village I thought about whether or not Fijians said "I love you" to each other in the same way that Americans and Europeans did. I'd never read anywhere that Fletcher Christian, or any of the other South Sea Island lovers ever said "I love you" to their dusky sweethearts. I liked Seini. She was a lively pleasure to be with, but love? I'm not even sure what it means in English.

Jonas was sitting in the middle of the floor when I returned to the bure. "Good afternoon, Max. Would you like something to eat? Some tea?" He gestured towards a serving tray nearby which held a teapot, a plate of sea biscuits and a jar of treacle.

"Yes. Thank you."

He patted the floor, "Come, sit down."

I changed my shirt and got my tin of Golden Virginia tobacco from my pack and sat next to him.

"You left very early this morning," he said, "Where have you been?" He looked over to me for an answer.

"I went for a walk to the pools."

He shook his head, "They are not pleasant in the morning. The afternoon is best. There is a waterfall up the stream, did you see it?"

He knows! Right? Maybe. "No, I didn't. I stayed around the beach, uh, looking for shells."

"I was getting worried about you so I sent my boys to look for you. Did you see them?"

"No, I didn't." The question jarred the Committees in my head into a rhetorical version of Dixieland jazz where everyone solos at once. 'Unless he has photos, I'm denying everything!' 'He probably knows where I've been and who I was with.' 'Hey! So what if he knows you've been loving up his daughter? She's an adult. It isn't a sin.' 'Says who? What do you know about sin?' 'Even if it's not a serious sin, it might be enough to warrant a wedding at the end of a spear.' 'Or a problem with an ex-husband or boyfriend.'

I fixed a cup of tea and opened my tobacco tin. I had tucked some papers in there and rolled up a couple of butts. Jonas watched the process intently without saying a word. I tucked the ends with a matchstick and handed him one. He smiled at me, nodded and inspected it for a few minutes, then I struck a match and lit it for him. My anxiety rush subsided somewhat as we doodled around with the tea and tobacco. Jonas took a couple of tiny, sample puffs on his new cigarette, "Good. Not strong."

"Yes," I agreed.

He sipped tea and smoked for a few minutes then said, "You said you lived in Hawaii, tell me about it."

I told him the embellished and edited history of my life running a "ranch" in Hawaii. He smiled a lot, and nodded encouragingly, so I kept the patter going for a long while. I had worked up a story-telling act over the past months, simply for entertainment sake. It was built around facts and only veered away from them when the story was embarrassing or dull.

"Do you raise coconuts in Hawaii?"

"Only for show around hotels and condominiums, not for copra. Do you raise vegetables?"

"No. Too much trouble with the animals and bugs."

"Especially the bugs. In Hawaii, they get their fair share of the gardens. But some people there are starting to grow vegetables in greenhouses and aren't losing any of their crop to the bugs. I imagine the same thing could be done in Fiji."

"You say the bugs don't eat the garden?"

"They can't because it is covered in plastic and planted in boxes of clean rocks and bits of lava. Then the garden is fed a liquid mixture of food every day."

"Does it take a lot of space?"

I got my notebook and drew him the plan of a hydroponics garden I'd seen in the *Whole Earth* catalog. We spent the afternoon discussing the idea. The boys came in, sat with us and listened in, but didn't say anything. It was nearly dusk when Jonas said, "That's enough for today. May I have these papers to look at?"

"Sure."

"Well, this is interesting, Max. We will talk some more about it later. Now, we go to the feast."

There were about a hundred people at the feast when we arrived at dusk. Some sat around the table cloth, others talked in small groups, children chased each other, girls waited on the table. Jonas and I stood around while he greeted friends in passing, then Seini came up behind us.

"Good evening, father," she said in a cheery tone.

"Bula, Seini."

"Hello, Max. Did you have a pleasant day?" She smiled slyly.

"Yes. And you? I haven't seen you all day?"

"I had to go to another village on an errand. I have to go to another one tomorrow, as well." Her eyes sent the unsaid message, "Get up early again."

I was trying to think of a clever way to tell her I understood what she meant when Jonas said, "Why don't you take Max with you?"

"Would you like to come with me, Max?"

"Sure, what time?"

"At dawn, in front of your bure."

"Right."

Seini smiled, I grinned, and Jonas appeared just plain pleased at the arrangement.

I woke up with a tickling feeling on my face and reached up to find a long, thin piece of grass. The tiny noise from the back steps told me that the Midnight Mosquito waited for me outside. I got dressed and walked onto the front porch where Seini stood, in dawn's early light, holding a teapot.

"Would you like a cup of tea before we go?"

"Thank you." Who would ever believe a village with room service?

She went inside, past the snoring body of Jonas. "He'll sleep late. He always does after a kava party." We sat on the floor and had a cup of tea, then quietly left the village and headed east along the road.

We followed the road over the sunny ridge and into the shadowy *Valley of The Pools*. It was about a mile and a half wide at its broadest stretch along the beach. The road paralleled the shore until it had to zig zag up the side of the next ridge. From there, it appeared as a sea of palm fronds.

"Too bad this valley is spooked," I thought, "It's an ideal place to live. It wouldn't take much to set up here for a few years. I could make a homestead easily enough."

"Penny for your thoughts," Seini said.

"Where did you learn that?"

"In school. I went to school in Suva and learned lots of English phrases."

I thought it was an American phrase, but never mind, "I was just thinking how this valley reminds me of Hawaii."

"Did you live in a place like this?"

"Yeah, a lot like this." I went on to tell her of my life on the "ranch" where the nearest neighbor was a half-mile away.

"I've never lived in a house that was off by itself. I only stayed in the village or in Suva. People around all the time."

"Do you think you would like it? Living apart from other people?"

"Maybe. If I was living with the right person." She smiled at me and changed tack, "I've got a surprise for you."

"What is it?"

"If I tell you, it won't be a surprise. You'll see."

"Where are we going?"

"To see a planter on the other side of the next hill," she pointed to the ridge on the far side of the valley, "I have a message for him."

We ambled along, talking. Finding out more about each other. As intimate as we were, I knew nothing about her.

"What do you do in Suva?"

"I work at the newspaper, the *Fiji Sun*."

"Are you a reporter?"

"Sometimes. I work in the office most of the time. Proofreading and compositing. Sort of a 'Girl Friday'." She laughed at her joke.

"It sounds like a fun job."

"I've been there for two years. I worked at the *Fiji Times* first. I stayed four years and learned a lot about writing and printing. *The Sun* started up and I joined it. Mostly because it was such a contrast to the *Times*. It seemed livelier, younger."

"Yeah. I like it because it has the Crossword Game and the Spot-The-Ball game. I could use a win of either jackpot. They're up to a few hundred dollars."

"What would you do with the money?"

"I'm not sure. But I know what I wouldn't have to do."

"What's that?"

"Go back to Hawaii."

"Oh."

We walked in silence for awhile, except for the guys in the Game Room of my head. 'Hey,' one voice said, 'We're talking like a few hundred dollars are the ticket to paradise.' 'Yeah, well at the present rate of expansion, we could coast here for a few months while we figured out what to do with our life.' 'True, true.' 'At least, we would have some choice as to when to return to the straight world.' 'Are we really going back to the straight work-a-day world?' 'Yeah.' 'Why?' 'I'm trying to remember. Oh, yeah. To make some money so that I can continue cruising the South Pacific. Right?' 'But we're already here.' 'This is no time for reality. We gotta stick to a plan.'

"Penny for you thoughts," Seini said.

"No."

"Come on, tell me."

"Okay. I was just tying to figure out what Jonas had in mind when he paired us up for today. I don't know much about Fijian courting customs."

"But you know a lot about Fijian lovemaking." She laughed and ran ahead of me.

I caught up with her where the stream that fed the pools crossed the road. She sat on a rock, splashing her feet in the cool water. I sat down next to her and did the same.

"So, why did Jonas suggest you take me today? Is it a normal drill for a father to approve a date for his daughter?"

"He probably want's to see me married," she laughed.

"How about you? Is marriage in your plans?" I asked.

She thought about it for a while, "Not right away. I like my life in Suva. Besides, being married would be too restrictive for me. It's impossible for a person to be themselves in a marriage. No matter how hard they try, there are always compromises to make."

"It sounds like something you have experienced."

"Oh, no." She giggled, "Just something I've observed. How about you?"

"Yeah, I'm an ex-husband. Not eager to give up my freedoms either. Come on, let's walk."

Along the way, I carved a Fiji racer from a palm frond and pushed it along the road with a stick. Seini smiled at my toy.

"Do you want to drive it?" I asked.

"I haven't done that since I was a girl," she hesitated, stopped. "Okay, give me the stick."

I carved another racer as we walked. The Committees talked quietly, taking in the sights and sounds of the morning. Reflecting on the conversation at the stream. How lovers always have to compare their agendas to see how close they match, just like travelers. The trip on the Lovemobile runs from One Night Stands to Eternal Rapture. New tickets are issued with each relationship and you choose your destination along the way. Marriage is only one of the stops. Friendship is one of the best. True friends more or less accept each other, warts and all, without demanding incremental changes in the other's behavior.

I finished my Fiji racer, found a stick and walked alongside Seini, seriously pushing a bit of carved, palm frond in front of me. Life is so easily enjoyable at times that the only negative part of it is the top four inches of my body. Sometimes, my mind can conjure up agonizing, worst-case scenarios at the drop of a hat. Which, in hindsight, have never occurred. It disguises cynicism as a look at the down-side. And being an insecure, temporary body on a relatively strange planet leaves a lot of room for pitfall thinking, especially since it can be somewhat backed up by a train of logic or past experience. On the other hand, wishful thinking forms the basis for most of my up-side scenarios. What are you going to believe? I don't know. When do you need an answer?

Look, this doom and gloom line always nags about the same things, the apparent lack of money or goal. The fact is that we've always had enough money and the objective is being taken care of. We're here, aren't we? Besides, how much is enough? It's not like sex where you can't get enough of the stuff until you just had some. The money lust is like rust, it never sleeps, but continues growing in scope and intensity, rarely decreasing. A car. A better car. A boat. A bigger boat. How many guys are working long hours at a job they hate to support a cluster of metal in a garage or own a plastic lined hole in a marina to throw cash into. Time, not toys, is the optimum trade for money. Just as the moments of timelessness are the climactic prizes of sex relations. Otherwise, it only amounts to a whole lot of exercise. But what about all those time saving devices money can buy? They're great if you don't spend all your saved time working to buy and maintain them when you would rather be doing something else. 'But if I go back to Hawaii and sell puka shells, we'll make enough money so that we won't have to spend time worrying about it.' 'Says who? The market could be flooded with pukas.'

I left the Black Hats and Wishful Thinkers to debate in my mind and glanced at Seini pushing her racer without even watching it. She looked at me, smiled and we both said "Penny for your thoughts," and laughed.

"It's your turn," I said.

"Fair enough." She stalled a few minutes before continuing, "I was thinking that if you want to, you could live in my village for as long as it took to decide where you wished to go next."

"Thanks very much. I'll think about that."

"You can stay with Jonas. He likes you."

"It wouldn't be so much fun without you as my guide."

"I'll be here. I decided to stay for a few months."

"Oh, but I thought you were returning to Suva." No immediate reply so I kept going, "Taking a new direction in life, huh?"

"Yes. My aunt is very sick and has no one to look after her. I must stay with her for awhile. She has no one else. That's why I'm staying with her now."

The Committee for A Life of Ease flipped when they heard that we could cruise here for a while. Hey, if we can't be happy here, we aren't going to be happy anywhere, maybe we ought to give it a roll for a few weeks. The Honolulu Plan has so many negative vibes that it doesn't feel like the right one. It's a time eater for openers. Go on, say "yes." We're not going to starve and you can repair the pressure lamps or something to earn your keep. Go on, tell her.

I looked over at Seini, "Yeah, maybe I will stay for a couple of weeks."

We crossed the valley and started up the ridge. The racers demanded too much attention on the rain rutted road, so we parked them and continued on to the crest where we stopped for a few minutes.

"Your surprise is only a little farther along."

"Some more pools or a waterfall, I'll bet."

"Well, you're wrong. Come on."

We followed the curvy road down the ridge for a couple hundred yards and stopped at a dusty, white sign board on a post by the road which said, "180th Meridian, Where the new day begins." An arrow pointed east over the word, "Yesterday," another pointed west over the word, "Tomorrow."

"Hey! This is a great surprise!" She looked at me curiously, like she couldn't figure out what the big deal was. To be truthful, neither could I. But it seemed like a significant place. Like crossing the equator or standing at the North Pole. I jumped across the imaginary line a few times to see how easy time travel could be. Hop from one side to the other and you are into the past or the future while at no time does your body leave the present. Interesting concept, time. We continued down the ridge onto a wide, coastal plain covered with coco palms, then took a path through the groves to a circular clearing with a large, wooden house in the center, its new, tin roof shining brightly in the noon day sun. We walked up to the screened verandah and Seini knocked on the door, "Mister Williams. Are you here?" A couple of minutes later a red-faced man in his fifties came out on the porch and opened the door.

"Well, well. Hello Seini! I haven't seen you since last year. Do come in."

"This is my friend, Max, Mister Williams. He's staying in our village."

"Pleased to make your acquaintance," he said with an accent which somehow crossed an Irish brogue with a Scottish burr. His medium height and weight, covered with khaki drill trousers and long-sleeved shirt, hid the workingman's strength which vigorously shook my hand. "Let's sit out here. I'll get us something cold."

He went into the house and Seini sat down. I walked the length of the verandah and checked out the house a little. Cement slab floor, single-wall, timber sides with large, paneless windows. The surrounding yard was clear of trees, to keep the coconuts, fronds and the trees themselves from falling on the house in a storm.

"Thank you, Mister Williams," I said when he returned with a pitcher of ice water and three glasses.

"Just call me Blue. Only my boys call me Mister Williams." How is the feast going, Seini?"

"Very well, Mister Williams. My father sends his regards and asks will you come tonight?"

"Yes, of course. Tell him I will bring the pig. My boys are cooking it now. It will be ready for tonight."

That seemed to be the main point of business and they gossiped on while I tried to figure out why redheaded men were called Blue, then he turned to me, "What brings you to Fiji, Max?"

"I like tropical island life. I lived in Hawaii for the past few years and became addicted to warm breezes."

"I know what you mean. I couldn't live in a cold climate again."

"You've been in the islands a long time?"

"Forty years. I started with a British plantation company in the Solomons, then did some scrapping of war surplus in the New Hebrides. The Yanks left lots of material there. Made a lot of money, but it's gone now. I'm running this plantation for five years. Not much to do right now, though, the price of copra being down so low."

"Well, it's a pretty place to not do too much. Mind if I have a look around? I've never seen how copra is made."

"Of course. I'll show you the place."

There isn't much to know about preparing copra. The nut is opened, then the meat is pried out and placed into a curing oven to evaporate the water and keep the meat from spoiling. Finally it's bagged and stacked, awaiting a rise in the market price. We finished the tour at the tool shed.

"You have a well equipped place, Blue," I said, "You could build a house with all the power tools you have."

"I wish I could think of something to do with them that would pay enough to keep my boys busy. I've had to let some of them go already. Ah, well. Let's go to the house and have some lunch."

We washed up at an outside spigot and returned to the verandah where a low, serving table was set up with a pitcher of iced tea, glasses and plates for three. A Fijian girl came into the room with a tray of sandwich makings. Tinned pilchards, pickles, hot mustard, bread and butter.

"Where do you get the bread and butter?" I asked.

"I make a trip to Waiyevu every three or four days. So I buy it from the Holiday Inn while I'm there. My refrigerator keeps it fresh."

During lunch he managed to bring me up to speed on his life.

"I served with Montgomery's army in North Africa. Against Rommel. Now, there was a commander."

"Montgomery?"

"No, the old desert fox, Rommel. After the war, I returned to England but it was a cold and miserable place, then. A friend told me about the job with the Lever company in the Solomon islands. I applied and got it, and have been in the South Pacific ever since."

"You have never been back to England?"

"No. I almost returned a few times, but something else always came up that sounded better. One thing leads to another and I'm still here today. I've lived most of my life out of England. I might have trouble fitting in," he laughed. "I visit Sydney every couple of years. It's a good city. I get along quite well, there." He stopped talking for a minute, he stared at his sandwich, lost in thought. "How was your lunch? Too bad I don't have any veggies. Hard to grow them here."

"I kept a small garden in Hawaii." Go along with the host's subject is my motto and for the next hour, we talked about gardening. I told him about the University of Hawaii tropical agriculture section where information and even seeds were given away, then gave him an outline of the hydroponics technique and wrapped it up with a magazine article claim that thousands of acres were farmed in the middle of the Arizona desert.

"That's amazing! I know what your Arizona desert looks like, from your John Wayne movies. Have you done this gardening yourself?"

"No. But I have seen a couple of small gardens built in Hawaii. The theory is simple. Raise a plant in a bug-proof greenhouse on a bed of crushed, clean lava and regularly feed it a prescribed set of nutrients mixed in water. This liquid fertilizer is recycled in a closed system, usually pumped up to a holding tank."

"What kind of veggies are they growing in Hawaii?"

"Mostly tomatoes, lettuce, cucumbers, string beans." The conversation had lost its edge for me, but Blue seemed to be taking mental notes on the process and continued his polite questions for awhile longer.

"Right, then," Blue said, "Tell Jonas that we will bring the pig round tonight. And, Max, why don't you come by in a day or two and we'll talk some more about this gardening idea?"

"Okay, I'll do that."

Chapter Twelve
The Plantation Project

We retraced our steps through the grove, onto the road and across the 180th meridian, leaving Plantation Blue in yesterday. In the Land of Tomorrow, we got our Fiji Racers and pushed them along the road to the stream where we parked to cool off in the water. Small talk occupied us along the way, but now even that shut down. Seini waded into the stream while I reclined on a hard, though shaded and somewhat comfortable rock and let my mind drift off. The rustle of the leaves overhead and the gurgle of water made the only sounds. After awhile, I felt like I had melted into the rock, couldn't tell where I ended and the rock began, and didn't care. The Committees must have been tripping out on some rare enzyme.

'I think we ought to stay here. Maybe make this our South Pacific base.'

'Why not? We could put up a hydroponics garden and save a primitive village from extinction.'

'Yeah, we would probably get a lifetime visa and maybe even a knighthood.'

'At the very least, an honorary degree from Suva Agricultural College.'

'Sure! We'd make enough money in veggies to return to the real world whenever we wanted!'

'With a girlfriend at each port.'

'A captain's paradise!'

'But we really don't like farming as an occupation.'

'Look, it's only short term. Three or four months and we'll know if it's going anywhere.'

'This visa runs out in a month. We'll get another three months visa and by the time that's used up we should be a partner in M'bouma Veggie Farms Limited and eligible for the lifetime visa.'

'Let's do it! We need some security to make us happy.'

It's this kind of thinking that distinguishes brain activity from electronic data processing. The mind can project how you are going to feel when certain conditions are encountered. Where the computer delivers absolutes, the mind submits fantasies and convinces itself to blindly follow through on its schemes, no matter how clumsily wired. That's power.

We left the stream and headed back to the village, stopping at the crest of M'bouma ridge for a breather. The beauty of a sunny, late afternoon view from a ridge anywhere in Fiji stuns me to one knee almost every time. The Committees "oohed" and "aahed" unanimously at the spectacular world of shape and color, simply ignoring the underlying mud and mosquitoes.

Back at the village, Seini stopped at her aunt's bure and I went on to Jonas'. He was sitting on the floor when I walked in, engrossed in the rough sketches and notes of the hydroponics garden I made the night before.

He looked up at me, "Bula Max. I'm glad to see you. I want to talk about the garden idea. Come, sit down." He patted the floor next to him.

I got my cigarette fixings and joined him. He took a pinch of Golden Virginia and mixed it with a bit of rope-twist tobacco into a foot-long cigarette. I held the match for him and when he had taken a couple of puffs, he propped the tip on a coconut shell ashtray

"I showed your idea to other men in the village today. They like it but think it will cost too much. What do we need? How much will this cost?"

Although my experience with hydroponics gardening was limited to a tour of a friend's greenhouse in Hawaii where he grew Maui Wowee, I could remember the plumbing setup for feeding the plants. The pump, check valves and holding tank were not available on Taveuni, the rest of the materials could be gotten locally. We had just completed our 'Needs List' when Seini came in the door carrying a tea service. During the tea break, Seini told Jonas about our visit.

"Did Mister Williams show you around the plantation, Max," Jonas asked.

"Yes, he did. It's very modern," especially for a guy living in yesterday, "I told him about the garden idea, as well."

"What did he think?"

"He liked it very much and wants to know more about it."

"It would be good if he joined us," Jonas said, "he has a lot of tools and experience in building this sort of thing. I'll talk to him at the feast, tonight."

We arrived at the feast at dusk, Seini joined the other women serving food while Jonas and I sat down and said "bula, bula" to the men around us. A few minutes later, the kids romping in the clearing next to the feast house suddenly changed their yelps and shouts to the call, "Mister Williams is here." A couple of boys raced to the feast house to be the first messenger of this important event. In the dusky background, Blue crossed the clearing followed by four men carrying aluminum washtubs heaped full with roast pork. Chattering children surrounded him as he walked. The men headed off to deliver their loads and Blue came into the feast house. He exchanged polite "bulas" with folks as he made his way to Jonas and I. "Bula, bula, Jonas, Max. Can I squeeze in with you two gentlemen?"

"Bula, bula, Mister Williams," Jonas answered.

I didn't know what to call him with Jonas there, so I just said "Good evening," and slid over to let him sit between us. The hubbub of Mister Williams' arrival quickly subsided and the conversations among the men seated around the table started up again.

"It looks as if you've got all the villages here tonight, Jonas," Blue said, "but then, M'bouma feasts are always well attended. It's an old grandfather of a village."

"Yes, everyone is here. They would not miss your roast pig for anything." The two men talked for a while, identifying the people there, reminiscing on previous feasts. Fijian fare doesn't vary much, taro, tapioca, wild spinach cooked in coconut milk, and fish are served both at home and banquets. Blue's donation set M'bouma's feast above all others. "Before you, Mister Williams, our feasts were very meager," Jonas said. He turned to me, "Mister Williams made an irrigation system for our tapioca and taro plantations."

"Man's gotta stay busy, doesn't he, Max? Leastwise, I do."

"Yeah, life can get boring when there's not much going on."

Women and girls filed into the feast house carrying pots and bowls of steaming food. The kids had come in and seated themselves in circles. When the table was completely set, everyone became quiet, then a man with a chiefly bearing said grace in Fijian for about ten minutes, accompanied by many "bulas" from the congregation. When it ended, everyone became very busy ensuring that everyone else had enough to eat. Fijians eat with the intensity of Chinese. No talking through the meal. When it was clear that everyone had finished, the women and girls took away the dishes and the men caught up on their conversations. The kids ran outside to play and the young adults tried to drift out of the picture, unnoticed. I was looking around for Seini with the fantasy in mind of a moonlight stroll when Blue said something to me.

"I'm sorry. I didn't catch that," I said.

"I've been giving some thought to your idea of gardening. I am intrigued by the possibilities."

My thoughts were light years away from watching plants grow and I answered with the first thing that came to mind, "I've told Jonas about it too."

"Oh? What do you think about the garden, Jonas?"

"It might work here, if the cyclone doesn't blow it down."

"Yes," said Blue, "it would have to be strong, that's for sure."

They aired their opinions, politely determining each other's interest in the project. I had never met a Fijian veggie farmer, the closest qualifier was a guy in Arovundi who had an acre planted in chili peppers which he sold to the Korean fishing boats. Villages usually maintained a few small, hillside plots of tapioca and some lowland taro patches, but little else. On Viti Levu, Indian farmers in the river valleys provided the fruit, veggies, and eggs to the market.

"Max has made some drawings of the plant house." Jonas said, "Would you like to see them?"

"Yes, I would. I'll come by in a couple of days, is that all right?"

He looked at me as though for an answer. "I'm not going anywhere," I said.

Kava pounders had been banging throughout our conversation and three, party sized tanoas were set on the floor. The kava making team brought in the water and mulch, then mixed the brew. When it was ready the chiefly man who said grace now droned a five minute invocation, punctuated by timed hand claps and a chorus of "Bula, bula" from the men. Then it was party time. The kava flowed, the bilo passed and everyone sat around mellowing out. The lanterns were turned down and placed on the floor. People talked in low tones. A guitar strummed somewhere. The eyes of the women and girls shined with amusement when the polite banter between boy and girl groups began. I got up to stretch and take a walk, my knees had nearly seized from sitting cross-legged and as I struggled to straighten them I had vivid memories of favorite chairs I had known. The last, real chair I sat in was at the Holiday Inn in Waiyevu. I limped out of the feast house and onto the edge of the clearing where a fallen tree had some branches to sit on. I found a place to perch, hopped up and let the circulation get started in my legs.

'What are we doing here, again?' asked the Committee of Common Sense, 'And don't give us that guff about being the savior of a village. You're not even a Peace Corps Volunteer.'

'Yeah,' said another voice, 'we need a clearer understanding than what the Motive Makers cranked up this afternoon at the stream. Knighted? With what, a machete?'

'I agree with you guys, the projections did get a little airy-fairy this afternoon but what it comes down to is this: we're going to talk to a couple of guys about making a garden,' said a voice from the Day-At-A-Time Group.

'But what about the return to Honolulu?'

'Look, we're not going anywhere for a few days, so we might as well do some constructive thinking and planning. Get stuck into the now.'

Maintaining a Just For Today Plan requires frequent, cranial locker room sessions. Like keeping a team in psychological shape for every game, especially when the players are on the road. I rejoined Jonas and Blue in the feast house, already feeling better after making up my mind to stop worrying and enjoy myself. The young men and women joined in another 'Battle of The Songs' with lots of embarrassed laughter and wise cracks. Kids stood in the shadows, quietly watching the courting customs they would need to know. Seini sat with a group of girls and openly looked over and smiled.

"Looks like Seini has got her eyes on you," Blue said.

"Can't get away with nothing in this village," I answered.

For a while, I joined a group of guys in the songfest, carrying a street-corner base line, "ba doom, ba doom." It must have been around three am when Blue left for home with his boys and Jonas and I returned to the bure.

I woke up around mid-morning and looked across to see Jonas sitting on his mat, sipping a cup of tea. He signaled to Ben nearby to bring me a cup too. We drank them, and a refill, in silence. It was the usual come down from a big party, but judging from the clear, balmy weather it was a nice day for it. I stood under the outside shower for several minutes during which I didn't see anyone or even hear a voice. But then it was Sunday, time for paying respects to another religious doctrine. Maybe the villagers were atoning for having partied after midnight. Or does Sunday begin when the sun comes up? Or do they somehow parlay the theory of the International Date Line into an extra few hours of Saturday night? A sort of Pagan Daylight Savings Time. I returned inside the bure and joined Jonas on the floor.

"The village is very quiet," I said.

"Yes, we enjoy this feast too much." A slight smile broke through his contrite expression enough to tell me that he wasn't too sorry about whatever missionary rules he might have broken. Besides, his appearance might have been because of the kava he drank. Drinking a lot of kava will not make a person drunk by any measure of the word, but overindulgence did leave me feeling shabby for a few hours the next day. Since it tasted nga-nga and the effects were just what you'd expect from drinking river water, I had no trouble controlling my intake to a few, small bilos. I don't know how kava affects the Fijians, but some guys really liked it and drank a gallon or so at a six-hour sitting. Even then, I have never seen a kava drinker become boisterous, challenging, lusty, brave, boastful or passed out. I thought it made me sleepy, but found out that was because I hadn't adopted the village custom of napping for an hour or so in the afternoon. By the midnight of a long day, I was ready to put my kickstand down, kava or no. So if it's not an ego booster, it must be an ego deflater. Traditional kava gatherings created a feeling of honest humility and camaraderie no matter how much is drunk. Most westerners are left wondering, "Why are we drinking this, again?"

Jonas napped during the day. His wife brought in some leftovers from the feast. Moses and Ben stopped in for a bite, then took off. I read a novel and slept. A rain squall drummed over in the late afternoon, partially waking me. When it passed the village became quiet as the moon. I opened my eyes and looked over at Jonas' side of the room. He was gone, but a tea service sat in the middle of the floor with an unlit lantern nearby. I got up to pour a cup of tea and saw a note on the tray, "go to church." I sat down to study this simple phrase. Who go to church? Me? You? I figured he was telling me where he went and helped myself to a cup of tea. The sketches, notes and lists that we had made for the garden were stacked nearby. I looked them over for a while, then got my notebook and began writing down the details of the project that came to mind. I wrote a letter to the University of Hawaii requesting information on hydroponics and agriculture in the tropics and had just finished up a to-do list when Jonas returned.

"Bula, Max. Did you sleep well?"

"Yes, and thank you for the tea."

"Some men will come here tonight. They wish to talk about the garden."

Later that evening, men began arriving in the bure. The conversation died away as if on cue and Jonas said, "Tell us about the garden, Max." I felt like a speaker on a budget seminar tour.

I found that if I told bare-bones stories I usually had to repeat them about an hour later so I gave a detailed and embellished description of what I knew about hydroponics. Jonas showed the sketches I had made and a few guys asked questions. The meeting broke up early, Jonas went to sleep shortly afterwards and I lay awake wondering what I was getting into.

The village returned to its normal routine the next morning. Plumes of cooking smoke rose through the trees, voices called out, people shuffled along the paths, somewhere a radio blared. Seini showed up with a breakfast tea tray of tapioca pudding. Later that morning, I heard a truck come to a stop on the road and the door slam. A few minutes later Blue strode into the village clearing and headed straight for Jonas' bure where I sat on the porch.

"Hello, Max. Jonas around?"

"Hi, Blue. Yeah, he's inside."

"Do you fancy having a talk about that garden idea? It's been on my mind since you told me about it."

"Sure. I think we can squeeze you in. We pitched the idea to some of the village elders last night. I don't know what their opinion is but Jonas still wants to explore the idea."

We went inside the bure. Jonas sat on the floor studying the garden plans.

"Good day, Jonas. I see M'bouma survived the feast."

"Bula, Mister Williams," he grinned, "Yes, but this old village has lived through much worse than a feast. Come, sit down. Look at the plans we are making."

We discussed the idea for hours. Blue suggested using the area in front of his house where it was clear of trees and the pump could be connected to the generator. The idea made perfect sense to Jonas since M'bouma had no electricity. "We can use coconut planks for the floor and frame and polythene sheet for the sides and roof. I have all that at the plantation."

Blue sketched up a new set of plans based on the measurements of his site, then figured up the amount of timber needed. He was pretty excited by the time we went over the needs list and checked off the items he could supply from the plantation. "We'll get a pump and a few other items from Suva and information from University of Hawaii on hydroponics in the tropics. Other than that, we're ready to go. I'll build it and your village will maintain it. What do you say, Jonas." He projected an Anglo-Saxon sense of urgency about decision making that Fijians rarely reach.

"I must ask the other men in the village about your idea. I can give you their answer in a few days."

"In the meantime, I'll start work on the project. Max, if you're free tomorrow I can pick you up in the morning on my way to Waiyevu and we can mail the letter to the university. I'll bring some plantation letterhead paper to use."

"That's okay with me."

I watched him for signs of "Captain Bamboo flu" which inflates a man's idea of his self-importance, but he seemed to be on a different plane of enthusiasm. One that came with finding a project which appealed to him. His positive energy caught me up and I found myself getting unusually stoked about raising vegetables.

Blue stopped a couple of times to gaze thoughtfully into the distance, probably visualizing the completed greenhouse. That evening Seini came and set the tablecloth and served dinner. After a final cup of tea, Blue got up to leave. "Right. See you tomorrow, Max."

"I'll meet you on the road."

In my head The Committee For Self Indulgence cheered, "COFFEE! REAL COFFEE TOMORROW!"

I stood on the porch the next morning, finishing a cup of tea and a smoke when I heard Blue's pick-up coming down the ridge. I walked out to the road to meet it.

"Good morning, Max," Blue said as he pulled up, "Hop in."

We drove off, nattering along the way about the weather, the island, and life in general then Blue said, "I'm very excited about the garden."

I knew that but didn't know why.

"I've been looking for some kind of project to get involved in. Especially with the copra market drying up. So to speak." He grinned at his play on words

"Do you think there's much money in raising vegetables?"

"No. There'll be no money to be made. Taveuni is a bartering island. Around here, food is as good as gold. I have enough money. The plantation company pays me well. I just like doing things, building things. What about you, Max? You don't seem like an obsessive gardener to me."

"To be honest with you Blue, I don't know how this garden thing started. I was only telling Jonas and you about it since it seemed like a topic you were interested in and the project took on a life of its own. I'm not sure how long I can even stay here."

"How long is your visa good for?"

I ran down my visa options and one topic lead to another so that by the time we arrived at Waiyevu he heard the story of my last year's walkabout and present indecision about where to go or what to do next.

"Well, you can stay here until your next visa run to Suva in July, renew your visa and come back until October, is that right?"

"That sums it up. Hey, there's the Holiday Inn. How about a cup of coffee? I'm buying."

I drank a quart of coffee while I rewrote the letter to the University of Hawaii. I gave it to Blue and lit a Pall Mall cigarette I had saved for a special occasion, like a caffeine binge.

"When do you think they'll answer, Max?"

"In about a month. Air mail takes a week to Hawaii. Figure ten days for them to turn it around and a week to return. We should include a money order for the return postage."

"I'll get one at the post office. You write a pretty good letter, Max, I could use you to help with some correspondence. Does that sound interesting to you? I couldn't pay you, but I could give you bed and board at the plantation. The house has plenty of spare room."

"What kind of correspondence?"

"Letters to shareholders, banks, creditors. Things like that. It's not my favorite job so I'm not very good at it."

I stalled with a sip of the coffee, a puff of the Pall Mall while the Committees concerned scrambled for a consensus. The offer of a room of my own formed the backbone of the decision. "I think I can do that. Thanks for the offer, Blue."

He bought a bag of rolls and a couple of loaves of bread at the Holiday Inn and I bought a pound of coffee from the chef then we walked to the Post and Telegraph office near the pier. After a few minutes a clerk faded into sight behind the counter.

"Will this letter get to Suva in a week?" I asked Blue.

"It'll be there in about five hours. Taveuni is a regular air-mail stop and the plane will be in, shortly."

After doing some shopping, we left Waiyevu and headed back to the plantation. On the way, Blue stopped at M'bouma while I told Jonas of my plans and collected my things. We met Seini as we walked out of the village.

"I haven't seen you all day," she said, "where have you been?"

"Waiyevu. I had to mail a letter to Hawaii," I said.

"Oh. Are you leaving soon?"

"No, it's to the university there for gardening information."

"Gardening information?" She hadn't been in any of the confabs about the project. Fijian women rarely take part in decisions regarding gardening. But then, the subject rarely came up in a village.

"Yeah. Jonas, Blue, and I are going to plant some veggies. An experiment, sort of."

"Vegetables?"

"You know, tomatoes, green beans. Things like that."

"Where are you going, now?"

"I'm moving in with Blue so that I can help with the project."

"You're welcome to come by anytime and see how we're getting along, Seini."

"Thank you Mister Williams," she turned to me, "I'll come over in a day or two."

It was late afternoon when Blue pulled up in front of the plantation house. I grabbed my pack and followed him inside where he showed me two vacant rooms. I took the one at the rear of the house with a west-facing window. I dropped my pack and sleeping bag, grabbed a towel and continued the tour of the house ending at the outside shower room. It wasn't really a room since it had no roof, but the tin sides provided a sense of bathroom privacy I hadn't felt since the Coconut Inn.

"Come up to the verandah when you have freshened up," Blue said.

I took a long shower, changed into a sulu and joined Blue on the porch, where a tea service was set up. I poured a cuppa, then sat in a chair, facing out through the porch screen, soaking in the ambiance of a plantation boss's lifestyle at sundown. The experience of sitting in a piece of padded furniture rather than cross-legged on a hard floor became a memorable occasion. We talked a while about general, short-lived topics then his housekeeper brought in a lantern and a tray of cold meats, cheese, bread rolls and butter. After the meal, Blue took the lantern and we walked outside to a small, tin shed which housed the generator. He got the two cylinder diesel engine going then flicked a switch and looked towards the house where two light bulbs flickered to life. He closed the shed and we headed back to the house. "I only run it for a couple hours a night. Keep the freezer cold and read for awhile. That's about all there is to do at night, here. Do you play chess?"

"Yes."

"Want to play a game while the generator is running?"

We played two games, winning one each. Afterwards, he gave me the outline of a letter he needed for the shareholders. "That's enough for today," he said, "I'm shutting the generator down. There's a lantern in your room, Max, light it up if you need it."

I fired up the lantern, tuned it to a low glow and caught up on my journal while sitting on a real bed. The downside was that there would be no midnight mosquitoes to wake me up. I missed seeing Seini but the affair couldn't have gone on much longer before the whole village got wise to it and that would no doubt trigger a decision crisis about our relationship.

The next morning, Blue and I began the planning phase of the project. Lunch was followed by a rest period which lasted until tea time around three. I worked on the letter writing until supper, then wrote in my journal until lights out. This pattern had become routine by the time Seini visited a few days later.

Chapter Thirteen
The Marriage Plot

During the mid-morning of the fourth day, Blue and I worked at the building site in front of the house when Seini strolled out of the coconut groves and into the clearing, "Bula, Max. Bula, Mister Williams."

"Hello, Seini," Blue answered, "I wondered when you were coming to inspect our project."

"Hi, Seini. Good to see you."

"You're just in time for morning tea," Blue said, "let's go to the house."

"What are you doing up this way, Seini?" Blue asked when we had settled on the verandah, "Anything special?"

"Yes. My father wants you to come to tea, tonight. Both of you, of course."

"What is today?" Blue asked, then answered himself, "It's Friday already. Sure, we can make it. We can all go in the truck later this afternoon. Right, Max?"

"Fine, by me."

We worked until shortly after noon, then stopped for lunch. Afterwards, Blue said, "I've got an hour or so to finish on the framing, but you might as well get a rest and talk with Seini." He walked out into the yard.

I know a good deal when I see one and headed for the shower, "I'll only be a few minutes," I said to Seini.

"Can I wait in your room?"

"Won't the maid be suspicious?"

"She's gone back to her village for the weekend." She followed me to my room.

"What about Mister Williams?"

"Don't worry," she smiled, "He's an old friend."

An "old friend?" The Committee of Relationships pushed that phrase through a list of suspicions and questions. From the first time I met Blue I sensed an undercurrent between Seini and him. She called him "Mister Williams," but her eyes said, "Blue." Theories popped into my head while I showered. 'Were they lovers?' 'If so, what does that mean today?' 'Nothing,' said a member of the R & R

Committee, 'All we're required to do right now is enjoy an afternoon interlude with a friend.' 'Sure, sure. We can think about it later.'

I returned to find Seini sitting on the edge of the bed and joined her. After a few minutes of small talk, we touched, embraced, and bounced off the walls for a while. Afterwards, we took separate showers and met on the verandah. We didn't say anything for several minutes. Just sat there with satisfied expressions on our faces. I could see hers and feel mine. Life is so pleasant when its needs are met. A roof, enough food, and a loving friend to share time with.

"My father knows about us."

"Oh?"

"Do you know what I mean?"

"Yes, I think so." I really didn't know what to make out of this news, the message was so out of place with my headspace that it seemed to come from another planet. I didn't probe the subject and she added no more.

That afternoon, we hopped into Blue's truck and drove to M'bouma. There, Seini went to see her aunt while Blue and I headed to Jonas' bure.

He appeared happy to see us and listened intently as Blue told of the progress on the garden. I watched Jonas for any signs that his attitude towards me might have changed. It had. Something in his glances towards me signaled that we were conspirators who shared a secret. I tossed around the idea of acting dumb and denying any reports of sleeping with his daughter. It's not the usual thing for guys to admit to a girlfriend's father.

Dinner was served by Seini's mother. She gave me the fish head, the best part. She knows. The entire village probably knows. After the meal, Blue left to visit with friends in the village leaving Jonas and I alone, sitting on the floor around the pressure lantern. We spent a few minutes rolling cigarettes and had a few puffs.

Finally he looked over at me and smiled, "You are making a good thing at the plantation. It will be a sound foundation for your life here."

"Yes, I'm hoping that this project will convince the Immigration Department to give me another visa. I have to go to Suva in a couple of weeks to apply."

He puffed his cigarette for awhile, then said, "You do want to stay in M'bouma, don't you?"

"Uh, sure," I said obligingly, suddenly feeling like I'd painted myself into a corner.

"I'll see what I can do," he grinned like a used-car dealer who just made a deal, then stretched out on the floor, and appeared to fall asleep though his smug expression never changed.

A few days later, Seini showed up at the plantation just as we broke for lunch. This time, Blue didn't ask her why she came, but instead acted as though he expected her. We small-talked through the meal then relaxed on the verandah for awhile. Finally, Blue stood up and headed for the screen door.

"I'm going back to work. You can stay and keep Seini company, Max."

"I won't be long. I have to start back to M'bouma, soon," Seini said.

"Max can take you in the truck when you're ready, the keys are in it. You'll have to watch him, though, he's a Yank and they drive on the wrong side of the road. Ha, ha." He went outside into the yard hollering, "All right, boys, lunch time is over."

"Let's go to the pools," Seini said.

That was enough hint for me. I changed into a clean sulu, gathered up a towel and we headed out the door. Fifteen minutes later, we arrived at the pools. After a bit of splashing around, Seini grabbed my sulu, peeled it off of me and ran into the bushes, laughing and teasing. I took off after her and we played Adam and Eve for a while. I caught her. We made love, then I ran off with her sulu and a new chase was on. It was Seini's favourite Fijian Romance Dance. I kind of liked it, too.

Afterwards, we relaxed at the edge of the pool. My mind casually explored the meanings of the words "frolic," "gambol."

"My father wants to know if you are going to marry me."

"Frolic" and "gambol" were quickly replaced with "uh-oh" and "careful."

In a stall for time, I said, "Uh, when does he have to know?"

"Max," she smiled, "You're so funny."

My mind screamed 'who's joking' but my mouth said, "I don't even know if I can get another visa to stay here. Ha, ha." Got to keep this scene light.

"Father says you can get a visa if you marry a Fijian and since you and I are more than friends," she let the sentence trail off. "Anyway, he's not expecting an answer today," she smiled at me, "he's only trying to help you."

I knew when to shunt the conversation, "Well, I better get the truck back to Blue. He may need it."

Jonas appeared on the road just as I pulled to a stop at M'bouma. "Bula, Max. Won't you come to my bure for a cup of tea?"

"I'd love to, Jonas, but Blue is expecting me back. He has some special projects he wants my help on. Next time, all right?"

I picked up on the signaling efforts between the father and daughter. Quizzical eyebrows, mouth scrunches and darting eyes.

"Thanks for the news, Seini. I'll give it some thought." I felt more secure now that the offer had sunk in. It was, after all, only a proposition and a practical one at that.

On Saturday morning, Blue and I set off for Waiyevu to do some shopping. As we approached M'bouma we saw Seini standing beside the road and pulled to a stop.

"Good morning, Seini," Blue called, "Want a lift to town?"

"Yes, thank you."

She climbed into the cab between us and we set off again.

"What are you going to town for, Seini," I asked, just to make conversation.

"I have to do some shopping and mail a letter for father."

"It must be important," Blue said, "I don't remember Jonas ever sending a letter."

"It's to the Immigration Department. He's trying to help Max get another visa."

"Oh?" Blue said. He glanced at me as if expecting an explanation, then went on, "I guess every little bit helps."

We split up in Waiyevu, Seini took off to do her errands while Blue and I poked around the town's hardware store and boatyard for materials we could use for the garden. Then we went to the Holiday Inn and settled down to drink coffee while we waited for Seini to join us.

"What's the deal with Jonas and your visa?" Blue asked.

"I'm not too clear on the details myself," I hesitated before telling him more, "but it has to do with being married to a Fijian."

He grinned, "I think I got the picture. Is Seini the Fijian he has in mind?"

"Yeah."

His grin broadened along with his knowledge, "That's an interesting turn of events. What's your ideas along this line?"

"Something tells me I'm not ready for marriage. For a whole bunch of reasons."

My discomfort amused Blue, "Ha, ha. So the old guy is trying to marry off his daughter, again."

"I'm not the first?"

"Sorry, no. Last year it was a Peace Corps bloke, ha, ha. Did he offer you the piece of land to settle on?"

I shook my head.

"That'll come soon," he looked up, "Here comes Seini."

We had lunch, then drove back to M'bouma. There, Seini asked us to stay for tea. Jonas greeted me warmly like a prospective son-in-law, then began talking with Blue about the garden project. That evening, a tanoa of kava was brewed and men began arriving at the bure. The talk centered around the garden project. Who would get the benefits, have the responsibilities, bear the setting up costs, manage the operation and make up the board of directors. Jonas put my name in as a member of the board since I "got the project going and wanted to stay in M'bouma."

That raised a few bulas of consent from the men and I was more or less elected. It might have been the effects of the kava or the energy of the meeting, but I felt positively about my role in the project and my Committees conjured up a future as the M'bouma Veggie King.

The meeting broke up late so Blue and I camped on the floor for the night. I took my old position by the back door. Sometime later, a soft tickling on my face awakened me. I reached up and caught the long, slender grass stem and gave it a tug. It tugged back. I looked around the darkened room for a few minutes. Blue snored loudly, and Jonas appeared to be asleep so I got up and tiptoed out the back door. I walked along the path and saw Seini standing in the shadows nearby. She motioned for me to follow her and we crept to the boulder pile at the base of the ridge. There, she dropped her sulu, grabbed me in a tight embrace, leaned back against a smooth rock and made love without saying a word.

"It seems you missed your mosquito," she said with a giggle, "you must not have one to bother you at Blue's house."

"You're the only one."

"Do you want to marry me?"

"Right now I do," I tried to lighten the answer with a forced laugh.

"How about next week? My father is waiting for your answer. He will give you some land to build a bure for us and see that you have everything you need."

"I'll have to think about it some more, Seini."

"Do you love me?"

I stalled on the answer, looking for a way to slip out of the trap. "Sure I do. But I have no way to support myself much less a marriage."

"When the garden is going you will have lots of money and my father will help us until then."

"I'm not sure that is a good way to start off."

"Why not? You will have plenty of time to pay him back, and anyway, the garden will be successful."

"I just wouldn't feel good starting off like that. You know what I mean, marrying a man's daughter and borrowing from him at the same time."

"Oh. Well, we will talk more about it tomorrow." She giggled and started fooling around again.

Sometime later, I sneaked back into the bure and slid into my sleeping bag. But I couldn't sleep, not with the Committees debating Seini's questions, and felt wrecked the next morning. Judging by the nudge-nudge, wink-wink smirk on Blue's face when he looked at me over breakfast, my appearance must have matched my feelings. I didn't bother to check a mirror. If Jonas noticed my tired condition, his smiling face and upbeat manner didn't show it. He chirped on about the garden and required only a little input from Blue or me to keep him going. I was anxious to leave and felt relieved when Blue said we ought to be going.

"May I ask a favor of you Mister Williams?" Jonas said. "It would take only a half-hour or so."

"Of course."

"I would like to show Max a piece of land where he could build his bure. It's only over the ridge."

"Sure, I'll take you there. I know where it is."

"Good. Thank you. I'll be ready in a few minutes." He left for the outhouse.

Blue looked at me with a bigger smirk than before, "He's setting you up for the pitch, mate."

We drove to the top of the ridge where Blue stopped. He knew the drill. We got out of the truck and stood on the road while Jonas scanned the *Valley of The Pools* as though he hadn't seen it in a long time.

"Look there, Max," Jonas said as he pointed, "Do you see the clear patch just to the left of the stream?"

It was the only clearing in view, "Yes, I see it."

"That is where you can build your bure. Close to the stream and the road and convenient to M'bouma and the plantation. We can build you a bure there in only a few days."

"It looks like a very good location," I didn't even want to say that but had to make some sort of comment.

He grinned at me, "I'm sure that you will like it. Shall we have a closer look?"

Blue saw me squirming and saved my bacon, "Perhaps some other time, Jonas. I have to get back and tend to the generator. It's been on its own for more than a day."

As we drove Jonas back to M'bouma, he waxed on about the life I could make for myself in Fiji, with his help. He mentioned that it might be lonely if I lived alone but tactfully avoided the issue of who I would share the bure with.

The following week I buried myself in the garden project. Blue didn't mention my predicament and after a few days, I didn't think much about it myself, until Seini waltzed into the greenhouse on Friday afternoon. Blue saw her first.

"Hello, Seini," he said.

"Hello Mister Williams."

"Hi Seini. How good to see you." I tried to sound enthusiastic but my heart wasn't in it.

"Hi, Max." She looked at me with an I-know-something-you-don't smile.

"She's a good excuse to stop working," Blue said, "Let's pack it up for the day Max."

"Sure thing." I sounded nonchalant but alarm bells went off in my head and the Committee of Foreboding went into a chaotic session creating scenarios of confrontation.

That evening after dinner, we socialized on the verandah. Blue and I played a couple of games of chess and explained the game to Seini. She soon grew bored and went to bed in the spare room.

"Looks like she's here for an in-depth talk with you, my friend," Blue said.

I answered with a nod and made a fatal move on the board.

Blue had me checkmated in a couple of moves, "Your game isn't up to par, tonight."

"I've got a lot on my mind."

"I can see that. I'll leave you to it." He lit a hurricane lamp then went out and shut the generator down.

I sat on the verandah thinking over my situation. The only problem with it was the marriage condition and how to settle it. Maybe Jonas and Seini would accept a postponement for a few months. Even if they did, I didn't think I would be ready for marital bliss. My fantasy of escape to the South Seas didn't include a wife. But then it didn't include a lot of things that had happened to me. I went to bed but the Committees wouldn't sleep, but instead stayed up listing all the possible outcomes and debating which way to go. Seini crept into my room a while later and, without a word, we made love. My mind wasn't into it but my body gave it's best effort.

The next day, I joined Blue and Seini on the verandah.

"Morning," was all I could say.

"Bright eyed and bushy tailed, today, are we?"

What's this "we" stuff? I felt like asking him if he was pregnant. Maybe he was an ex-nurse. Maybe he meant him and Seini. She fit the description. "I didn't sleep much."

"Thinking about your chess game, were you?"

"Something like that. Good morning, Seini."

"Hello Max. Would you like some tea?"

"Thank you." She fixed a cup just as I liked it and brought it to me. "What's the plan, today, Blue? Are we going to Waiyevu?"

"Yes. We'll take Seini to M'bouma on the way."

"This evening you'll come to my father's bure for tea."

I looked at Blue for a way out of that.

He rolled his eyes, "Jonas wants an update on the project."

I wanted to go back to bed but we left a few minutes later. An ominous feeling began to settle in my head where the Committees maintained silence. Not calm, just silence. Except for one diabolic optimist who said, 'It's a nice day for it.' It's curious how foreboding sharpens my senses to the world around me. While we drove I watched the soft pastels of the western sky dissolve into sky blue as the sun cleared the ridges and changed the gray of the valley into green.

We stopped to let Seini off. "Don't forget to come for tea tonight." I wish I could. I better get some kava root, a bottle of beer and a foot of tobacco for Jonas. These are the usual offerings for deal making in Fiji. I wished I had a tambua, a sperm whale tooth which is submitted along with a major request, getting out of a marriage for example.

In Waiyevu, we stopped at the post office. "I've got some replies from the companies I wrote to in Suva," Blue said, "Let's go to the Holiday Inn and read them."

We ordered coffee and then he read the letters aloud. "Seems like they have everything we need," he said, "This strengthens your case for having to leave next week. You'll need some spare time to check the equipment out."

"Blue, there's a chance I might not get a visa and have to leave Fiji without returning here. I'm worried about the letter that Jonas sent to the Immigration Department."

He thought about it for a minute, "Me too. I have an idea that Seini knows what was in it. Did she say anything more to you about it?"

"No. Do you have any guess as to what he might have written?"

"Offhand, I'd say it has more to do with Seini than the garden project, and it probably has conditions. If it was an endorsement, he would have given it to you to deliver in person."

"You've got a point, there."

"Do you still want to continue with the project?"

"Sure, but not under the threat of marriage."

"Then let's just act as if you will get another visa."

"And if I don't?"

"I'll give you a letter of credit and some cash for expenses if you will inspect the equipment that we need and send it to me. You can return in a few months when Seini will have moved back to Suva or found someone new. It's happened before."

"Sure. Maybe I should return to Hawaii for a bit of summer, sidewalk selling in Waikiki. I need some cash."

As we left Waiyevu the Cut-and-Run Committee took charge of the thinking process and outlined an escape plan. The only dissenting voice was the Take-A-Chance Gang, 'Here we go again, back to the old, second rate ideas.' I fell asleep in the midst of their debate and awoke when we arrived at M'bouma late that afternoon. They were still at it.

"Sleep well?" Blue asked.

"Better than nothing, I guess. Let's go see Jonas."

We left the truck on the road and walked through the village. Saturday is the Fijians social day and women strolled around visiting each other. Men squatted in front of their bures like watchful roosters. A group of boys lounged under a tree drinking kava, banging on homemade instruments and singing along with the music from a radio. People waved and called, "Bula." A soft breeze rustled the leaves of the towering breadfruit trees, constantly shifting the shadow patterns and colors of the scene. It worked its magic and quieted the Committees.

"I hope a deal can be worked out with Jonas," I said, "I really do like living in Fiji, just don't want to get married to do it."

"I understand, but Jonas must have his reasons. There's a lot of customs and culture that we don't know about. He might be pressured by the chiefs of the village, the church, his wife or daughter. Just play it straight. Don't promise anything you're not prepared to do."

We arrived at Jonas' bure, left our shoes on the porch and went inside. Jonas was sitting on the floor, facing the door.

"Bula, Mister Williams. Bula, Max."

We returned his bulas. He patted the floor next to him. I fished the kava, tobacco and bottle of beer out of my pack and we sat down opposite him.

"This sevu-sevu is for you, Jonas," I said as I presented the gifties to him.

"Vinaka vaka levu, Max. Thank you very much." He sniffed and examined the kava root for a minute, then pronounced, "It is from Kandavu. It is good quality." He put it aside, "Now tell me about the garden."

I let Blue field that question. I wanted some time to think and he could stretch a single sentence up to five minutes duration. I took out my tobacco and offered it to Jonas. He smiled, took a pinch then began to construct his cigarette. So far so good.

"...We finished covering the greenhouse and next week Max will go to Suva for the pumps and valves we need."

"So soon?" said Jonas, "I thought Max would be here for another two weeks. Seini said they are going to be married and it would be much better if this were done before he went for his visa. Then he could get a longer visa, and one which would allow him to work here. As you know, Mister Williams, non-Fijians are not allowed to work here without a permit. It is a very serious offense."

The news that Seini assumed we would marry didn't surprise me so I didn't say anything, just concentrated on the tip of my cigarette.

"True. But don't you think that sometimes a law like that could be overlooked, especially when it is beneficial to the nation?" Blue said.

"Yes, you're right. However if someone turns Max in for working, I am the one who will be blamed. Do you understand my position?" he said as he looked at me.

"Of course," I took my cue from Blue who was nodding his head in agreement, "I don't want to make problems for you. But on the other hand I'm not really suitable for marriage, now. I don't have much money to live on."

"I will give you land and help you to build a bure. You can live off the village here until you get settled and the garden begins producing. You will have very little need for money."

I stalled, tapping my cigarette into the coconut shell ashtray, "This is happening very quickly. I feel it would be in our best interest to put our efforts into the project, first."

He nodded and smiled politely.

Jonas nodded but didn't look entirely convinced. He looked up when his wife entered the room with plates and silverware, "Would you like to wash up for tea?"

No one mentioned the garden or marriage for the rest of the evening. Only a reminder from Jonas as we were leaving, "Let me know your final decision before you go to Suva, Max."

I could have told him right then that anything short of marriage was all right, but instead thanked him for the chance to make up my mind.

Seini came out of the shadows as we walked back to the truck. I stopped while Blue went on ahead.

"Did you and Jonas get things settled?" she asked.

"Yes. I have until next week to make up mind about his offer."

"I'll come and see you on Monday."

"I don't think that's a good idea, Seini. Not until I decide what I'm going to do."

"We are going to marry, aren't we?"

"Look, I'm much too tired to talk about this right now. I'll be back in a few days." Even in the dark I could see her spurned look and took her hand, "I'll see you then. Okay?"

"It might be too late. I have other suitors, you know."

"I'm sure you do. You are an attractive, fascinating woman."

That didn't soften her, "Then why don't you marry me?"

"Because I don't want to marry anyone, right now."

She turned and walked off.

"Rough day, eh, cobber?" Blue said as I got into the truck.

"The only good part is that it is over with."

Chapter Fourteen
Where Do I Sign?

For the next five days I worked on the greenhouse, played chess, and worried about the visa-marriage situation. I decided not to have a last meeting with Jonas or Seini and on Friday, Blue drove me to Waiyevu. I got out at the pier.

"Good luck, Max," he handed me an envelope, "Here's the list of suppliers, a letter of credit, and a hundred dollars for your expenses. I hope to see you in a week or so but if your plans change drop me a line and let me know."

"Sure thing, Blue. Thanks for everything."

The same boat that brought me waited at the end of the pier. The few passengers already aboard had taken the lower deck. I went to the upper deck, unrolled my sleeping bag and slept for the entire crossing, waking only when the boat's engine slowed down to enter the mangrove swamp. Then it slid to a stop on the mud and the passengers climbed out.

"Where is Loa?" I asked the skipper.

"Follow those people through the mangrove," he pointed to the departing passengers, "When you reach the road turn right. It's only two kilometers from here. You can't miss it."

Yes, I can, I thought, but this day was on a roll. A couple of hundred yards of plodding through swamp muck followed by an hour of road strolling and I saw some spires of smoke that marked a village and cut through the bush to the cluster of huts called Loa. A few minutes later I knocked at Ratu Nemia's bure.

"Bula, Max," he said when he saw me, "Come in." I followed him. "Please, take your pack off and sit down. I'll just put some water on." He returned a few minutes later, "Tell me, what have you been up to?"

Through several cups of coffee, I told him the whole story of my M'bouma life. His face showed puzzlement at the garden project, and amusement at the Seini entanglement.

"It's good that you didn't go back to say goodbye. Fijian women can be very possessive. Ha, ha. But then, so can any woman."

I caught the bus at six am the next day and eight hours later arrived in Savusavu. There, I headed immediately for the docks but the *Adi Moapa* wasn't in port. I went to the boatyard to look for Harry.

"He's gone to Suva," said a co-worker, "Don't know when he'll be back."

"When is the *Adi Moapa* due in?"

"Not for two or three days. That old bucket broke down in Levuka, again. It always breaks down there. I think the captain has a girlfriend."

I headed for the Holiday Inn but stopped at a Chinese food shop along the way. The place had no menu so I looked at the food a nearby couple had in front of them, pointed at the man's plate and said, "I'll have one of those."

The waiter shuffled off and the man looked up at me and smiled. I guessed him to be a year or two past sixty, probably English. Then he said, "You must be new here. This is the only meal he cooks," and his melodic accent had me guessing all over again.

"What is it?"

"Oh, some sort of Chinese pork and noodles thing. It's good and filling. Take my word for it. We come here all the time. Don't we dear?"

The Indian woman at his table agreed, "Yes, very often." She appeared to be a few years younger than the man and while he was slender, she was plump and filled the green sari she wore. "Where are you from?"

"Hawaii. I'm just doing a walkabout around the islands. I've been on Taveuni for the past few weeks and am now trying to get to Suva, but I have to wait for the *Adi Moapa*."

"Yes. That terrible old boat is overdue again. It is not reliable," the man said. "Won't you dine with us?"

"Thank you." I moved to their table.

"I'm Henry Johnson. This is Yasmine, my wife." During the meal they asked the usual questions, not prying, just curious.

When we finished, the woman said, "Where will you be staying? At the Holiday Inn?"

"No, I can't afford that. I was hoping there was a guesthouse nearby."

"There are no guesthouses at all," Henry said, "not enough call for them." He studied me for a minute. "You can stay with us until the boat comes in. We have a spare room right now."

"Thank you. I can pay you something for it."

"Don't be silly," the woman said, "It will be good for Henry to have some company. He misses talking to his old mates from work."

"I retired from the sugar company a few months ago," Henry said, "I would have kept working but the company has a policy to enforce."

"Will you return to your home country?"

"This is it. I was born in Fiji, the son of a mining engineer. I have never been out of the country. I always planned to travel when I retired, but this is the farthest I've gotten from Suva. I'm too old now. I don't feel like being on the move. Come, let's go home now."

We left the food shop and walked to a new, Japanese pickup truck. I hopped into the back with my pack and we set off away from town. A couple of miles later, Henry pulled off onto a dirt track and into the yard in front of an old, wooden house. I followed them inside and Henry showed me to a bare room.

"It's not much," he said, "You may want to change your mind and stay at the Holiday Inn."

"This will be fine, thank you."

"Get your towel and I'll show you where to wash up."

I pulled stuff out of my pack, looking for a towel. Henry noticed the folding chess set I carried. "You play chess?" he asked.

"Yes. And you?"

"I haven't played a game since I retired. I would love to play a game. This evening, perhaps."

"Certainly."

I crashed and when I awoke the room was dark. From somewhere in the house Indian music screeched from a scratchy radio. In the brightly lighted dining room I found Yasmine setting the table. "You're just in time for some curry," she said, then turned her head and called, "Come on, Henry." He walked in from an adjoining room.

We sat down to a meal of curry and rice. Afterwards, Henry said, "Now we can play chess, yes?"

"Please play with him," Yasmine said, "He has talked of nothing else since we came home."

"Sure. I'll get my set."

"Never mind, mine is set up already."

He led me into the screened verandah, except for different furniture it was the same as Blue's. "Is this an old plantation house?"

"Yes. It was the foreman's quarters. I bought it a couple of years ago to retire in."

"I stayed in one very similar to this for a few weeks on Taveuni."

"What were you doing there?"

"Setting up a hydroponics garden."

"Oh. Well, let's play chess."

He played serious, no talking chess and won two games in a row. "You play well," he said, "Let's take a break."

Yasmine sat nearby while we played but now got up and brought in a tea tray, complete with sea biscuits and treacle, then returned to her chair.

"Tell me about hydroponics gardens," Henry said.

I gave him an overview of the project at Blue's plantation.

"So, once again man has worked his way up to another pinnacle of supremacy," his lilting speech contrasted his smug expression, "and without help from a God."

Yasmine threw a look that said 'don't start that again', but she was behind him and only I saw it.

"Do you agree with me?" he said.

"I'm not clear what the point is."

"Simply that the concept of God is irrelevant to human existence."

"Oh?" This guy jumps right into the deep end of the conversation pit. "You would get an argument on that from several billion people."

"Yes. Even my wife disagrees with me," he glanced towards her, "but then Indians have many Gods."

"Are you saying that there is no God, or that God doesn't matter?"

"Either way. Theology has no place in the affairs of man. Man creates his own peace, his own chaos. If there is a God, he's abandoned mankind as though it was a useless thesis. The world is a mess."

"Maybe that's mankind's fault," I said.

"Indeed, it is. But we're not doing badly considering where we started from. If God was involved, all things would be perfect, wouldn't they?"

"I suppose so, if the element of individual free-will was removed. But then what would be the purpose of a planet full of robots?"

"On the other hand, what is the purpose of a planet full of beings whose self-will has run riot?"

"You'll have to take that up with someone who is more knowledgeable than I am, Henry. Right now, I can't even play a winning game of chess."

"Yes. Let it go Henry," said Yasmine, "He always has to talk about God."

That's probably because you don't have television, I thought.

The next day we visited a friend of Henry's who was dying of cancer. We drove to the man's house and parked in a yard along with several other vehicles. Inside a couple of dozen people were spread throughout the house. Yasmine joined the women sitting in the front room while Henry and I went to the sick man's room. There, four men sat or stood around the bed, talking and joking with the invalid, a Fijian man in his late fifties.

"Hello, Henry," croaked the man, "Thank you for coming."

"Hello, Samuel. I see you are in fine spirits."

"Not too bad for a sick man. Who is this with you?"

"This is a friend, Max. He's from America."

"Bula, Max. Nice to meet you."

"Bula, Samuel."

Henry introduced me to the other men, then said to Samuel, "He plays chess."

"You are lucky to find a chess player. I have not played for a long time but I would like to play once more. Maybe you will come and play with me, Max?"

"I'll only be here for a few more days," I said.

"So will I. Perhaps you can come tomorrow?"

"Yes, of course."

The conversation drifted to other subjects and after awhile I excused myself to go out for a smoke. On the back porch a tanoa was set up and a group of men stood around it, talking, one of them offered me a bowl of kava. I accepted it and they went back to their quiet conversation about the state of the copra market. A while later, Henry, Yasmine and I returned to their house.

We settled into a chess game after dinner. Henry moved thoughtfully while I made some unorthodox plays. They seemed to throw his game off and I won the game.

"You made some unusual moves," he said "Where did you learn those?"

"They were new to me as well. I didn't have much of a plan, just made some impulsive moves that worked out."

"I didn't know how to counter them. Didn't know what you were up to."

"I just felt like taking some chances, Henry."

"Hmm. I learned to play chess by reading books, studying games and defensive strategies. You seem to switch your tactics without reason or a constructive buildup."

"I guess I have simplified my game down to one move at a time. It doesn't seem to pay when I try to figure out your long range plan so I just try to figure out how to counter the immediate threat or advance a piece."

"Maybe that's my problem. I always try to plan everything to the last detail. I've planned my whole life like that. Never took a chance. It has worked out but it doesn't seem fulfilling. Now I'm stuck here in retirement waiting for the end. It's safe but boring. I don't even have any great memories of my life. There's nothing exciting about having worked in a sugar mill. There were so many things I wanted to do when I retired but now I don't have the drive to do them. My friend, Samuel, has lived a life full of change and adventure. I have known him for years. He has worked for many companies and traveled all over the South Pacific, has been both broke and well off, married twice and raised two families. I used to tell him he was irresponsible, foolish. Said he would end up a wastrel. But in fact, he is richer in all ways than I am."

"He seems well adjusted to his situation."

"He has always been like that. Happy go lucky. When things didn't go his way, he set off in another direction. I could never be like that."

We didn't play another game. Henry was thoughtful, maybe even a little down, so I excused my self and went to my room.

The next day I took my chess set and walked over to visit Samuel. He was alone except for two women puttering around the house.

"Hello, Max. I'm glad you came to visit. I see you brought the chess set."

I set up the board on the edge of the bed. "Henry tells me that you've traveled a lot," I said. "Have you been to New Zealand?"

"Oh, yes. I lived in Auckland for a couple of years, in Ponsonby."

"I lived there last year."

"Really? Do they still call it the Coconut Grove?"

"Yes, but there are mostly Cook Islanders and Samoans living there now. Not too many Fijians."

"There were mobs of us there a few years ago. We used to go to the Glue Pot, the big pub on Jervois Road. Do you know it."

"Who didn't? No television but a fight every night."

"That's the place. Boy, I had some good times there."

"I finally won a game against Henry, last night," I said.

"I beat him all the time. He plays the same games. Uses the same tactics for the situations which develop. Once you know this, it's easy to go around them."

Although he occasionally wheezed and panted as he struggled for breath, and he was obviously in pain, his attitude was that of a man who was convalescing, not dying. He won easily and managed to laugh as he checkmated me.

"What method do you use to play chess," I asked him when the game was over.

He thought for a moment, "Nothing you can formalize. I mean, I play to checkmate the king, but the plans I make to do that are always subject to change. I plan, but if it doesn't work out, I scrap it and make another one. It's no good to make a plan you can't change.

It must be one which goes along with the conditions which you can't change. Knowing what you can and cannot change in life is the key to living. When things don't go your way, accept that and work with the things you can. I never think that my plans will turn out as I expect, because in reality, they rarely do. And when they do they don't seem so good. I like a life of surprises. Dealing with life as it happens is much more exciting than following a plan which is not working."

The *Adi Moapa* arrived in port the next evening and Henry drove me down to the docks. The crew was still loading cargo when I went on board and claimed my berth by throwing my backpack on top. Then I walked back to the galley where I found the captain.

"Bula, captain."

"Bula, Max. I wondered what happened to you. Good to see you were not eaten. Ha, ha."

"Well, I attended a feast but lucky for me a missionary provided the main course. When do you leave for Suva, captain?"

"Tomorrow morning, very early. But first we will make a stop at Koro tomorrow night."

We talked for awhile then I went to my bunk and crashed. It was still dark when the boat's engine started. I woke up to see that during the night a load of passengers boarded and occupied all the bunks and some of the floor space. I went to the top deck and sat on the bench in the open air as we departed Savusavu. As the lights of the town dimmed in the distance the stars in the east disappeared with the dawning of a new day. I stayed on the top deck all day, except for the occasional foray into the galley for a cup of tea or something to eat. It was easy to slip into the rhythms of life on a boat. Sleeping, reading, writing in a journal, daydreaming. Until a boat voyage is completed and the passenger is on shore, there is really nothing to worry about except sinking. Sure a person can concern himself with shoreside problems but can't do much about them. I'll decide what to do next when I arrive in Suva.

That afternoon, the captain anchored on the lee side of Koro and the crew began ferrying passengers and their belongings ashore. They were contract workers who came to harvest the copra and they brought a lot of personal gear with them. One guy even carried his innerspring mattress. The captain and engineer stayed ashore again. I think they had a girl in every port. The crew pilfered some of the cargo of kava and ground it up in a tin can using a wrench as a pestle. We played cards well into the night.

We were underway early the next morning and I stayed in the wheelhouse with the captain. The day progressed normally until we came to the channel between Ovalau and Koro where the tradewinds were able to build up a steep sea which smacked the side of the boat. Suddenly a loud, wrenching sound came from the stern. The wheel flopped around loosely in the captain's hands and a look of concern came over his face.

A crewman came running to the wheelhouse, "Captain, the rudder has broken!"

They went aft and in a few minutes the engine was shut down. The boat wallowed so much that I was forced to leave the wheelhouse. I made my way aft past the frightened stares of the other passengers. In the galley, hatch covers were pulled up and the captain stood in the opening examining the rudder gear which was swinging wildly, dragging a broken chain. It took three hours to repair during which practically everyone became seasick. Once again underway, the boat sailed out of the channel and into the calm, reef sheltered waters. I rejoined the captain in the wheelhouse.

"We will have to anchor in the reef for the night. It's too late to make Suva today. I hope you don't mind."

"No. It doesn't matter to me. I don't have an appointment to meet."

I went to the top deck and studied the passing reef. We cruised in a channel about one hundred yards wide rimmed on both sides with the light colored water covering the reef. Every so often, the deep, blue water marking a narrow pass cut through the reef. The captain turned into one of these side channels and parked the boat as though on a city side street. When the boat was securely anchored and the motor shut down, everyone on board settled in for an afternoon nap.

I had the top deck to myself and let my senses enjoy the day, reliving the excitement of the broken rudder and the peace of the anchorage. The tradewinds blew steadily yet kicked up only small wavelets on the reef. This kind of adventure could go on for a few more days. I wasn't looking forward to the decisions which awaited me in Suva.

We left the next morning and by noon were coasting along the shore of Viti Levu island near the seaplane base. Then the captain rounded the point and entered Suva Bay arriving at the Queen's wharf around one o'clock. I got my kit together and headed for the Coconut Inn.

"Didn't think you were coming back," Ken said when I checked in to the hostel.

"It wasn't a sure thing," I said.

"What happened to the English girl you left with?"

"She stayed in the villages." I told him what happened to me and he had a big laugh about the near-miss marriage.

"There was a Peace Corps fellow through here last year with the same problem. He had to leave the islands. Couldn't get another visa."

"I'm going to Immigration tomorrow to see if I can get another one."

"Good luck."

At the Immigration office the following morning I was interviewed by an Indian man in a starched uniform and grim expression. I gave him my passport and he got my file from a cabinet. He opened it, read for awhile, then looked at me. "What were you doing in M'bouma?"

"Nothing much. Just showing some friends how to make a vegetable garden."

"I have a letter here that says you were quite involved in a project. Is this true?"

"Well, no. I mean, I didn't have a lot to do with it."

"This letter, from one of the elders of the village, says that you were a director and that you would become a shareholder in the project when you married a certain woman named Seini. Do you plan on returning to this village if you stay in Fiji?"

"I'm not sure. Probably not if it means I have to get married."

He looked right into my eyes for a few moments then said, "There's something funny going on here. Do you have any money?"

"About two hundred dollars."

"That's not enough to guarantee you can take care of yourself. We require at least that much for one month and you want a three month visa."

"Can I get a one month visa?"

"Out of the question. You might stay longer and become a liability to the country."

"I still have an air ticket back to Hawaii."

"What's to keep you from cashing it in and leaving my office with the expense of sending you home? Don't ask me any more. The answer is no. You make sure you are gone from Fiji when your visa expires next week!"

I left the office and went to a milk bar to think it over. So much for Plan A. Now to see what Plan B has to offer. It hadn't occurred to me that I could cash my ticket in. I thought there was some kind of restriction on it so I headed to the Qantas office where a clerk assured me that I could have the cash by the end of the week. I traded the ticket in, figuring that the cash would give me more options on which direction to go. New Zealand was out of the plan. I had to be out of the country for six months before I could apply for a visa. Maybe

Australia would take me. As a last resort, I could always buy another ticket to Hawaii.

That afternoon I went to the yacht club to check on Mike and Harold but their boat wasn't there. I found out from a yachtie that they had left a couple of weeks before but didn't say where they were headed. Seems they left an unpaid bill with the club. I checked the bulletin board and saw a "Crew Wanted" ad for a boat bound to the New Hebrides. I took down the information but the New Hebrides offered even less opportunities than Fiji, what's more, the yacht was anchored in Lautoka, the port on the other side of the island near Nadi.

"How did you go with your visa?" Ken asked when I returned to the hostel.

"I didn't get one. I have to be out of the country when this one is up, in ten days."

"Where will you go?"

"Back to Hawaii. I'm tired of all the hassle."

Over the next few days I bought and shipped the stuff that Blue ordered for the garden. Then the check from Qantas came through. I was burned out from dealing with new situations that were beyond my control and ready to return to Hawaii and a visa-free life. Finally I was ready to make plane reservations and was headed out the door of the hostel when Ken stopped me.

"You've got some mail," he said.

It was a letter from Megan in the New Hebrides. She had seen Mike in Port Vila and heard that I was in Fiji. She told me of her experiences over the past year and ended with "Come on over here. Love to see you." The Committees conferred on that idea all night. None of them were crazy about going back to Hawaii and were grasping at straws.

'We have a few hundred dollars now that the air ticket is cashed. That's enough for awhile.' 'Just reserve a seat for Hawaii. Don't buy a ticket yet.' 'Maybe we can get on that yacht in Lautoka.'

I caught the bus for Lautoka the next morning. It rolled out of town on the Queen's Road, crawled over the mountain ridge to the west highballed along the flat coastal plain trailing a plume of dust, retracing the route I took when I first arrived in Fiji ten months before. Then, I took my time, hitchhiking and walking, taking it all in. Now, I couldn't get to the destination quickly enough. I wanted my future to be settled. But the bus stopped at every little village as it loaded and unloaded people and cargo. I was too keyed up to sleep and arrived in Lautoka, dead tired. The bus driver told me of a guesthouse in town where I got a room and slept until noon the next day.

Still tired and hungover from too much sleep, I went to the docks and sat on the edge of the pier near the dinghy dock looking at the anchored yachts, trying to see which one was *Vixen*, the boat looking for crew. A man in a dinghy rowed up to the dock and I asked him if he knew *Vixen*. He pointed it out to me, then left. It had a dinghy tied up alongside so I waited. Finally, a woman came out on deck and I hollered "*Vixen*. Ahoy, *Vixen*." She looked over at me and waved then got into the dinghy and putted over to the pier. I met her at the dinghy dock.

"Hello," I said, "I saw your notice on the bulletin board at the yacht club. Are you still looking for crew?"

She climbed up to the dock, a slim woman in her early forties dressed in shorts, polo shirt and a wide brimmed hat shading her well tanned face. "No. I'm sorry. We just took on a new guy yesterday."

"Oh. Just my luck."

She looked me over for a minute, "Well, tell me something about yourself. Maybe someone else will need crew. Is it important where you go or when you leave?"

"The where isn't critical but I have to be out of the country in a few days because of my visa."

"Have you done any sailing?"

I told her about my experience.

"You know more than the guy we signed on. Too bad I didn't meet you before but I had to make a decision since we are leaving in three days. Leave me an address or phone number where I can get a hold of you in case something comes up. I'll check with the other yachties."

I gave her the phone number of the guesthouse and watched as she headed back to the boat. From a distance, *Vixen* looked great. A white ketch about fifty feet long with a hull that glistened and brightwork that sparkled. A posh yacht.

I gave it up on the way back to the guesthouse. I wasn't going to get a boat. Might as well buy the ticket to Hawaii tomorrow, I thought.

I didn't sleep much that night. Partly because of the dejection I felt over not getting the crew position and partly because the guesthouse was part whorehouse with drunken sailors and hookers yelling in the halls. Lautoka's claim to fame is that it is one of Fiji's biggest sugar ports and has enough bars and duty-free shops to prove it. I packed up the next day and checked out, then headed down to the road for a bus to Nadi and the airport. I had walked a few blocks when I reached for my harmonica. I couldn't find it and remembered that I left it in the room. I went back to the guesthouse.

"I thought you left," the clerk said.

"I did but I forgot something in the room."

"Well, you got a phone call from a woman on a boat. I told her you had already checked out."

I got my harmonica and hurried down to the pier. I waited for an hour or so until I saw the woman came out on deck, then called, "Ahoy, *Vixen*."

She saw me and putted over to the dinghy landing.

"I thought you left," she said, "I'm glad I got a hold of you. Our new crew member went on a drunk last night and got beat up. He's in the hospital. Can you make the trip with us?"

"Where do I sign?"

THE END

ABOUT THE AUTHOR – CAPT. ROBERT HEIN

Known by family and friends as 'B 'n B' the 'dynamic duo', Robert and Bianca Hein have sailed together from the Atlantic to the South China Sea. They have been shipwrecked, chased by pirates and narrowly escaped being tattooed by New Guinea natives.

B 'n B met on Maui, Hawaii in 1978. Bianca swam out to the ketch Robert was the captain of on his birthday, looking for a crew position, and they have stuck together ever since — like 'two peas in a pod, like a barnacle to a boat, like gum to a shoe'.

www.ingramcontent.com/pod-product-compliance
Lightning Source LLC
LaVergne TN
LVHW050639100826
845148LV00011B/1908

9780974050232